JOSEPH IS LEAVING

A NOVEL

JOSEPH IS LEAVING

A NOVEL

GEORGE A. STEHLING

SUNSTONE
PRESS

SANTA FE

Sunstone books may be purchased for educational, business, or sales promotional use.
For information please write: Special Markets Department, Sunstone Press,
P.O. Box 2321, Santa Fe, New Mexico 87504-2321.
Printed on acid-free paper
∞
eBook 978-1-61139-6133

Library of Congress Cataloging-in-Publication Data

Names: Stehling, George A., 1939- author.
Title: Joseph is leaving : a novel / by George A. Stehling.
Description: Santa Fe, New Mexico : Sunstone Press, [2020] | Summary:
    "Historical fiction about a young farmer from Germany who migrated to
    Texas in 1845 with hopes of settling on a 320 acre land grant"--
    Provided by publisher.
Identifiers: LCCN 2020038218 | ISBN 9781632933126 (paperback) | ISBN
    9781611396133 (epub)
Subjects: LCGFT: Novels.
Classification: LCC PS3619.T44836 J67 2020 | DDC 813/.6--dc23

LC record available at https://lccn.loc.gov/2020038218

WWW.SUNSTONEPRESS.COM
SUNSTONE PRESS / POST OFFICE BOX 2321 / SANTA FE, NM 87504-2321 /USA
(505) 988-4418

PREFACE

In the mid-nineteenth century, the poor economic conditions in Europe enticed many of its citizens to migrate to a place called Texas. In this fictional story, a young farmer from Germany named Joseph, accepted the challenge. He left not knowing if he would ever see his family again.

After a treacherous journey on the sea and after being stranded on the shallow shores of Texas, Joseph soon learned that Texas was still an untamed wilderness. He managed, however, to get all his possessions into the interior of what was now the State of Texas with the help of an ox-driven cart. There he helped other immigrants create a new town. He also met and married a young lady named Jenell. In later years, one of their twin children was captured by Comanche raiders. That led to an intensive search for the missing child.

As a descendent of the German pioneers that settled in Texas, I tried to depict the characters and environment as accurately as I could. The immigrants were mostly hard working, fun loving, and pious people looking for a better life. Some never reached their destination due to very harsh conditions, but the survivors persisted and etched in many of the customs and traditions of today.

The book has twelve chapters. I believe that the reading of the first will leave you anxious to read the next. Also, I want to take this opportunity to thank my wife Janice and my daughter Debbie for all the support I received during this entire process.

1

Jacob was in the barn on a crisp fall day preparing it for the long winter ahead. The barn had been in the Schmidt family for many years and cleaning and repairing it was nothing new. While inside he could hear a lot of noise on the roof as his brother, Joseph, was searching for and repairing any possible leaks.

Suddenly the noise got much louder. He heard a rolling, thumping sound but then there was abrupt silence. He ran outside and found Joseph lying on the ground motionless. Fortunately, he had rolled off the lower side of the barn where the ground had been softened by heavy rain.

"Joseph, Joseph, wake up," he shouted while shaking him. He was relieved to hear him groan. He then grabbed a bucket of water and threw it on his head.

"I'm all right," Joseph sputtered. "I don't think I broke anything, and I just need a little time to catch my breath."

"What happened?" asked Jacob.

"My hammer started sliding down the roof and I made a mistake by reaching for it and found myself following it all the way to the ground," he said sheepishly.

Jacob closed the barn, got a nearby bench, and brought Joseph a tin cup of water. Joseph thanked him but reminded him that he had already had a bucket of water. Jacob then questioned Joseph, "You've been acting a little differently lately and it seems you are not concentrating on what you are doing. Is anything wrong?"

"I'm fine, but I've been thinking a lot about my life here on the farm. I like our animals and crops and my work here, but it's the same routine that we, and everyone before us, have always had. I'd like a bit of a challenge...something new and different," he replied.

"I have to agree our grain harvest is low this year and we lost a lot of potatoes to the blight," Jacob responded. "We'll be talking about the year eighteen forty-five for a long time, but we will eventually recover and start making some money again."

"That's true, but I am restless, and the farm may not be large enough should I get married and have children. If I had another way to make a living, you could better support your son, Guido, your wife Dorothy, and the baby she is expecting. Our parents find a lot of comfort in having you and your family on the place," he answered.

"You must have something on your mind because you're starting to lighten up a little bit. What is it?" Jacob asked.

"Do you know that my friend Franz and his wife and daughter have left Germany and are headed for Texas where they will get a lot of fertile land for settling there? I've heard that I might qualify for up to three hundred twenty acres. I can only imagine how much and what I could produce on that much land."

Jacob was surprised and almost speechless but seemed to understand Joseph's hopes and dreams. "I have heard a little bit about that, and I think some noblemen down on the river have something to do with it. If you are serious about it, I suggest you get more information before you discuss it with our parents because it will be a matter of great concern to them," he said.

Joseph thanked his brother for helping and listening to him. He was very sore and bruised from the fall but knew he'd get over it in a few days. He was too excited about the possibility of boarding a ship for a distant land to think about the pain.

Joseph knew, however, that there was much to be done on the farm as well as a commitment to help an elderly couple finish the remodeling of an old house. It was now late in the afternoon, so he gathered a few vegetables in the garden and returned to the house.

Before he got into the house, he could smell the aroma of fresh bread. His mother, Barbara, was preparing the evening meal. She was a good cook and had a knack for stretching whatever meat, fish, or fowl she had to feed the family and their frequent guests. She was tall, thin, and always looked neat in her mostly handmade dresses. The ribbon in her hair and the wearing of an apron seemed to make her many chores much easier.

Joseph could hear the rocking chair squeaking as he entered the house. His father, Gustav, was resting after having split some firewood for the woodstove. He was strong and robust but needed a walking cane for a limp he could not hide. He, like Barbara, had many friends and relatives in their vicinity and in the nearby town of Baumberg. When something newsworthy happened there or in the German states, he often had an opinion about it and didn't hesitate to express it to anyone that would listen.

The next morning after a quick breakfast of sliced cold meat, cheese, and fresh milk, Joseph left on their old work horse to finish a job for Hans and Martha Hibner. They lived in an old house on a sizable tract of land near the forest by a river. Since they had no children, Joseph occasionally had opportunities to earn some extra money by helping them. There he had cut trees, worked livestock, and did carpenter work.

There were times, however, where there was time left at days end to do something besides work on their place. Joseph enjoyed swimming in the river, hunting game birds, or riding one of their spirited horses.

This day, however, was not as productive as usual. Joseph still was sore from yesterday's fall and it started raining at mid-day preventing him from doing some finish work on the outside. He could not complete any work indoors as Mrs. Hibner was entertaining some unannounced guests.

Recognizing that the job could not be completed this day, Mr. Hibner came out on the porch with two cups of coffee and invited Joseph to have a seat. Still wet from the rain Joseph anxiously accepted the offer.

"Your work is looking good, Joseph," he said. "I don't think the rain out here or the talking by the women inside will stop anytime soon. I'll be happy to pay your wages now and you can finish another day when you have some extra time."

Joseph wanted to accept the offer for pay but replied, "I appreciate the offer, but I might have a better use of the money when I finish the job, but most of all, thanks for trusting me to come back soon." Joseph was anxious to discuss his ambition to leave for Texas, but he felt that his parents should be the next to know.

It was obvious to Joseph that Mr. Hibner wanted some company, so Joseph decided to stay for a while. He knew that he had traveled a lot and liked talking about his experiences.

"How old are you, Joseph?" he asked.

"I am twenty-three and my brother, Jacob, is three years older. We all wanted a larger family, but my mother could not have any more children. She especially wanted to have a baby girl," he answered.

"I understand that. You sure have a lot of work experience for your age and you come from a hardworking family," he replied.

"There always is something to do on the farm and we learned a lot growing up. My father has always said that all of humanity is dependent on the land and that we must take care of it. We did almost everything having to do with producing meat, dairy products, fruit, and vegetables. And it seems there is always something to remove, repair, or build and we can't afford to hire anyone to do it, especially now," Joseph said.

"Well, I've been around about forty more years then you have, and I can tell you that economic conditions are really bad now. Martha and I couldn't have any children at all, so we moved around the country a lot before we returned and settled back here on my parent's home place. We really enjoyed our adventure but now it sure is nice to be back on this beautiful place in this beautiful country," he replied.

"It sure is nice," Joseph agreed. "You have the meadows, trees, river, and this solid old house."

"Yes, we are very fortunate, but many people are not. Many citizens are suffering because of the shortage of potatoes...in Ireland it is even worse. I have never heard of so many people coming down with disease and a good number have died," he stated.

"Maybe that explains why my mother is always asking us if we have any fever," Joseph said.

"That could be," he replied. "She is probably being cautious since you work in the fields."

He continued, "Perhaps it's a good thing that you stayed on the farm because so many factory workers these days are getting low wages, and some have no work at all. Many of the linen weavers are still using out of date hand looms and can't compete against our neighboring countries that invested in better equipment. Our rulers need to listen more to the people to get back on our feet. Many are traveling to other countries looking for a better life."

"What countries are they going to?" asked Joseph.

"I suppose some are headed for nearby countries but a lot of them are sailing to the United States of America looking for more opportunities. I hear that the trip there is very uncomfortable and sometimes dangerous," he replied.

"Is Texas a part of the United States of America?" asked Joseph.

"I am not sure, but if not, I believe it will be some day because that country has been adding territory westward for some time. I haven't read or heard anything about that recently," he stated.

"I sure have enjoyed the coffee and the visit on your porch, but I should be going now. I will be back in about a week to finish the job," Joseph promised.

"I'm looking forward to it and allow a little extra time so I can introduce you to Sunrise," he said with a smile.

"Who is Sunrise?" Joseph asked.

"He is our new horse. I had to trade two horses to get him. He wants to run faster than I want to go so I thought you might want to give him some exercise while you're here," he said.

"It would be my pleasure and I'll be looking forward to it. For now, I'm glad I'm leaving on our plow horse because I've become a little stiff from my fall yesterday. I'll be ready when I return," he promised.

Joseph slowly mounted the plow horse and headed home. All the way he thought about his plans to go to Texas and what he should do to prepare for the trip. He didn't know what his expenses would be or what belongings he could take but most of all he did not know how his parents, who nurtured him for twenty-three years, would take the news.

As usual, Jacob and Joseph got up early in the morning to milk the cows, gather the eggs, and tend to the animals. Other family members frequently helped with these daily chores and on this day, it was Jacob's wife, Dorothy, who was assisting them. She liked the outdoors and knew that her mother-in-law was keeping an eye on her son, Guido, who had just turned four years old. She also knew that she would not be as productive when it got closer to the birth of their second child.

She asked Joseph, "How are you this morning?"

"You know, I was just going to ask you the same question. I am good and I'm getting better," he answered.

"That's good news. I wouldn't be out here working if I thought it was harmful to me or the baby. I like to watch things grow and help whenever I can. By the way, are you seeing anyone these days?" she asked.

Joseph was surprised at the question. "Not at this time. Why did you ask?"

"When I went to town the other day and I ran into my friend, Dora, and she asked about you," she replied.

"I know Dora. Her brother, Fritz, and I have been hunting together for a long time. I think she was just being friendly, and she is seeing someone else. Besides, I'm not interested in any relationship at this time. Now I just want to be free," he said firmly.

Joseph was relieved that the bell at the house rang announcing breakfast was ready. The family sat down and Gustav recited the blessing.

Guido looked up at his Uncle Joseph and asked, "When are you going to play with me?"

Joseph hesitated and then said, "Guido, why don't you and I do something when I finish my work this afternoon. What would you think if I gave you a ride in the wheelbarrow and we can go down to the creek? Then we can pick enough wild berries so you mother can bake some fresh pie for us."

Little Guido was overjoyed and clapped his hands in approval. Dorothy looked at Joseph a little scornfully but said she would bake the pies soon. The others thought it was a splendid idea.

Jacob looked at Joseph and said, "I'm glad the sun came out this morning. It would be a good day to continue the work on the barn. This time, I'll repair the roof and you can work closer to the ground."

Joseph answered with a laugh, "Sounds good, Jacob. Let's get started."

Gustav said, "I'm going to grab a hoe and work out on the field". He then asked Joseph, "Do you have any plans tomorrow?"

"I can be flexible tomorrow. What do you have in mind?" he asked.

"It's about time I get with Peter and Wolfgang and play some Skat. You can watch us play or see what's going on in town. After that we can buy a little feed and be home before dark. What do you think about that?" he asked.

"That sounds good. I'll get the wagon ready when you're ready," Joseph replied. He was elated because it might give him a chance to get some details in town about emigration.

"It seems that everyone has a lot of work planned for today," Barbara said injecting herself into the morning discussion. "I am going to wash clothes because it is starting to stack up. Then, since the sun is shining, I'm going to hang it on the line to dry. I hope that everyone is careful today, so I don't have to worry so much."

"We will do just fine," Gustav said as he left to get the hoe.

Everything went well on this beautiful day. Guido was the happiest of all as he got to ride on the wheelbarrow and helped pick a bucket of wild berries. At the end of the day everyone in the family was tired from the day's activities and slept well.

The next morning Gustav and Joseph Schmidt left for Baumberg in their horse drawn wagon. It was a pleasant morning, and both were ready for a change in their daily routine, but they were saddened by the current conditions on the farms they passed on the way. Historically, the fields here produced bumper crops, but now the land showed signs of the damage done by insects.

Gustav knew and greeted many of the people they met on the way and tipped his hat to any women among them. He was cheerful and tried to remember the names of as many people as he could. Traditionally, the weather was the most important topic of discussion among the locals, but these days, the poor harvests in the area dominated most conversations. When parting, he would try to assure them that times would soon get better.

The tavern where Gustav and his friends played cards was on the opposite side of town. Everything was open for business but there were very few people on the streets. Shop owners waved at Gustav and Joseph as they passed hoping they would come in to buy something.

Peter, who owned a shop in town, was the first to arrive at the tavern and saved their favorite table. The establishment had been in business for many years and was considered a hangout for older men who liked playing cards and perhaps having a beer or two. Wolfgang, another farmer, arrived as Joseph found a shady spot to leave the horses and wagon.

It did not take long for the three to start playing their favorite game of Skat while Joseph watched. For a while they would forget the problems of the world and engage in discussions about a wide range of topics that would overshadow the card playing. They would ask how each other's family members were doing but wouldn't listen to the answers. One might start talking about the high price of food and clothing but be drowned out by another who complained how slowly they were playing their cards. Then another would check the time and ask if it was too early in the day to order a glass of beer.

Joseph got his father's attention and said, "I'm going to walk around town and see what's going on. I'll be back in a few hours."

Without looking up, Gustav replied, "The exercise will do you some good."

Joseph was not sure he could find the emigration information he wanted in Baumberg. If not, he would have to travel to a larger city at another time. He headed for the market square area where most of the businesses and governmental offices were located.

He stopped at a sidewalk cafe for a cup of coffee and sat down at a small table where someone had left a newspaper. To his surprise and in it he spotted an article about a society that could provide transportation and land for those wishing to move to Texas.

He said to himself, "This was too easy...I can't believe it." With great interest he read the rest of the article. It was a detailed announcement containing the requirements needed for receiving the free land, the cost expenditures associated with it, and the suggested items to take along.

Joseph was elated. He wandered around town for a while wanting to tell everyone he met about his intentions but remembered that his parents should be the next to know. He returned to the tavern where the Skat players where still playing and talking over each other. The subject matter, however, had become a little more serious.

Peter complained about the raising of taxes when times were so bad. Wolfgang was concerned about the shortage of work in the factories near the navigable rivers. Gustav was worried about the costs of supplies they had to purchase on the way back to the farm. Joseph, for the first time ever in this tavern, stepped up to the bar and ordered a glass of beer. His father was surprised at that but gave his wink of approval.

After the card party, Gustav and Joseph stopped to buy the necessities they needed for the house and farm. They had an enjoyable day, but Gustave looked tired as they headed home. Joseph decided it would be best to tell Jacob what he had learned before he would approach his parents. On their return to the farm Joseph told Jacob that he would like to talk to him privately and later in the evening.

Before dark, the two brothers took a walk around the farm pretending they were checking the animals. Joseph then told Jacob about the newspaper article he had found and that he would start making the necessary plans to leave for Texas.

"Joseph," he said, "You are talking about a very big change in your life and it will not be easy, but with your ability and determination I think you can do it. We are all going to miss you here. When are you going to tell our parents?"

"I think Mother will take it the hardest. I think I should tell Father first. Hopefully he can then help console her," he responded.

"I agree with that. Dorothy and I will also be available to assist in any way we can," he promised.

They slowly and quietly returned to the house.

The sound of the chickens awoke Joseph the next morning. He was behind on his work, so he quickly spread some molasses on a large piece of bread and went to the barn.

While working, he started thinking about the preparations for the voyage ahead. Uppermost on his mind was the hundred and twenty dollars that had to be deposited with the society before leaving. He had some savings, and a little money coming to him for work he had completed for others, but it was not enough to cover the expense for the trip.

Then he heard the barn door squeaking as it was being opened wider. It was his father who was mumbling that he'd have to grease its hinges.

"This is the time," Joseph told himself. He placed two stools near the entrance of the barn and said, "I have something important I want to talk to you about. Please have a seat."

Gustav lit his pipe, sat down, and asked with a smile, "Do you have a new girlfriend?"

"No, I do not," he replied nervously. "You know how much I like this land and our nice home, but I am thinking about farming at another place."

"I do not think you have the money to buy a new place. Also, I do not know of anyone around here that can afford to hire anybody during these difficult times."

"I want to go to Texas where there is lots of fertile land available. Some noblemen down on the river are anxious to settle a large land grant they have there."

"You must be talking about a society headed by some princes and counts. We talked about that yesterday at the card game. We were wondering why they were doing that. You know sometimes things are not as good as they sound."

"I can get three hundred and twenty acres free by improving and occupying it for three years. My leaving would also make it better for Jacob and his growing family."

Gustav stopped puffing on his pipe for a while. Joseph could tell that many things were going through his Father's mind.

He finally looked at his son and said, "Forgive me for pausing, but I'm thinking that after you board a ship I may never see you again. But I know what you are made of and I saw that gleam in your eyes. It would be wrong for me to tie you down. You have my blessing and best wishes to follow your dream. We will all be waiting for your first letter from Texas."

"Thank you for understanding. I will think about you and our family, farm, and this beautiful country every day. I think I should tell Mother this afternoon," he replied somberly.

Gustav paused again. After a while he said, "Maybe I should tell her first. It might be less shocking. You can wait outside on the bench and when we're ready I will call you in."

It was now late afternoon. Jacob, Dorothy, and Guido were going for a ride in the wagon. Earlier Jacob had informed Dorothy about Joseph's plans and they decided it best that Gustav, Joseph, and Barbara should have privacy at this time.

Gustav asked Barbara to sit down at the table to discuss something important.

"What is it, Gustav?" she asked, a puzzled look on her face.

"Joseph is leaving," he replied.

"Is Joseph going hunting again with his friend, Fritz?"

"No"

"Well then, is he going to that big fest in Baumberg?"

"No"

"Why don't you just tell me what Joseph is up to?"

"Joseph is planning to go to Texas because he has an opportunity to get a big piece of land there free. He will just have to pay for travel, shelter, and other expenses."

"How far is that?"

"It's thousands of miles away and might take more than two months to get there by ship."

"So, when is Joseph coming back?"

"That is the hardest question to answer. He wants to settle down there like so many others from Germany."

Barbara started trembling. She got up and started pacing around the table. She picked up a small towel and said, "I think you are trying to tell me that we will never see him again." She started weeping, using the towel to wipe away the tears.

Gustav called Joseph in. He hugged his mother and tried to assure her that everything would be fine. She was so shocked she could hardly speak. She settled into the rocking chair as Jacob, Dorothy, and Guido returned from their ride.

Dorothy opened the pie safe and pulled out a berry pie she had baked earlier in the day. She served Guido some milk and made coffee for the others. Barbara, with tears in her eyes, politely accepted a cup but kept on rocking.

It was an unusually quiet evening in the Schmidt house. Barbara remained in the chair as the others turned in. She could be heard rocking and sobbing most of the night.

Everyone was a little slower in getting started the next morning, but on the farm, there is always pressing work to be done. The men went to do the outside chores while Dorothy stayed inside to care for Guido and to try to cheer up Barbara.

Dorothy looked at Barbara and said, "You know, we could use some fresh air today. Why don't you, I, and Guido get in the wagon and go see your sister, Edna. We can take her some leftover pie."

"Well, I suppose your right. Ask one of the boys to get the wagon ready. I don't think I can get anything done today anyhow," she responded.

They arrived at Edna's house while she was busy in the garden. She was very pleased to have company and welcomed them in.

"Edna," Barbara announced, "Joseph has big plans. He has decided to get on one of those big ships and sail to Texas. He will get some free land there and start a large farm."

Edna was surprised and said, "Texas is on the other side of the world. That's going to take a long time to get there. Well, I guess I can't blame him since we have so many problems here now."

"I am really worried about it."

"I can tell. You look tired and your eyes are swollen. Maybe we should have a glass of wine. I know you prefer red wine and I happen to have some. I wish Emil was still alive so he could join us. Dorothy, do you want some too?"

"No, but I really do appreciate the offer. I believe Guido and I will go outside and play with your dog for a while," she answered.

Barbara and Edna sipped on their glasses of wine. They had a lot of things to discuss but Joseph's plans always crept into the conversation. They also reminisced about Emil who passed away suddenly over a year ago.

At noon Edna served some lentil soup. They then finished the leftover pie.

Wanting to extend her visit, Edna suggested that Guido take a nap. He went to bed reluctantly but soon fell asleep. It allowed the three of them to talk and spend more time together.

On their return home Barbara started thinking about what she could do to help Joseph for his voyage.

On Sunday morning the Schmidt family heard the bells ringing as they arrived at St. Paul's Church. After the service they greeted some of their relatives and friends as so many times in the past. They discussed Joseph's plans to migrate to Texas and heard that there was another family in Baumberg planning to move there. The news made Barbara feel better about Joseph's leaving.

Later in the day Jacob and Joseph went for a walk down the road from the farm. Jacob said, "I know you will be traveling on a light budget. My finances are not so good now, but I will be able to take you and your belongings to Fluten when you are ready to go. It will take a few days and I'll make sure the wagon is in good condition to prevent a break down on the way. Dorothy fully agrees."

"Thank you so much," Joseph said. "That takes a lot off my mind. Now I can concentrate on rounding up the hundred and twenty dollars I will need for the expense."

Gustav came walking up the road and told Jacob he was wanted at the house. He then took the opportunity to ask Joseph how his travel plans were coming along.

Joseph, eager to get his advice and help said, "I have to provide personal information about myself including evidence of my profession and a birth certificate. When I get everything together, I'll submit my application to the society."

"Your experience here should help you get approval," Gustav said.

"I agree. Next, I will round up the hundred and twenty dollars I need to cover the cost of transportation to the colony, some sort of shelter, and some equipment to work the land."

"These days, that is a lot of money," his father said.

"I'm working on it," he answered. "I have fifty-five dollars in savings and Hans will pay me twenty dollars when I finish their job this coming week. Also, I will go by and see Lewis to collect the twelve dollars he owes me for a recent job, and Wilhelm, who owes me fifteen dollars for a job I did this summer. That will put me over a hundred and I can find a way to gather the rest."

"Lewis will pay you when he finds out what you are using the money for. Wilhelm can be somewhat of a scoundrel and will delay paying you for as long as he can. Let me talk to your mother and we will see if we can help you somehow," Gustav promised.

The next morning, after breakfast and completion of some of the daily chores, Joseph and his parents sat down at the table to discuss the funds required to obtain the Emigration Certificate. Gustav said that they would advance to him the fifteen dollars Wilhelm owed as they could eventually collect it from him when he needed more help on his farm. Barbara complemented Joseph for all the improvements he had made on the home place and that he should not be burdened with debt while starting a new life in Texas. They told Joseph they would give him forty dollars putting him above the required amount. Barbara knew the extra dollars would help him somewhere along the way.

Joseph was overwhelmed. He expressed his sincere gratitude to his parents but knew they would have to make sacrifices to give him the money. The support of his family meant so much to him during this transition period.

Then he asked if Wilhelm was related to them. Gustav answered with a chuckle, "Yes, he is somehow related to us. He is probably a third cousin. If he paid his debts on time and didn't drink too much, we could say he was a second cousin."

The next morning, Joseph packed his hand tools and saddled the plow horse to return to the Hibner house. Their wagon horses were younger and could travel faster, but he thought the old horse deserved some lighter duty for a change.

Hans Hibner saw the horse and rider coming down the road and welcomed them.

"Mr. Hibner," Joseph hollered, "I have some exciting news. I am getting ready to move to Texas. I'm still working out the details, but I will receive a large piece of land when I get there. Then I will clear and cultivate its fertile soil."

"Well, that is good news and I know you will be good at it," he replied. "Martha and I will miss seeing you. By the way, you can call me Hans like everyone else."

"Okay, I will if you wish, Hans."

"You can get started now. The weather is good, and the birds are creating a lot of chatter. We will settle when you are finished and then you can take Sunrise for a ride on the meadows."

Joseph glanced at the work that had to be done. "It looks like I'll be riding Sunrise at sunset," he said with a grin.

With a lot on his mind, Joseph finished the outside repairs by noon. Martha provided a lunch for him while trying to learn more about his trip abroad. She said she and her husband had enjoyed their work and travels in the German states but that they were now anchored and happy to be settled in their restored house near the river.

Inside the work was basically finished but the baseboards and trim needed some attention. Moving the furniture out of the way took almost as much time as the actual repairs.

Joseph finished the work earlier than expected. Martha and Hans then invited him to have a seat at the table for some cake and coffee. They voiced their happiness with the work he had done and paid him the remaining twenty dollars they owed.

Martha asked Joseph, "Have you started packing for your trip?"

"No, but I will start very soon. I thought it best to make the trip arrangements first," he answered.

"Well, Hans and I are not going to do any more moving. We have an old but good trunk you can have for your things if you need one," she offered.

Joseph's eyes lit up. He said, "I moved a trunk when I was working on the baseboards. It was big and seemed very sturdy. Are you talking about that trunk?"

"Yes, we would like to give it to you because you have helped us so much," she replied.

"I would be delighted. It looks like it would be perfect for my needs and I thank you so much. I will be able to pick it up next week," he said.

"I have a better idea," Hans said. "We have not seen your folks in a long time so we would like to bring it to your house. That way you can take care of your other business."

"That's great. They will enjoy your company and appreciate your kindness as well," he answered.

Hans then announced that it was time to meet their pride horse Sunrise and take it for a ride. All three went to the corral to see the tall, handsome stallion. Hans opened the gate while Joseph was inspecting and saddling him. He slowly mounted the horse and left the corral at a slow pace. It did not take long, however, for them to pick up speed and disappear out of sight as Hans and Martha were watching. After a while horse and rider returned at a full and fast gallop.

Hans looked at Martha and asked, "Who do you think enjoyed that the most...the horse or the rider?"

"I believe it's a tossup," she answered. "But I enjoyed it to."

When back in the corral Joseph said, "I hope they have horses this good in Texas. I need to go home now but this sure has been a good day. Thanks again."

The evening meal had started by the time Joseph arrived. After he gave thanks Gustav said, "We have some good news for you. Lewis must have heard about your trip. He brought your twelve dollars here and he hopes to see you before you leave."

"That sure was thoughtful of him," he replied. "I have good news as well. Hans and Martha gave me a nice trunk for storing my things. They said they have no more use for it, and they will bring it here soon so they can see you again."

"That's good, because Gustav and I have already been talking about the things you need to take along," Barbara replied. "You have both personal and necessary possessions that you need to pack carefully so you don't break or lose them. You will appreciate them most after you get there safely and settle down."

Dorothy nodded in agreement. Jacob wondered how Joseph would be able to get his possessions into one trunk...he knew that he wanted to take some tools and a gun or two.

It became too quiet around the table for Guido and he started getting restless. He was too young to understand what was going on. Joseph had a lot to do on this October morning. He did not want to shirk his responsibilities on the farm while processing his application to emigrate. But, with the help of his parents and cooperation from some references, it was soon completed and submitted. From what he had heard, he expected quick approval as the German noblemen were anxious to establish a colony on the land grant in Texas as soon as possible.

He also realized that he had not seen his friend, Fritz, for a while. He saddled a horse and road to his house where he found him sitting on a stump whittling something out of wood.

"Hey Fritz, how are you doing?" Joseph asked.

"Oh! I guess I'm all right," he responded while looking up, "But Mother is not feeling well these days. We, especially Dora, are taking care of her the best we can."

"I hope she starts getting better soon. What are you making?"

"Right now, I'm making a toy boat for my niece. I like to do this when I have spare time and maybe someday, I will be good enough to make something that I could sell."

"I am sure you will because you have the talent and desire to do it. Talking about boats, have you heard I'm going to Texas?"

"Yes, I have. You know that news travels fast around here. I wish I was going with you, but I can't leave Mother and Dora by themselves. I wonder if Franz and his family are in Texas yet!"

"I wish I knew. I hope to run into them when I get there. Have you been hunting lately?"

"No, I have not had time to go but I brought my pistol along. I thought we would at least do some target practice."

"That sounds good. I'll tell Dora so she and Mother don't get startled by the noise."

Fritz and Joseph fired a few shots at insignificant targets. Fritz's old dog was not disturbed by the sound of gunshots and just walked up slowly and sat down between them.

Sensing that they probably would not have time for another hunt together, they exchanged somewhat exaggerated hunting stories from the past. Fritz told Joseph that he would see him again before he left. The sun was setting so Joseph saddled up and headed home. Thoughts about the land in Texas and preparations for getting there were on his mind as he rode along.

A few days later Joseph returned from Baumberg after taking care of some routine matters. He heard some voices inside the barn and found his father and brother examining a wooden box they were making.

"What are you making that for?" he asked.

Gustav answered, "Hans and Martha brought your trunk here today. It was nice to see them again. The trunk is big but maybe not big enough for all the things you may want to take along. Barbara already made up a long list. So, Jacob thought it would be a good idea to have a second place to store things like tools, bridles, and boots. You know Jacob is a pretty good blacksmith and he can make the hardware for it."

"That's good," Joseph said. "I had the same concerns. I sure hope the society approves my application. Everyone has been so nice to me and I sure don't want to return everything."

Joseph was on his way to the house but noticed his mother, Dorothy, and Guido off in the distance. He went down to meet them. Barbara, as usual, looked pretty in her long dress, apron, and bonnet.

Dorothy said, "It is such a nice day that we decided to go for a walk and get some fresh air."

Guido wanted to show Joseph how fast he could run and did until Joseph caught him and returned him to the ladies.

"We were just talking about you," Barbara said. "I think you already know that Hans and Martha brought the trunk here today. It is in good shape and will help protect your belongings. I've already started putting some things aside for you."

"Thank you so much," Joseph said. He then added with a warm smile, "I sure wish it would be possible to take along a year's supply of your delicious home cooked meals. Then I would spend more time in the fields."

"Thank you. I'll take that as a compliment. What is your next step?" she asked.

"Soon I should get my papers from the nobleman. Then I'll check it and return it with the deposit," he replied.

They walked and talked some more. It started getting a bit cooler, so they turned and headed back to the warmth of the old farmhouse.

The next morning, after the customary duties were completed, Joseph left the farm and headed for town. Jacob was busy getting ready to heat, hammer, and shape metal for the box hardware. Gustav was checking the fields and pastures making a list of things that they needed to do before winter sets in. Barbara and Dorothy were busy inside making and storing food preserves for the cold months ahead. Guido was playing on the floor with his homemade toys.

Later the evening meal started without Joseph as he had not returned to the farm. They then heard hoof beats, loud steps on the porch, and the door bursting open. It was Joseph.

"I got it. I got it. They approved my application," he shouted.

"When are you leaving?" asked Jacob.

"On November tenth on a Brig named Guenther. I want to be at the port in Fluten the day before to make sure I don't miss the boat," he proclaimed.

Everyone started speaking at the same time asking and answering all sorts of questions. Guido looked bewildered as he gazed around the room wondering what was going on. There was abundant happiness and sadness in this old farmhouse on this evening.

Dorothy, realizing that reality was setting in, stood up and said, "I think we should have a going away party for Joseph and invite some of his family and friends. The Saturday before he leaves would give us enough time to prepare for it. Everyone is accustomed to bringing a dish or something."

"I agree," said Barbara. "Maybe I can talk my sister Edna into bringing her accordion so we can have some music."

Barbara's endorsement of Dorothy's proposal settled it before the father and the two sons could say anything. They, however, were in favor of it and nodded their approval. All of them hoped the weather would cooperate.

Dorothy organized the party. She and others spread the word by personal contact and word of mouth. Barbara did some extra baking, but her thoughts were all about Joseph's pending departure. Gustav started gathering makeshift tables and benches for the yard under the large tree.

The weather was about as good as it gets for the month of November. Before noon, family and friends started arriving at the Schmidt farm with food and drinks for everyone. For a day they would try not to think about the food shortages in the country.

Small children were herded into the house and the older ones ran and played games outside. After the initial greetings, the women tended to circulate from group to group talking about their children, aging parents, and Joseph. Martha stated that Joseph should be able to find a nice girl in Texas because of his good looks and ambition. The men talked about the weather and likely perils that Joseph might encounter while on the sea and in Texas.

Edna did bring her accordion but, because of the cold, could not be coaxed into using it until Jacob started a fire under the big tree. She played traditional German folk songs that prompted some of them to sing whenever they could remember the words.

Peter gave an eloquent blessing and asked God for Joseph's protection while on the journey. The meal choices were many and included soup, schnitzel, sauerkraut, and cake. At the conclusion of the meal, Dorothy gave a toast with a glass of homemade wine that Wolfgang had furnished. Everybody gave Joseph their best wishes.

Surprisingly Fritz, who was generally shy, stood up with a package in his hand. He said, "Joseph, we spent a lot of time together and I know you are accustomed to finding whatever you want. But I don't think you are going to find and cut down a Christmas tree in the middle of the ocean. I made something for you and maybe you will have room for it in your trunk."

Joseph hurriedly opened the package. He then carefully removed a Nativity scene consisting of three small wood carvings representing Jesus in the manger, Mary, and Joseph. He raised them up high so all the guests could see the good workmanship.

Joseph looked at Fritz and said, "Now, for sure, I will be able to celebrate Christmas day. On Christmas morning I will remove these beautiful works of art from my trunk and put them on display. After that, I will make sure that they make it safely onto the shores of Texas. Thank you very much. Also, I want to thank all of my family and friends for this day which I will never forget."

Many in the crowd were still misty eyed as the tables were cleared and the leftovers carefully put away.

Later and inside the house, Guido was showing off his wooden toys to his young friends. Outside, Edna sat closer to the fire and resumed playing her accordion. More guests, holding beer steins, joined in the singing. When she started playing an old favorite, Schnitzelbank, the children gathered around and participated.

The festivities started breaking up as it was getting colder and many had a good distance to travel. Before departing, Peter told Fritz that he could stop by his shop in Baumberg any time to discuss the marketing of any wood carvings that he might want to sell on consignment. That surprised Fritz and he said he could expect him soon with some samples.

Joseph was tired that night but had trouble sleeping. He lit a candle and started making two separate lists of the things he wanted to take on the trip. One list was for the more breakable items and documents and the other for the more durable things and heavier clothing. His departure date now was less than a week away and he wanted to make sure he did not forget anything important.

The members of the Schmidt family were indoors on Sunday afternoon due to persistent rain showers in the region. It was quiet until Barbara got up from the rocking chair and told Joseph, "This is a good time to pack the trunk and I am going to help you."

"I agree, and with this audience how could I forget anything. Jacob and I will be leaving the day after tomorrow to make sure I check in on time," he replied.

Barbara and Joseph placed the trunk on the floor in the middle of the room. The others, even Guido, sat silently and watched.

Barbara cushioned the more fragile items, like the heirlooms and nativity set, with the linens. The plates and flatware were placed inside the iron pot and covered with the heavy lid. A small sausage stuffer, coffee pot, beer stein, cups and a bowl followed. A bible, prayer book, documents, and stationary were left near the top for easy access. Blankets and clothing filled the remaining space.

When the lid was closed, they all sat down and stared at the trunk.

Then Gustav said, "Well, we might as well go to the barn and pack the box. The boys have everything ready."

When the rain stopped everyone paraded into the barn. Barbara praised Jacob's work on the moving box which was mounted on some sawhorses.

Due to the space limitations of the box, the handles of some of the longer tools, like the scythe and spade, had already been removed. A mallet, broad axe, hatchet, and hammer followed. Rope and leather were used as fillers. The pistol and the dismantled rifle were wrapped in some heavier clothing. Additional hats and shoes were then crammed in. Gustav then checked to make sure that the lid would close. Jacob and Joseph lifted the box and confirmed that it was indeed heavy. Jacob tested the lock to demonstrate that it worked and handed the keys to Joseph.

The sky cleared on Monday and everyone on the farm stayed busy after the festive weekend. In the middle of the afternoon, Barbara summoned Joseph into the house.

"Joseph," she said, "We are going to have my special stew tonight. You have to help me and watch everything I do so you can make it in Texas."

He answered by saying, "That is a good idea. I've been good at eating it and today I will learn how to make it."

"That's good, and you should write it down because you may want to impress somebody with it someday," she said.

"That could be, and I will tell her the recipe is secret and that it came from the best cook in Germany," he said with a grin.

"When that happens," she added, "Please write me and tell me about it."

"I will. I will," he promised.

Early Tuesday morning, Joseph milked the cows and fed the animals on the farm. He had many fond memories about this old home place and hoped that someday he could see it again. But now it was time to say goodbye.

By now Guido knew that Uncle Joseph was going away on a very long trip. He did not eat his breakfast and could not be coaxed into it.

Joseph asked Guido and Dorothy to go with him to the barn area to watch Jacob hitching up the horses and wagon. He thanked Dorothy for all she had done for the family and farm. He also asked her to be sure to tell Guido and their next born child about Uncle Joseph who was living in Texas. She said she would and then gave Joseph a final hug. He then cheered up Guido by taking him on a wheelbarrow ride around the barnyard.

Joseph could smell the pipe smoke when returning to the yard. His father had brought two chairs from inside and was sitting and waiting under the big tree.

He motioned for Joseph to have a seat and then asked, "Do you have any more room in your moving box?"

"Not much," he replied, "But I could switch something into the trunk. Why do you ask?"

"I suggest you take some seeds along should they not be available near your land. I packaged an assortment for you that might become useful and thrive on your property," Gustav said.

"I'll find room for them. I should have thought about that myself," Joseph said.

"That is all right. I know that you have had a lot of things on your mind. You have done very well," he added.

They paused for a moment. Then Joseph said, "I want to thank you for all you have done for me from when I was small, until a minute ago, when you mentioned the seeds. I will plant them in Texas soil and watch them grow. I intend to improve and protect the land for myself and future generations just as you have here in Germany. You, this family, farm, and country will cross my mind every day."

"I am very proud of you and Texas will be so lucky to have you as a citizen," Gustav replied. "I believe you will encounter some difficult times, but you know how to face those challenges and keep on going. Your faith will help you and God knows where Texas is. I will comfort your mother and together we will wait to hear from you. Goodbye son."

Gustav and Joseph were both teary eyed as they opened the box and found room for the seeds. Jacob helped Joseph lock and load it on the wagon. Gustav returned to his chair. Dorothy and Guido were returning from the garden and joined Gustav near the tree. Joseph walked slowly towards the house.

As expected, Joseph's mother was in the rocking chair when he entered. He pulled up a stool beside her and held her hand. She kept on rocking for a while and then stopped.

She reached in her apron pocket and pulled out a rosary he had never seen before. She said, "I got this rosary from my grandmother years ago for helping her during her last days. I think it would be a good companion for you on your voyage."

"That is very thoughtful of you," Joseph said with a warm smile. "I will take the rosary, and all of the goodness and kindness that I have seen in you and carry it with me to my next home in Texas. I will be busy preparing the land to raise crops and livestock, but I will always find time to think about you and my family. Jacob is waiting. I must go now."

Joseph helped his mother up and led her outside to the chair next to Gustav. Jacob and Joseph went into the house to get the trunk and loaded it on the wagon. Dorothy brought the food that had been prepared for the trip to the port in Fluten.

Jacob, after assuring Guido that he would return in a few days, said goodbye and got in the wagon.

Joseph's departure was much more difficult. They could hardly speak so they all just hugged each other. Barbara, Dorothy, and Guido were crying. Joseph, Gustav, and Jacob were trying not to.

The two brothers left in the horse drawn wagon. Before getting out of sight, Joseph turned around and waved goodbye.

2

On the outskirts of Fluten, Joseph knocked on the door of the house of Olga Beyer, a longtime acquaintance of the Hibner's. It was late in the afternoon and only two days before Joseph and his possessions were scheduled to board a tall ship and leave the shores of Germany.

Although Olga had never met Jacob and Joseph, she welcomed them with open arms. "I received a letter from Martha and Hans, and I am so pleased you could stop by," she said. "The town is full of people and I insist you stay here."

Jacob replied, "That is so generous of you, but we would like to pay you."

"No. I am glad to have company because my husband passed away a year ago, and our children live too far away to come often. Please bring in your things," she insisted.

They brought the box in first and sat it on the floor. When they walked in with the trunk, she stopped and stared at it and said, "That trunk looks familiar."

Joseph watched her, smiled, and said, "You probably saw it when the Hibner's owned it. They gave it to me because they have settled down and knew I could make good use of it."

"That doesn't surprise me because they are so nice," she replied. "Your things will be safe here while you take care of your business tomorrow."

Knowing that her guests were tired and hungry she prepared a hot meal. Olga was pleased to have made new friends and hearing more about her old friends, Martha and Hans.

As Jacob and Joseph left early the following morning, Olga handed them a sack containing bread and smoked herring for their lunch. Having lived in this port city for many years, she was able to give Joseph directions to the agency where he would complete the transaction to reserve a place on the ship.

The brothers traveled down some narrow streets and nodded at an occasional resident along the way that included sailors and fisherman on their way to work. As they made their way to the Market Place they marveled at the large mansions and tall gabled buildings. They soon started seeing more and more individuals and families with stacks of bags, trunks, and other supplies indicating they were going to take an ocean voyage.

Thanks to Olga's precise directions, Joseph and Jacob easily found the agency headquarters. People there were standing in a line that was moving very slowly. There was speculation from those in line that it was held up by someone who did not have the proper credentials or fees. An emigrant behind him said he regretted that he didn't come a day earlier. A child nearby said she could not wait to see the big boat.

Finally, the line started moving. Joseph's papers were in order and he paid the remaining balance. He then received the Immigration Certificate and a statement giving him credit to help cover expenses such as those relating to the cost of surveying on the land grant.

He returned to Jacob and announced, "I'm finished with the paperwork and tomorrow I'll be on my way to Texas. Now it's time to see the tall ship."

"That's exciting," Jacob said, "But now I'm really hungry. Let's eat the herring and bread." All the benches were occupied so they ate while walking to the harbor.

From a distance Joseph spotted the masts of a ship. Soon he saw three ships but only one showed any activity on it. After further inspection he discovered that it was his ship that was being loaded with food, water, and other supplies. Anxious emigrants were being told to clear the area and not interfere with the loading.

Joseph walked among the onlookers to see if he recognized anybody but he didn't. He then approached a couple with a young girl and introduced himself.

"I'm James," the man replied, "And this is my wife Meta and our daughter Lucy. We're pleased to meet you."

Joseph asked, "Are you boarding this ship in the morning?"

"Yes, we are. We're going to Texas," James answered.

"So am I. Have you been on the ship?"

"No. We will have to load our things and board tomorrow. Yesterday we were surprised to watch them unloading cotton. We heard that the spaces are small but we're not complaining. At least we know the ship got here so it must be seaworthy."

"It sure looks like a good ship. Those two tall masts should catch a lot of wind. Have you seen Captain Harris?"

"Earlier I saw a man board the ship. He walked around the deck, looked up at the riggings, and then went below. He may have been the captain."

"We will find out tomorrow. My brother, Jacob, is waiting for me. It was nice meeting you," Joseph said.

Olga was anxiously waiting for her two guests. She wanted to know how things went, and on their arrival, poured beer into three decorated steins. She was pleased to hear that things went well in town and said she was thinking about traveling to the Baumberg area in the spring to visit her old and newfound friends.

Jacob said, "That is wonderful. We will look forward to it and it will give us a chance to return the hospitality that we have received here. I'll tell the others and you can let us know when you can come."

After another delicious meal Jacob and Joseph turned in for the night. Both were restless and had trouble sleeping.

Jacob thought about all the good times they had together while growing up on the family farm. He also realized that his own workload and responsibilities were increasing, and that he would have to plan and perform well for his family, parents, and the farm.

Joseph's thoughts were many. Tomorrow might be the last time he would ever see his brother or the country that he grew up in and loved. He was a little worried about the uncertainty of crossing such a vast ocean but found comfort in knowing that many ships had completed the voyage. He tried to visualize what the land in Texas looked like and how the weather would be. He thought about his Father, Dorothy, and his nephew, Guido. He also suspected that his mother was sitting in the rocking chair and praying for his safety.

Joseph and Jacob arrived at the harbor early on the departure day. Many of the emigrants were already there with their possessions gathered around them. As the crowd grew so did the anxiety among the passengers and the impatient behavior of the crew members who were trying to keep order.

The possessions that were not considered necessary for the duration of the trip were crammed into the body of the ship. That included Joseph's box containing his work supplies. He was not yet allowed on the ship, so he just watched as it was carried off.

It was now time for Joseph and Jacob to say goodbye. They were so overwhelmed that they could hardly speak. They were glassy eyed and wondered if they would ever see each other again.

The crew members were separating the emigrants from the other family members when Captain Harris appeared before them. In a loud voice he announced,

"If you can settle down you can start boarding as we call your names and check your papers. Then you can carry your own things to your quarters and if you are lucky get a crew member to help you. The weather looks good and don't interfere with the sailors because they have a lot of work to do. If you cooperate, we will soon be on our way. If you don't, the others will have a little more room on the ship."

In a somewhat orderly fashion the passengers, with whatever they could carry, made their way into the body of the ship. There they found small open berths at two different levels. Everyone would have someone either above or below them. The bedding was sparse.

Joseph located the berth that would be his home for the next two months or more. There was room for himself, his trunk, and not much else. Infants were crying and adults were complaining as the families were trying to settle into their small niches.

On and above the deck was a lot of noise and activity as the sailors were preparing the ship for departure. There were larger ships on the sea, but the two square rigged masts looked very impressive in the morning sun. The aft mast was slightly taller than the foremast. They and the other smaller sails were designed to improve the speed, direction, and safety of the vessel.

The seafarers were ready to set sail. The passengers were allowed on deck for a short while to wave goodbye to their relatives and friends. Joseph and Jacob waved their hats to each other. Then Captain Harris, who was behind the steering wheel, gave the order to release the ship for its long voyage. Slowly the ship moved away from the onlookers and out of the harbor.

Joseph gazed at the coastline as the vessel headed for the open water. There were commercial fishing boats scouring the waters for a catch. The birds of many colors and sizes were following them and competing and diving for the scraps that fell from their nets.

Eventually, too soon it seemed, the landmass of Germany started getting smaller. He tried to withhold the tears in his eyes as it went out of sight. It was a moment he would never forget.

Soon the sea started getting a little rougher and the passengers were ordered below deck. Agile sailors were high above the deck climbing and grasping the lines for the changing conditions ahead. Captain Harris was barking out instructions to the entire crew.

Below deck the travelers were still trying to get situated. They were happy to be on the way but were grumbling about the shortage of space inside their berths.

When Joseph returned to his lower berth, he noticed that Ernst and Andrea, an older, couple, were having difficulty in getting into their upper berth. He asked them if they wanted to switch...they were delighted to do so. Due to the small isle space and the swaying of the ship it was not an easy transition, but it was accomplished. Then Joseph jumped into his upper berth and took a nap.

It was quite when he awoke as many of the passengers had gone up to the deck to get some fresh air. He joined them and looked around. There was water, lots of water, in every direction. He spotted James with his wife, Meta, and daughter, Lucy, and approached them.

"Did you folks get settled in?" he asked.

Meta answered and said, "We did, but we're a little crowded. Our space is a little small for us three and our things, but we knew we would have to sacrifice on this trip."

"You sure have a lot of spirit and you will do well in the new country. I have a little space left next to my trunk that you can use for something. Just bring it over so the three of you can stretch out a bit," he said.

"That's kind of you. Thanks a lot, because it will be a very long trip," Meta said. "We need to get Lucy out of the wind now. We are looking forward to seeing you later."

Joseph strolled around the deck of the craft thinking about all the things that were happening in his life and looking for someone to talk to. He tried to stop a sailor who told him not to bother him because he had some important work to do. He watched him as he climbed up the rigging taking with him some small tools.

On the starboard side of the ship were some passengers suffering from seasickness. Joseph also saw a man trying to comfort a crying woman who was by his side. He approached them and asked, "Do you need any help?"

"No, there is nothing you can do for us now," the man replied.

"Do you mind telling me what the problem is? Is she sick or did she get hurt on the boat?" asked Joseph.

"No, No, none of that," he answered. "We are just talking about what we have done. I couldn't find a job, so we decided to emigrate like so many others. To do it we had to get rid of our house and almost all our possessions. After all these years, all we have now is the few things we have stored below our feet on this ship that does not like to be still."

"I can see why you are scared and upset but this is a solid ship. The captain can be a little cantankerous, but he has been exploring the high seas for a long time."

"It is encouraging to hear that, but we still have to start all over when we get there."

"That will be the good part. You, I'm sure, have your skills and each other and it is never too late to start over. I also know we will make many new friends along the way."

"For a young man you sure are sure of yourself. I think we already made a friend in you. By the way, my name is Oscar, and this is my wife, Freda."

"I am Joseph Schmidt and it won't be long before I will be farming in Texas. Who knows maybe I will be lucky like you, Oscar, and find the right girl like you did!"

After that, Freda stopped crying, stood up, and without a word gave Joseph a hug.

Joseph started thinking about food, but it was not until late in the afternoon when he saw any evidence of anything to eat. He knew that food and water would have to be rationed but was relieved to learn that beef, potatoes and tea would be served on this, the first day.

The first night on the sea was a long, cold night for the passengers. It was an unfamiliar environment for the children, but they were covered up and kept warm by their loving parents. The parents managed by pulling out some of their extra clothing and blankets that they had brought along. It would take time for all of them to get used to the coughing, snoring, and talking while in the belly of the ship.

At daybreak Captain Harris was again at the helm of the brig shouting orders to the crewmembers. They were all presently on duty because of a storm they thought was coming their way while they were in a long, large channel. The passengers below had been warned and were in or near their timbered berths.

The storm blew in and a heavy rain soon followed. The sailors were on the deck and horizontal beams waiting to modify or repair, as best as they could, any damage to the sails. The ship weaved back and forth and the force of the wind, swept water across its decks. Courageous sailors hung onto anything that was fixed and within reach.

But soon and much to the relief of the passengers and crew, the storm passed on by and the ship settled down in calmer waters. The crew started checking the masts and cordage for breaks and tears and the morning sun started drying out the crew, deck, and rigging. By the time they were nearing a narrow part of the channel the square sails, filled with the wind, were likely visible from the British coastline.

The passengers were allowed back on the deck. Lucy, who was five years old, was holding hands with her parents, James and Meta, as the deck was very slippery. They were able to see land.

Lucy looked at the land and then at her father and asked, "Is that Texas?"

"No. I wish we were there, but we will not see Texas for a long time. We will all have to be patient until we get there," he answered.

Days passed and the ship had cleared the channel without major incident. They were moving steadily in a somewhat southerly direction.

The weather was calm and a suitable time for cleaning the deck. The sailors were on their hands and knees scrubbing the hard to remove scum and algae that had accumulated. It was a messy task and they were relieved when the job was done but they realized the importance of a clean deck for themselves and others during rough seas.

They preferred inspecting the riggings of the ship. Seasoned sailors carried tools, large needles, and twine with them as they made their way along the spars and rigging of the ship. Less experienced sailors were anxious to learn the many techniques of sailing so that they could continue to make a living and see the world.

It did not take long for Joseph to become restless. He was not accustomed to being idle while others were working. He ventured out on the deck and watched the sailors that were on duty.

A sailor, looking older than the others, was inspecting the large tapered beams that held up the sails. Another was handling the ropes that stabilize the tall masts. As they worked and talked to each other he heard many unfamiliar words describing the different areas and parts of the ship. He also heard some words that he hoped the women and children on the boat would not hear.

Joseph sat down on one of the raised compartments on the deck of the ship and gazed out over the water. Joseph asked a sailor, "How are you doing today?"

"I'm fine," the sailor said. "I'm just going to rest a bit before my next watch. My name is Leo. What is yours?"

"My name is Joseph. I was a farmer in Germany and soon I will be a farmer in Texas. Can you make the boat go a little faster so I can get started?" he asked jokingly.

"I would if I could because I'd like to make this a fast trip. My wife is expecting a child soon and I hope to be home for the big event. I just could not afford to stay home," Leo said.

"I can understand that," Joseph said. "I bet it's hard to be away for months at a time."

"It is for me but not for some others. Not all sailors have strong family ties and they are content at layovers in different places around the world. Also, there are a few that got in trouble and don't want to go back to where they came from. We all like the sea and the adventure. I'm sure you like the dirt and the harvest."

"You are right about that. If we all liked doing the same thing everyone would be in trouble."

"It's time now for me to report for my watch. It sure was nice talking to you."

"I enjoyed it too. I'm staying here a while longer. I prefer the openness here to the darkness below."

In the evening Joseph, and sometimes others, enjoyed watching the panoramic views of the setting sun as it nestled behind the ever-changing formations of the clouds above. He felt a correlation between the craft he was on and the colorful clouds because both were so influenced by the same winds. The ship, he thought had an advantage, as the mighty sails could be turned to change its direction.

As the days went by, the passengers were looking for ways to pass the time. Many had agricultural backgrounds but there were other professions as well that generated lively discussions. Konrad was a carpenter and was sponsored by an entrepreneur, Alfred, who was on the ship with his wife, Maxine, and their three children. Gertrude was a seamstress. Anton worked as a blacksmith. Martin had bank experience and Petra had worked in her father's shop.

Planned or not, they all brought their customs and family traditions with them. There was some serious competition between the women and the men for what little aisle space there was. The men wanted to play Skat, but the women that were making a quilt for an expectant mother, usually out maneuvered the men.

The children had a difficult time as they had little to do below deck and were watched too closely on the deck by their parents for fear of falling overboard. They, like everyone else, were missing their longtime friends that they probably would never see again. Some of the children had some of their smaller toys with them and shared them with their new friends.

On a cold and breezy December morning, Joseph opened his trunk just for something to do. He noticed the stationary and thought about writing home. "But what is the point!" he thought to himself. "I can't mail it now so I may as well wait until we land so I can tell the whole story about my ocean voyage."

Instead he pulled out one of his prized possessions, a compass he had brought for himself on his twentieth birthday. He lifted its lid and watched the needle wobble back and forth.

By the middle of the morning the wind slowed down and Joseph went up to the gangway to test his compass. There he ran into, Daniel, who was Captain Harris's most trusted assistant.

"I would like to speak to the captain," Joseph said.

"I think Captain Harris is very busy this morning. I'm sure I can help you," Dan suggested.

"No. This is very important, and I'd like to see him myself."

"You stay here. I'll go and ask him if he has time for you."

Dan went to the captain's quarters and found him drinking coffee. He told him about a passenger who wanted to talk to him.

Captain Harris scratched his bearded face and said, "If it was an emergency, he would have told you. You can just tell him I am busy now. If what he wants is that important, he can come and see me on the afternoon watch. I will be at the helm then."

Joseph was a little apprehensive as he later approached the captain while he was steering the ship.

"What is it? I hear you have a problem or something," the captain said in a brash manner.

"I think we are going in the wrong direction," Joseph firmly said.

"We are! What makes you think that?"

"My compass tells me we are still going south. I think we could reach Texas faster if we turned west. Where I come from, the shortest distance is a straight line."

The captain looked at him in disbelief, raised his voice, and said, "I've been on the high seas since before you were born and I am not going to change course. Your choice is to stay on the ship with the rest of us or find a different way to get to Texas. I don't even know if you can swim or paddle a boat...the sharks would sure like to see you try it."

"Is there something wrong with my compass?"

"No. I think it is a good compass. Your problem is that the water all looks the same to you. To me and my crew it is different."

"What do you mean?"

"It is hard to explain to someone that has always had dirt under his feet. By now you probably know how important the wind and the wind patterns are to the sails because I've seen you studying them. But also, there are strong currents in the ocean like the currents in the big rivers of Germany. Sometimes you can see them and sometimes you can't. They can have patterns as well."

"Can you tell me more?"

"Yes. I too have made mistakes over the years and found myself in places I did not want to be. On this trip the best way to get there is the way we are going. We will turn west when the wind and the current conditions are in our favor."

"Thanks for the lesson. I understand but now I feel a little bit like a fool."

"You are inquisitive and strong. I think I could make a good sailor out of you," the captain said as he toned down his voice.

"Maybe not," Joseph replied as he looked at the towering masts. "Not long ago I fell off of the roof of our family barn."

The captain laughed and said, "My replacement is here and I'm going back to my quarters."

Joseph stayed on the gangway after his enlightening discussion with the captain. He watched Dan, Leo, and the other crew members lift, lower, and redirect the massive sails to get the vessel going in the right direction. The splashing of the water against the hull of the ship and the howling wind made it difficult for them to hear each other.

The salty air and water were a constant menace to the riggings and the surface of the ship. There was a sailor high above the deck, suspended on ropes, inspecting the lines leading up to the towering masts. On the deck, another sailor was cleaning and sorting out his tools so he could climb up again to perform his duties. Their vessel must be prepared for whatever weather they might encounter on their long voyage.

Surprisingly, Captain Harris showed up again. He slowly walked around the deck touching, as if to inspect, various surfaces and cordages while still looking out over the horizon. As he passed the sailors much of the idle chatter subsided. If something was not correctly done or not ready, they would soon hear about it.

He looked up at the sky again and then went down to the passenger's quarters. Some of the emigrants noticed him and sat up in their berths. The parents tried to quiet down their children. Gertrude and Meta greeted him. Petra, who apparently was not feeling well, forced a smile. The captain simply nodded to them as though he understood their discomfort and returned to his quarters without saying anything.

Soon afterward, he summoned Dan to his quarters. "Dan," he said, "I just inspected our ship. On the outside it is ready for what lies ahead but inside the living conditions for our emigrants are very poor. We should remember we are hauling people and not cotton or merchandise. The weather is good now and this is our opportunity to do something about it. The crew and some of the passengers would help clean it up. Also, we must make the best use of the food and water we do have."

"Captain, I hear you loud and clear. We will get organized now and start at the break of day," he replied.

The next day was a busy one. The captain and his staff helped man the sails to free up some of the sailors to help below. The passengers were receptive to all the commotion and it helped lift their spirits. Joseph concentrated on moving trunks and other heavier items so all the surfaces could be cleaned. The women were especially eager to help the ones that needed help the most. When the work was completed, they were rewarded with larger portions of sausage, rice, and tea.

Dan reported to the captain early the next morning. He said, "The work went well, and the emigrants are happier. I am grateful for a woman named Katharina who has worked for a doctor and took an interest in those not feeling well. She mentioned that an older gentleman was running a high fever and a young girl was suffering from a bad headache."

"Let us hope they all get well. We still have a long way to go," he replied.

Another long week went by. Joseph spent lot of his time on the deck at night wanting to know more about the moon and the stars. The sailors often ignored his questions because they were busy or did not know the answers. Leo tried to be helpful, but he was more concerned about his wife and the baby they were expecting.

Joseph overslept the next morning. After a cup of coffee, he went up to the deck to check on the weather. It was getting very cloudy, but he noticed something different. He pulled out his compass and learned that they were traveling west. He turned around and saw Captain Harris at the helm grinning back at him. Joseph waved back his approval and felt that they were now making more progress.

As Christmas neared and the space between himself and his family increased so did his thoughts about the home he had left. His Father might now be wondering what he could give to his wife, Barbara, on Christmas morning. She might be in the kitchen baking cookies for the family. Jacob, Dorothy, and Guido could be in the pasture looking for a suitable Christmas tree. He wished there was a way that he could send them Christmas wishes from the middle of the ocean but there was none.

On December 25th, 1845, Joseph sat up in his berth. Some of the others were already milling around and drinking coffee. He opened his trunk and found the three wood carvings of Jesus, Mary, and Joseph. He borrowed a wooden crate from his friend, James, on which he displayed the nativity scene as he had promised his friend, Fritz. Because of the wind and the subsequent tilting of the boat the small statues fell over many times but there was always someone close by to stand them up again.

There were very few gifts exchanged among the adults, but all the children received a little something from their parents or from their new friends. In the afternoon and inside, Gertrude gathered the children and led them in the singing of Christmas carols. The crew heard them and invited them on the deck to sing them again.

Captain Harris heard them too and saw the calming effect they had on his crew. When they finished singing, he sent word to Gertrude that he would have some lemonade and cookies delivered to them as soon as they were finished.

For the remainder of the day the passengers and the crew members mingled and exchanged stories about the past and hopes for the future. A few of the emigrants remained in their berths due to illness. In the meantime, a moderate wind coming from the stern was slowly taking the Guenther and its occupants closer to their destination. In the evening when things got quieter, Joseph rewrapped the statues and manger and carefully put them back in his trunk.

More days and nights had passed when Joseph received word that the captain wanted to see him and Dan. On the way to his quarters Joseph wondered if he had done something wrong. but he was relieved to find the captain in good spirits.

"Joseph, do you know if any of your people have any musical instruments?" he asked.

"I know Meta has a Concertina. Also, I heard that Martin may have a Tuba on board. That's all I can tell you," he answered.

"Good. Do you know what day today is?" the captain asked.

Joseph paused for a moment and said, "It must be the last day of the year. Tomorrow we will begin the year eighteen forty-six."

"Your right," he said. "Maybe we should celebrate again and have some music with your people and ours. We have a sailor with a fiddle and another with a harmonica and together they should make good enough music for this ship in the middle of the ocean. If the weather holds out, you and Dan can get the bunch together. I will furnish some wine."

Joseph and Dan looked at each other and told the captain they could put it together.

The news spread quickly that there would be a New Year's Eve celebration on the ship later in the day. The musicians met on the bow of the ship to discuss what tunes they knew and could play and then practice them. They decided that Meta would serve as their leader.

The party started an hour before sunset when the wine was distributed. They assembled near the entrance to the emigrant's quarters so that those unable to attend could hear the music. Meta, in good humor started by saying, "We are going to play for you, but we are not accepting any complaints and remember you did not pay an admission charge."

The musicians enjoyed playing their instruments and the audience appreciated their effort to entertain them. On some of the tunes they were able to sing along. James had made a harness for their little Lucy so she could not go astray. The music was not perfect but for the time and place it was fun. A sailor, perched high on top of a beam, shouted out that he was noticing a lot of insects and rodents leaving the ship. Everyone, including the band, laughed.

For the next several days Joseph noticed that Captain Harris was seldom seen outside of his quarters. Joseph was interested in seeing some of his nautical instruments but was told that he was too busy. Dan, when confronted, said there was some concern about the ocean currents and the weather.

Joseph then noticed that the sky was getting greyer and the clouds were drifting faster. Then he saw a sailor scrambling down the rigging and into the captain's quarters.

Joseph returned to his berth wondering if he should tell the others when Dan unexpectedly came rushing into their quarters.

"I need everybody's attention," he shouted. "There is a big storm ahead and it looks like it is coming our way. Protect your children and those that are sick the best way you can. Put away or fasten down anything that could fly and hurt someone. The entire crew is on duty and I'm joining the captain at the helm." He then quickly left.

The emigrants did not need any further encouragement to do what they were told. They cushioned the young and crowded around them. Katharina was tending to the sick when she noticed Petra had a bad skin rash. Joseph tied his trunk to the berth framework and then helped others secure their belongings. The crew members listened to the thunder as the storm was approaching.

"The lightening can really put on a pretty show but when it is coming your way it starts looking ugly," Captain Harris commented as Dan joined him at the helm.

"I agree. I can't wait until I see it go the other way," Dan answered as the wind started howling.

Rain came down in sheets making it difficult to see or move around. The large rolling waves caused the ship's bow to rise and then slam down on the water. The fierce winds swept water across the decks making passage on it very difficult. Wet and slippery riggings, and having to keep an even keel, made this storm very challenging.

Inside the emigrants were frightened and hanging on to whatever they could. On the berth below him, Joseph could hear Ernst and Andrea praying and shivering so he jumped down to comfort and shield them. It was too dark and turbulent to see if there was a greater need among the other passengers. There was no choice but to wait, hope, and pray that the storm would pass.

Joseph heard loud voices above as the waters finally calmed down. Inside there were grimaces of pain, sighs of relief, and a stench all about. The emigrants got up slowly to inspect their surroundings. Fortunately, their hasty precautions prevented serious injury, but Katharina was already treating the cuts that some of them had received. Other conditions included bumps to the head, bruises to the body, and cases of nausea.

Anton, the blacksmith, and Joseph were the first to go up to the deck. They saw the crew members hustling around the deck as though they were assessing damage to the ship. Dan was among them.

"Dan, how does it look?" asked Joseph.

"Not good. Not good at all. We lost Leo. We can't find any evidence of what happened to him."

"No. That can't be. He is such a skilled sailor."

"Joseph, it was such a bad storm. We think he was thrown into the sea when the ship tilted to the port side."

"His wife will miss him the most. They were waiting for the arrival of their first child."

"We will get word to her as soon as we can."

"Let's go looking for him. I'm sure he is a good swimmer."

"We can't. We have repairs to make before we can go anywhere in this current. We have been driven off course."

Joseph went to the stern and gazed at the choppy waters. Anton reported the tragedy to the others below who were greatly saddened.

All on board were anxious to get things back to normal and get back on their way. The passengers cleared and cleaned their quarters and the crew did what they could in the moonlight.

At daybreak, Konrad the carpenter, Anton the blacksmith, and Joseph the farmer approached Captain Harris and volunteered to do anything they could to help recover from the storm damage and the loss of Leo, the sailor.

The captain was taken by the offer, tried to hide a tear in his eye, and said he would have the staff come up with a plan.

Konrad, Anton, and Joseph reported to the deck early the next morning. None of them were accustomed to maritime work but they felt they could do some of the more basic tasks to free the experienced crewmen to concentrate on the difficult ones.

The deck was slick, so they started by scrubbing off the algae. They then became useful in helping the sailor's sort and haul the large spools of rope, cord, and cloth needed to replace or repair the damaged riggings. They were amazed at the many kinds of knots the sailor's used to secure the pins, pulleys, and masts. Most of the time was spent mending the sails while kneeling or standing on the deck of the ship. Performing the tasks on a surface that was continuously moving back and forth and or up and down was difficult but necessary. By the end of the second day the volunteers were no longer needed. Captain Harris then invited them into his quarters and offered each of them a tall schooner of beer.

"Thanks for your help," he said. "Please don't mention the beer to anyone because out here there is no way to replenish my supply. We are behind schedule but in a few days, we should be back on course. Not long after that we'll be in the gulf and closer to your new home.

They then heard loud footsteps and a knock on the door. It was Dan.

"Captain, I regret to inform you that we have had a death on the ship. A woman named Petra lost her battle against a high fever, probably typhus. The emigrants have her body wrapped in a quilt that they made for her on the trip," he reported.

There was complete silence for a few moments. "Then the captain asked, "Does she have relatives with us?"

"Yes. Her husband's name is Bruno and she had an unborn child."

"Give Bruno my condolences. It is now too late and breezy. Suggest a burial in the morning. Soon she should be moved to a more suitable place for the night"

Emigrants and crewmen gathered on the gangways at mid-morning. Petra's body, with child, had been wrapped in an unfinished homemade quilt and then in sailcloth containing metal weights. It was then placed on some joined wooden planks.

Bruno, with his head down, was supported physically and emotionally by the friends around him. The men had removed their hats and the women were crying. Martin, the banker, said some prayers and gave an eloquent eulogy. Then the planks were tilted, and the bodies of Petra and her infant slid into the sea.

After a long pause Captain Harris asked for everybody's attention. He announced, "As soon as we can we will serve a meal so you can remain here if you wish. Also, and Bruno agrees, we have not yet had a remembrance for Leo who died while trying to protect us from the weather. You may join us before sunset later today."

The meal consisted of pork, potatoes, and tea. It was well received by the mourners.

Nearing the end of a serene day, they gathered again. This time it was to mourn the disappearance of Leo who was lost at sea. There was no body to bless or fresh flowers to broadcast. Leo's sailing tools were perched on a bench near the ship's railing.

Dan read some prayers from a small book. Captain Harris talked about Leo's dedication to his family and to his career as a sailor. He said he would get word, his wages, and a monetary gift to his expecting wife as soon as he could.

The tightly wrapped bag, including a mallet, knife, and twine, were then tossed into the ocean. As the sun went down so did the tools of his trade.

It had been a sad day for everyone on the boat. Joseph was unable to fall asleep. In the moonlight he went to the stern of the ship to watch and pray the rosary that his mother had given to him just prior to his departure.

Another week passed. The ship had proven it could survive a big storm, but it was now over two months since it had left the shores of Germany. It was becoming more obvious to the emigrants that the food supply on board was depleting because of the smaller portions they were receiving. The water had long lost its good taste and it too was carefully rationed. Worried parents were often seen sacrificing some of their portions so that their children would have more to eat.

Consequently, many of them lost weight and their strength. As time slowly passed, more emigrants became sick with fever, skin rash, and other ailments. The elements and the crowded conditions on the ship made recovery difficult. The hero below deck was Katharina. Having worked for a doctor for a long time, she was able to help many of the passengers with their medical problems. She was fully aware that she could become a victim of their diseases.

Heavy footsteps awakened Joseph the next morning. It was Dan announcing, "We are now in the waters of the Gulf of Mexico. We still have a long way to go but if the weather cooperates, we will be at our stop in Anchor Bay in a few days.

There was a flurry of questions, but Dan answered all of them by saying, "I have to go back to the helm. I can assure you that we are all anxious to set foot on dry land."

His quick visit created a lot of excitement among the passengers. Perhaps it was the best medicine the ill and homesick had received thus far. Everyone was talking at the same time about what they would do, see, and eat at the layover. Children wondered what games they might play while there. Some went on deck to see it they could spot any land but there was nothing visible but water.

After things settled down a bit, Joseph went to see Captain Harris. In a grumpy voice, he asked, "What do you want this time? Are you going to tell us we are going to slow, to the wrong country, or what?"

"No, I just was passing through and thought you might want to give me a sample of your rum and a fresh steak since we'll soon be in Texas," Joseph replied with an uncertain smile on his face.

"Well, just come in but, I won't give you anything. You'll be lucky if I don't throw you overboard," the captain managed with a laugh.

"You know I was just kidding but I do have a favor to ask of you."

"What is it?"

After we buried Leo you mentioned that you would get word of his death to his wife, Monika, as soon as you could. It was good to hear that. I would also like to let her know that Leo and I had become good friends and that he always talked so highly of her. If I prepare a letter to her will you send it along with what you are sending her?"

"That is the easiest question you have asked me on this whole trip. Of course, I will. Leo was a good man and a good sailor. She will be in shock when she gets the news, but I think she would appreciate your letter and show it to her child when he or she gets old enough to understand."

"That's good. I will give you the letter before we get to Anchor Bay," he said while scanning the navigational instruments in his quarters.

The captain just watched him for a while and then began explaining the uses and functions of each instrument. He noticed that Joseph was especially interested in the handheld telescope on his table.

"I don't suppose I could look through your telescope!" Joseph asked.

"You can look through it here where I know you won't drop it in the water. Give it a try," the captain replied.

Joseph picked it up. He looked through it but all he could see was water and the setting sun. He thanked the captain and returned to his berth.

There still was some daylight, so he reached in his trunk for his stationary and composed the letter.

January 30, 1846

Dear Monika,

My name is Joseph Schmidt and I am traveling to Texas on the ship that your husband, Leo, worked on. It was painful to lose him at sea. Leo and I became good friends on this long voyage. We talked a lot about his work, and he taught me to tie knots that I had never seen before. But most of all he talked about you and how much he missed you. He did not want to come on this trip but felt an obligation to provide for his growing family. He hoped he would be at home for the birth of your child.

There was a nice service for him on the ship. Everyone here attended and prayed for him. God bless you and your infant.

Joseph

Captain Harris was surprised when Joseph arrived at his quarters the next morning with the completed letter. He said, "I did not expect you so soon. Maybe this letter is just an excuse to ask me some more questions."

"I had the time to do it, so I did it. But I do have an easy question."

"What is it?" asked the captain with a snicker.

"How big is Anchor Bay and how long are we going to be there?"

"That sounds like two questions to me. The answer for both is I don't know. I never had a reason to go there. But I know that some of the waters are shallow and we will use caution going in. Now, if you excuse me, I have some planning to do."

When returning to his berth, Joseph heard the pleasant sound of Meta playing her old Concertina. At the same time there was a game of Skat in progress and some women were mending clothes. But after just a few minutes Dan came down and asked Joseph to meet Captain Harris the at the helm.

"Joseph," the captain said, "The wind and waves have calmed down. Now would be a good time for you to try my telescope. Here it is."

Joseph beamed as he took the shiny object to the port side of the boat. After adjusting it he hollered, "I think I saw some birds in the distance."

"That's good. Why don't you take it to the starboard side and see if there are any more!"

"I don't see any more birds. Wait. I think I see something. I see land. That's right. I see land."

"You've just discovered Anchor Bay, Texas. You can tell the others, but we need to make sure we do not have an accident on board."

The remaining one hundred sixteen passengers soon would get their first glimpse of Texas.

3

The crowd on the deck grew as the Guenther approached the shores of Texas. Land was visible from both sides of the ship as they made their way into the port. Their spirits lifted as the water calmed and the vessel settled down on the smoother surface. The older children who were allowed on deck watched the many species of birds and fish that seemed to be welcoming them to their new land.

Overhead the sailors were scrambling as the ship was making a turn to the left. The waterway narrowed and they spotted another tall ship that was anchored and motionless near the harbor. Some smaller craft were tied to long piers that stretched out into the bay.

The emigrants were relieved to be near dry land and in safer waters. The crew dropped anchor near the end of the longest pier and the riggings were secured.

Captain Harris appeared in front of those that had gathered. He announced, "I am here for the first time myself. The town looks smaller than I expected. We will check out the accommodations and your procedures for entering this country. Dan and I will take along two volunteers."

Alfred and Joseph were the first to raise their hands and they were selected to assist them. Then the captain added with a laugh, "I'll make sure no one goes into a saloon."

A small boat was lowered, and the four men rowed to the end of the longest pier. Joseph's legs felt wobbly as they walked the long distance to the shore. It felt good to finally step on dry land.

Captain Harris and Joseph, separated from Dan and Alfred, went to the wharf where many bales of cotton were stacked and ready to be shipped abroad. A dock worker named, Alex, directed them to the immigration station.

The clerk there, Sam, was polite and said, "Good to have you folks. It has been busy lately. You Germans must be looking for something. If it's more space, we have lots of room for you in Texas. Did you know that Texas is now in the United States?"

Joseph was surprised and asked, "What do you mean?"

"I guess you haven't heard," he replied. "Texas just became the twenty-eighth state of the United States."

"Is that good or bad?"

"I think that it is good for all of us. Just bring your people up here and we will make you part of it."

Dan and Alfred wondered around town searching for the necessities they would need for the remainder of the ocean voyage. While in a general store they were introduced to a Dr. Logan, an elderly gentleman. Having seen the conditions of some of the previous immigrants in town the doctor asked about the passengers on the ship.

Alfred answered by saying, "My wife and three children are fine now but there are others suffering from all sorts of ailments. I'm sure they, and those helping them, would like to consult a doctor."

"You can tell them that I will help them if I can while they are still here. They can come to my house or I can come see them on the ship. Also, I am retired so if they can't pay me, I won't worry about it," he said.

The captain and Joseph thanked him for the generous offer and said they would spread the word to the ailing passengers and crew.

Weather wise it had been a pleasant day but suddenly the air got much colder and a strong wind blew in from the west. They had to hold on to their hats as they returned to the ship. There they found the passengers eagerly waiting for a report.

Dan was the first to speak. He said, "I am afraid accommodations in town are almost non-existent so it will be necessary for most of us to sleep on the ship. There are a few eating establishments, but we will also arrange to bring fresh food and water to the ship. In addition, a Dr. Logan said he could see anybody with medical problems while we are still here. Alfred or I can tell you how to locate him."

"As you may know by now," Captain Harris added, "this port has been busy exporting cotton to other countries and the town may not be ready for the many immigrants that are coming this way. We will have to do the best we can. You have the time to get something fresh to eat and process your credentials for entry into the country. When this cold front goes on by, we will have more favorable weather for our trip to Ensenada."

After a brisk walk on a windy morning Joseph was admitted into the United States of America. His name, age, origin, ship's name, gender, occupation, marital status, and date of arrival were carefully recorded at the place of entry. When he was finished, he felt another step closer to the land that soon would be his.

Not wanting to return to the confines of the ship he decided to do some exploring as he had been given the directions for the shortest route to the beach on the Gulf of Mexico. There he made himself comfortable on top of a sand dune to watch the sea gulls and the waves washing ashore.

His thoughts were many. He wondered how his family was doing, should he now consider raising cotton on his land, and would he and the other immigrants be affected by the annexation of Texas to the United States. He then waded into the water and decided it was too cold to go for a swim. He was surprised and got excited when he spotted a large fish swimming in the shallows.

On his return trip to the harbor he ran into Anton and Konrad who invited him to join them for a beer. They found a small, smoky place that apparently was a stop for the fishermen and marine workers of the area.

It did not take long for the three immigrants to voice their opinion about the quality of the beer. Anton said that German beer was better, Konrad said it wasn't as strong as German beer, and Joseph agreed with them, but said that he could get used to it.

Then Joseph noticed Alex, the dock hand, standing by the bar. He invited him to come and join them at the table.

After they all got acquainted, Alex said, "I sure have seen a lot of your people coming through here. Some stay and get entrenched here, some decide to travel north from here, but many like you go on to the port in Ensenada. They all seem anxious to start their new life in Texas."

"Have you been in Ensenada?" asked Konrad.

"No, but I hear from the returning crews that they have a lot of problems because the town is small and not well equipped to handle the boatloads of people coming in. I'm sure you will soon find out," he said.

"Alex, when do you think we can get going?" asked Anton.

"In about two days the weather should be much better, but your captain will decide when you move out of here," he answered.

"How's the fishing there?" asked Joseph.

"It should be good. Find an old timer that can give you some hints on how to catch them. You have to be smarter than the fish."

The next day was a busy day for everyone. The west wind was still blowing but families were on the banks of the bay to walk and play while they had the opportunity. Others were just walking around town to help get a feel for the country and to purchase anything they could afford and might need for the rest of the ocean voyage.

Katharina remained on the ship tending to those who could not leave the ship. She was replacing a bandage on a small boy when she heard footsteps behind her.

"Hello Katharina. I am Dr. Logan. I heard about you from a couple of the passengers that came to see me. Do you need any help here?"

"I am so glad to meet you. The trip in these small quarters has been difficult for us and especially for those not feeling well. Thank you so much for coming to see us," she answered.

"Well, let us just visit with each of the sick or injured and do what we can. I would like for all of them to feel good and enjoy their new country."

For the rest of the day, the doctor and Katharina walked up and down the aisle treating wounds and administering the limited medications they had for the symptoms they encountered. Katharina called each of them by name and then Dr. Logan and the patient joked about each other's funny accents...theirs German and his Irish.

When he finished, he praised Katharina for what she had done. The passengers thanked them, but the smiles on their faces would have been enough gratitude. As Dr. Logan was leaving the ship Captain Harris silently gave him two bottles of French wine...one red and one white.

When returning from his hike Joseph was surprised to see Ernst and Andrea waiting for him on the deck.

"Joseph," Andrea said, "We want to thank you for having switched berths with us. It made the trip much easier. Ernst and I have decided we are not going on to Ensenada or up into the interior."

Ernst added, "We found a place to stay here and believe it will be better for our health. You're a fine young man and we hope we will cross paths again."

"I am surprised, but I understand. I have seen a lot of the town and surrounding area and you will like it here. Now, from one Texan to another, I wish you the best of health and good wishes," he said.

"That's not all."

"What else?"

"We are not the only ones staying in Anchor Bay."

"Who else is staying?"

"Karl has found a job here with someone that overhauls boats. You know, he has lived in Fluten and has some experience doing it. He will be able to support his wife and son here."

"Again, I am surprised, and I will congratulate them when I see them."

When Joseph arrived on the deck the next morning, he discovered that Alex's weather forecast was accurate. The wind had died down, the sun was rising, and it was getting warmer. The crew was busy preparing the brig for its final leg of the trip to Ensenada.

The passengers on board and the ones staying behind were saying their goodbyes. Sam, Alex, and other new acquaintances from their stop were on the banks and pier to see them off.

Slowly the Guenther pulled out of the harbor and into the pass that would lead them back into the Gulf of Mexico. There was less fear of the ocean as the longest part of the journey was behind them. Now there were fourteen crew members and one hundred eleven passengers on board headed into the deeper waters of the gulf.

The passenger's quarters were a little less crowded since five passengers had elected to stay behind. John, the oldest son of Alfred and Maxine, and some of their things were moved into the berth that Ernst and Andrea had vacated. The layover and the medical attention that the immigrants received had a positive effect on their overall health and morale.

While the immigrants were speculating about their futures in the new State of Texas, Captain Harris was in his quarters thinking about how he could get them there safely. During the stay he had met with some of the local boat captains to discuss the Texas coastlines and he was concerned about the many shallows and sand bars they had mentioned.

He called Dan and the key members of the crew to his quarters for a conference.

"Gentlemen," he said, "During the layover you were probably at the biggest port in Texas. The next one will be even smaller and harder to get to. The land is flat and does not rise much going inland and does not drop much going out to sea. High winds and currents can cause the water to roll up on the beaches and inlets and change the shape of the land and depth of the water without any warning. That means we need to be alert and ready when we go through a small pass and on into the port area. Be sure you are at your stations and keep your eyes open. I hear shipwrecks have occurred in the vicinity so watch closely so we don't hit any wreckage. Do you have any questions?"

"No," said Dan.

"Good. I'm glad you understand. The people that came in on the larger ship you saw in Anchor Bay had to be unloaded and transferred to smaller boats and taken to Ensenada. Our ship is smaller and better, and we can deliver these German people ourselves. Again, do we have any questions?" he asked.

"No," they said.

"Oh, I almost forgot. We had an unusual request from one of the passengers and we have to remember they paid your wages," he said.

"What is it?" asked Dan.

He cleared his throat and answered, "We were asked if we were able to bring in this ship without doing a lot of cursing."

The staff was surprised, broke out in laughter, and said they could and would.

Early the next morning Captain Harris was at the helm of the ship. Other than a squall off in the distance the weather was peaceful. The captain saw Joseph coming and asked, "Do you have any questions for me this morning?"

"I sure do. About the letter I gave you to send to Leo...did you ever get it sent?"

"I sure did. It left Anchor Bay on a ship headed back to Fluten. I sure hope that Monica has some family around her when she gets it. You don't have any dumb questions today!"

"Well if you insist, I do. How come they call this the Gulf of Mexico when we have not seen anything but Texas? It seems it should be called the Gulf of Texas."

"Wow! That is a tough question. I come from the other side of the world and they didn't consult me when they named it. Perhaps you should find out and let me know."

"What is your address? Is it the Atlantic Ocean?"

They both laughed. Then the captain said, "I need to go get something. Here, hang on to this steering wheel until I get back. It won't take long."

Joseph was flabbergasted but grabbed the wheel hoping he didn't have to do anything besides holding it steady. He didn't realize Dan was watching him from a spar above.

The captain returned with a telescope in his hand. Joseph was wrong in thinking that that was a hint that land was in sight.

Joseph looked at it and said, "This is not the same telescope I saw before. This is not as shiny."

"I have accumulated more telescopes than I can use. I thought you might need one since you will be in the big State of Texas and might have a use for it. It's now yours to keep."

"Thanks a lot. I don't know how to thank you."

"You really earned it when you helped the crew after the big storm. I don't have any here for Anton and Konrad because they worked hard too. I'll give them some money to even it out."

The next morning and after a cup of coffee, Joseph went up to the deck to check on the weather and their progress. He noted that all hands were on duty suggesting that they were getting nearer to their destination. He watched the sailor that had climbed the highest thinking he might be the first to see land.

Not much later the sailor hollered something as loud as he could and pointed in a northerly direction. It must be the long narrow island that would escort them to the feared pass. As they got closer Joseph could see birds dancing in the sky through his new, but old, telescope.

The passengers were soon ordered below deck so they wouldn't be in the way of the crew or distract them during the critical entry into the bay. They were disappointed but understood.

It was especially difficult for Joseph to be below when there was land to be seen. He could feel the ship moving slowly, making turns, and leaning to the side. He was hoping and praying that they would not feel a sudden jolt.

Finally, the ship settled down in the water and the passengers were allowed back on the deck. There were some smaller vessels and barges moored in the bay. There was a functional pier and the remnants of another.

The immigrants, after traveling thousands of miles, were surprised to find Ensenada in such a low-lying area and surrounded by small bodies of water. The small number of buildings and houses that were there looked badly weathered and in need of repair.

A contingency of the crew and passengers boarded two small boats and rowed to the pier while the others watched and waited. A small group of people came to the end of the pier to meet them.

A man extended his hand to Captain Harris and said, "My name is Frank. Welcome to Ensenada but I can already tell it's not what you expected. We can show you around but unfortunately it won't take long."

"Where are the facilities for all these people?" asked Alfred.

"I thought I would be well on my way to my free land by this time, but I'm stuck here like many others. We have not had the transportation to get us out of here. It's been wet and cold, and many are sick. We've already buried some of them," he answered.

"Many of you look even thinner than we do. Where are you getting your food?" Anton asked.

"Sometimes a boat comes in with some food and supplies. We're getting some from the small villages around here but they themselves have little to spare. When we're lucky we eat fish. Fresh water is another problem," he answered.

Frank showed them around town. Some men were seen making additions to a house with scrap material. They walked by some rustic barracks on the outskirts of town. Tents of different shapes and sizes were scattered about.

There wasn't anything the immigrants could do except to make the best of it. With the help of the crew they started lightering the passengers and possessions ashore. Trunks, boxes, and bags were placed on the sandy shores until the owners could find a place for them and themselves.

During all the turmoil, Joseph had another important thing to do before the ship would leave. After another look at the shallow bay and his current environment he sat on his box and wrote home.

February 9th, 1846

Dear Mother and Father,

We arrived in Ensenada, Texas today. The ocean voyage was rough, but the crew and the ship got us through it all. I had some sea sickness but some of the others had more serious problems. One lady died of typhus and a sailor was lost in a storm.

I sure miss you and the home cooked meals, Jacob and his family, and the farm, but I have already made some good friends. The crew members I may not see again, but many of the passengers have the same destination as I have. Now I will find a place to sleep tonight.

Since I don't have an address yet, I will write again as soon as I can get it delivered to you. This letter I will hand to Captain Harris who is returning to Fluten and then he will forward it to you.

Love,

Joseph

Joseph sealed the letter and returned to the ship.

"Captain Harris," he said, "You look a little tired. Are you feeling well?"

"I'm fine but in a bit of a dilemma. I should be on my way to Anchor Bay to pick up a load of grain, but I am concerned about my immigrant's living conditions... they have suffered enough."

"You have a job to do. We have a lot of faith and we will manage somehow. I have just one more favor to ask of you."

"I'm not sure I should ask what it is!"

"I would appreciate your taking this letter with you to Fluten and then mailing it to my parents in Baumberg."

"That's easy. I can do that."

"Also, I want to thank you again for the telescope. I can't wait to find a hill or mountain so I can look out over the countryside."

"You do that. In the meantime, I am going to stay here in the bay another day so we can bring your people the food and water we can do without between here and Anchor Bay. There we can stock up again for our return trip."

"That is very generous of you. Now, I need to go back on land to find a spot out there for myself and my possessions. Thank you for getting us here safely and I hope we meet again."

"I hope so too."

Joseph walked the town again and watched the others trying to find a suitable place to spend the night. He spotted Oscar and Freda who had found some room in a house that had a covered porch. Near them they had enough room for his trunk and the box. He could sleep on the porch that night.

As promised, the crew members from the ship delivered food and water to the immigrants the next morning. The immigrants were very appreciative and some of them followed the crew members back to the pier to say and wave their goodbyes.

Joseph had mixed emotions. He was happy to be on dry land in his new home country but was worried about those suffering from disease and malnutrition. Surely, he thought, this should not be happening as Texas had been promoted as a land rich in soil and with many rivers flowing to the sea.

Joseph got a good night's sleep on the porch as the house had protected him from the wind. After a meager breakfast he walked about town hoping to find out more about the predicament that he and the other immigrants were in. Some of them had arrived well before them and many others were still on the way. He felt his possessions were secure under the watchful eyes of Oscar and Freda. He also needed to locate a more suitable place to stay as his permission to stay on the porch was for one night only.

It was warm for February and there was considerable activity in this small coastal town. He overheard some men talking about a boundary conflict between the United States and Mexico. He heard a woman tell another that two more immigrants had died of cholera on the day before. Only moments later everything got much quieter. The men took off their hats as a group of people passed them by... they were carrying the body of a child that was wrapped in a blanket, lying on a stretcher, and following a trail leading out of town.

Joseph followed the procession. They passed a crudely made cistern containing several inches of discolored water. He prayed with them before he knew the child's name was Emma. There were many other freshly made graves in the area. The smaller graves were lined up in a separate section.

On his way back, he came across a small tent that had been abandoned and probably because it was badly torn. He untied it, shook out the sand, and wrapped it up and took it with him. He found Gertrude, the seamstress, to see if she might have some string and large needles. She did and wanted to help. Together they sewed it up good enough, they thought, to withstand the persistent winds coming from the bay.

They finished it before nightfall. Joseph said he would eventually repay her with some fresh fish. He then erected the tent behind the house where his possessions were stored. He assumed that this would be his home until the wagons arrived to take them to the land grant.

Katharina, other immigrants, and Ensenada residents were kept busy tending to the sick and trying to prevent the spread of any disease. Joseph helped others improve their shelters, collect water, and search for food sources. He tried fishing on the banks of the bay but caught only enough to provide Gertrude, Oscar, and Freda with some small trout.

He thought he could improve his chances by venturing out to one of the many inlets and small lakes in the area. He was creeping through some high weeds and saw a school of fish in the shallows. With his long pole he dropped a bait in their midst and immediately caught a large fish. It was a red drum about as long as his arm.

With a cord, he staked it out in the water and tried again without success. The school of fish had gone so he quietly went further.

He noticed some splashing in the distance and first thought it was another large fish or an animal that jumped in the water. He looked closer and realized that it was a struggling child trying to call for help. He ran up the bank, dove into the water, swam as fast as he could, and pulled up a small boy. There Joseph was able to touch the sandy bottom, but the boy could not.

He was carrying him to the bank when a man, likely his father, ran up and hugged the boy and said something in Spanish. While still trembling, the man said "gracias" over and over while shaking Joseph's hand. He introduced himself as Miguel and his son as Pedro. After Joseph introduced himself, Miguel motioned for him to follow him.

Miguel and Pedro led Joseph to their house on a small bluff. Nearby were some pens and a barn with some chickens and other animals. His wife, Carmen, rushed out and hugged her wet son. Miguel started a fire in the yard and told her that Joseph had saved Pedro's life after his slipping and falling into the water while he was looking for their dog.

When they dried out, Carmen invited Joseph inside for some cabrito, spicy beans, and tortillas. It was the best meal Joseph had had in a long time. The dog returned to finish the leftovers.

The sun was setting so Joseph motioned that he must go. Departures were given in two languages and Joseph left to pick up his fish that he had staked out earlier in the day. It was getting dark and he could not find it. He returned to Ensenada believing that no one would believe either story.

Later on, in the middle of March, Joseph and Konrad were working on the front porch of a house belonging to a settler. The porch roof had fallen during a storm and they were there to help raise it up again.

They stopped working when they heard some wagons coming their way. When they got closer, they could see teamsters guiding and coaxing their ox driven wagons and carts into town.

"Look," Joseph said. "They must be coming to pick us up."

"Don't get too excited," Konrade told Joseph. "I don't see too many of them... maybe a dozen or so."

"Maybe that is just the start. There could be more."

"I hope so. Let's finish fixing this porch and then we'll find them and ask them."

They hustled to where the teams had stopped. Many anxious immigrants had already gathered around them and were asking a lot of questions.

The freighter, rather than trying to answer everybody individually, jumped on the stairs of a warehouse and said, "I don't have the answers to all of your questions. I know you need more wagons but I'm hearing that the military is paying more for their use. These oxen travel slower than the horses and mules, but they will get some of you up to the interior. We just need a little time to feed and shod them and a little rest for ourselves. We will leave early on the third day, but you must keep in mind that we will bog or break down if you overload the wagons. The earliest arrivals to Ensenada will have the first choice."

As forecast, on the third day the ones that had been there the longest loaded their families and their most valuable possessions in the wagons. They then headed in a northwesterly direction and soon they were out of sight.

Ironically, another shipload of immigrants showed up and anchored in the bay the same day. Joseph joined Frank and the group that would welcome and help them unload. They learned that their journey on the sea had been about as difficult as theirs.

They were also faced with about the same problems that those before them had had. It was warmer but the shortage of shelter, food, and water did not fare well with those that were already in poor health. Also, the wet environment made it difficult for them to escape the dreaded mosquito.

There was a gentle breeze coming off the bay on an April morning while Joseph was fishing on the pier. Oscar saw him out there and went out to see if he was catching any fish when he already knew he was not.

"How are you?" Oscar asked.

"I was just thinking about some of the things that have happened to us. We came to the Republic of Texas but now we are told that we are in the United States. I've heard we may go to war with Mexico. Also, we are not getting the transportation that we were promised to get to our land. I hope we don't get any more surprises," Joseph said.

"I can add to your list that Freda and I sold everything we had to get on this land that is barely above the level of the sea. But we can't give up like you told us one time," Oscar said.

"Oh, I'm not giving up. I'm just very anxious to walk on my own land and then I want to grow food and raise animals."

"You will get there and so will we. I did hear that some of the German immigrants have signed up to join the forces that are heading for Mexico. I hope the dispute gets settled so they can come back and finish what they started."

Just then they noticed Beth, Martin's wife, coming out on the pier in a hurry. She told Joseph that Martin had shot a large deer and he needed help in bringing it in. Joseph followed her directions and soon found him kneeling by the deer while grinning from ear to ear.

They tied the deer to a pole and marched into town much to the delight of the ones watching. They took their time in slaughtering it so they wouldn't waste any meat. There were many observers to whom the meat was distributed so that they could prepare venison soup or stew for those that needed it the most.

Joseph woke up the next morning thinking about Martin's success in harvesting a deer and the joy it brought to the hungry immigrants. He decided to stay in the tent until the occupants in the house got up and started milling around.

When they did, he went in and opened his wooden box. He removed his rifle and then locked it up again. He then opened his trunk and withdrew his compass and canteen. He told Freda he was going hunting. She wished him luck.

When Ensenada was out of sight, he started looking for deer tracks but didn't find any. There were, however, many other tracks left by large birds and small animals. He sat down on a sand dune near a marsh to watch and wait.

He started dozing off when he was startled by the arrival of some herons. While watching them he noticed something sticking out of the water behind some tall weeds.

He carefully waded out to it and found a partially submerged cart that looked like the ones he had seen in Anchor bay. Apparently, he thought, it had been abandoned long ago by someone that got stuck while trying to cross the marsh. He pulled on it, but it had been there too long. He studied the area so he could find it again and then left.

He continued to hunt but lost his concentration. He found some berries to eat with the bread he had brought with him. It started getting late, and with the help of his compass, he headed back to town. On the way he spotted the house belonging to Miguel and his family. On his return Freda and the others looked disappointed that he didn't get a deer.

He left again the following morning but didn't take his rifle. Instead he took a spade and a lariat. He headed back to where Miguel and his family lived.

Carmen was hanging clothes on the line when she saw someone coming. She soon recognized Joseph by the shape of his hat. Pedro and the dog ran out to welcome him.

Miguel heard them and came from the barn to join them. After they all greeted each other Joseph tried to describe why he was there by using some motions and gestures. Miguel looked confused so Joseph led him to his barnyard where there were chickens, hogs, milk cows, and an older looking ox.

Joseph grabbed a worn harness that was hanging on a fence post and motioned for Miguel to put it on the ox and follow him.

When Miguel saw the stuck cart in the marsh, he finally determined what Joseph wanted. He watched Joseph loosen the mud around the wheels with the spade and then tie one end of the lariat to the cart. Miguel then tied the other end of the lariat to the ox's harness.

While Joseph pushed on the cart Miguel urged the ox onward and the cart was dislodged and pulled up on the bank. It was obvious that the cart had deteriorated but Joseph felt that with a little work it could become useful again. It was decided to leave the cart there until it could be cleaned up and minor repairs made. Major repairs could best be accomplished by having it done at a more suitable place. The two men returned to Miguel's house and then they parted.

Joseph then left for Ensenada. When entering the town, he met his friend, James, and his daughter, Lucy. Lucy was admiring the birds and throwing rocks into the water.

"Hello Joseph," he said. "We have more bad news. One of the new arrivals died this morning and is now being buried. Another is in serious condition with a high fever and Meta is trying to cheer him and his family up by playing her Concertina."

James continued, "I may have some good news too. There is a rumor going around that more wagons are on the way."

"I hope and pray that it's true and not just a rumor. There has to be a better place to recover."

The next day Joseph and Miguel returned to the cart leading the ox behind them. They repaired some weaknesses in the structure so it could be moved. The ox, harness, and cart were joined together well enough for the return to the barnyard. There they examined it some more and determined that they could complete the repairs the next day with the scrap material that was stacked behind the barn.

That night, around a campfire on the beach, Joseph told the others about the abandoned cart he had found.

Anton asked him, "How and where are you going to pull that thing?"

"I'm not sure yet. I'm going to start looking around for a mule, horse, or ox as soon as I can. Then maybe I can make some plans," he answered.

"Does it float?" asked Konrad jokingly. "If it does, maybe you want to paddle it back to Germany!"

Joseph laughed and said, "I have had enough saltwater for a while. The next place I'm going is to my land right here in Texas."

Suddenly a rain shower broke up the peaceful gathering around the fire and everyone returned to their shelters.

The next day Joseph and Miguel inspected the cart again. Most importantly the wheels, frame, and axle were in good shape. Old wood from the barn was used to replace rotten boards. It took longer to cut and replace some of the corner stakes and spindles.

The sun was settling behind the clouds when the work was done. Miguel then tried to tell Joseph that he knew of someone that might have a draught animal to sell. Joseph didn't fully understand and indicated he would be back in the morning.

After a mostly sleepless night Joseph returned to Miguel's house. This time he took his rifle for hunting and some money should he find a draught animal to buy. On his arrival the ox and the cart were already prepared to travel. Prior to their departure Carmen, with Pedro's help, prepared a delicious meal for them consisting of eggs, tortillas, and milk.

Miguel, while holding the reins, walked on the left side of the ox. He told Joseph he could sit in the cart, but he preferred to walk. Their progress was slow but after a few hours they came to a house and a large corral. Felipe, a friend of Miguel, came out of the house. After discussing something in Spanish they all walked down to the corral. There were no horses or mules in it but there were some cattle. Among them was an ox that was about three years old. Felipe fitted a single yoke on the ox and led it out of the corral.

He lifted each of the hooves for Joseph to see and then motioned that he could have the animal and a yoke for eighteen dollars.

Joseph did not know what the animal was worth. Was it a good offer or not? He motioned that he would like to switch it with Miguel's ox to see how the ox and cart would match in size. They made the exchange and Joseph could then tell that the yoke and cart were a good and straight fit.

Joseph paced around and thought about it. He would have preferred a horse that he could ride like he did back on the farm. But he also realized that the ox might take him to his destination and then be useful to work his land. He reached in his pocket and peeled out the money and gave it to Felipe. It made all three men happy.

On the way back Miguel led his own ox back while Joseph would learn the techniques of making an ox and cart go where he wanted them to go. This much younger ox was not as gentle or cooperative as was Miguel's older ox. Miguel laughed but knew that Joseph would eventually get the hang of it.

Back at the house Carmen and Pedro were outside anxiously waiting for their return. They admired the ox and the cart. Joseph thanked them for their hospitality and all they had done for him. He reached in his pocket and handed Miguel ten dollars for the work he had done. He refused it so he handed it to Carmen who turned it down. He then reduced the amount to one dollar and handed it to their son, Pedro, who was overjoyed.

Then all three watched as Joseph left with his rig. They all hoped they would see each other again.

On the way back to Ensenada, Joseph got tired, stopped, and sat down on the edge of the cart. As he was thinking about his purchase, three deer stepped into a small clearing to browse on some short green weeds.

His rifle was propped up against the tree several feet away. Realizing the breeze was in his favor he slowly moved toward the tree and picked it up. The deer got nervous and they were in an alert position when he fired at the largest one.

The shot alarmed the ox and all the deer disappeared. After the ox settled down, he reloaded and went to see if there were any signs of having hit the deer. There were signs and he soon spotted the carcass by some heavy brush. It was a big buck. He dressed it and loaded it onto his cart. The money he had received from his parents before he left Germany was already paying off.

Joseph with his ox, cart, and big deer created quite a stir when entering the town. The people knew Joseph would share the venison but were uncertain about his plans for the rig. He felt like he was in a parade as he passed them by.

It excited his friends and several of them pitched in and did the butchering and the distribution of the meat. Anton offered and took the ox away to get it fed and watered. Joseph and Martin had a friendly quarrel about who had brought in the largest deer thus far.

Fewer people in Anchor Bay went to bed hungry that night. Some of the men stayed up and gathered wood to build a fire. They just wanted to talk and maybe the fire and smoke would keep the mosquitoes away.

"Joseph," Oscar said to get his attention. "I don't have much to do tomorrow. Why don't I take your ox in the morning and find a place for him to graze?"

"That's good. That will give me time to do some other things. I've been gone from here the last several days," he replied.

James then asked, "Does your ox have a name?"

"No, but that's a great idea. Let me think. I don't want to just call him Ox because that's too short. How about a long, distinguished name like Tex! he said with a laugh.

"That's perfect," said Konrad.

"That settles it," said Joseph. "Just be nice to Tex because I paid a lot of money for him."

As the evening progressed the subject matter got more serious. Alfred said, "I guess I am lucky. So far, my family hasn't had any serious medical problems. I just hope we all can get on the next caravan."

Everybody agreed and then he continued, "It may not seem like it, but I think this town is going to grow quite a bit. We are seeing more activity now than when we got here. The other day I saw some lumber being unloaded from a boat. Some more immigrants showed up and they were unloading larger things including furniture. We're also seeing more soldiers and supplies coming through."

It was quite for a while and then Konrad asked, "Joseph, what are your plans?"

Joseph hesitated for a moment and said, "I will head out the day after tomorrow. That gives me a day to get ready for this last leg of the trip. It hasn't been, and it won't be easy, but soon we will all see better days."

After that there was silence as everybody gazed into the fire. Joseph was exhausted and left for his tent.

He overslept the next morning. He went to the house and was successful in finding a cup of coffee. With it, he wandered outside and studied the tent. It had deteriorated from the sun and the wind considerably since he had it. He decided he would take it along to cover his trunk and box during bad weather.

Joseph walked around town to say goodbye to his friends and acquaintances. Some of them suspected that he would leave and some already knew he would. He tried to give encouragement to those that were sick by mentioning the milder and dryer weather of late. Some expressed their concerns as he would travel alone through an untamed wilderness.

He strolled out to the end of the pier to take a last look at the body of water that brought him to Texas but could be so harsh and unpredictable. On his way back he stopped for a while on the banks of the bay to watch the children playing. Lucy and some of the others ran up to him and gave him a hug.

On April 23, 1846, Joseph got up at daybreak and strapped Tex to the beams of the cart. He then took down the tattered tent, folded it, and put it in the cart next to a container of water. He led the ox and the cart around and in front of the house.

Freda prepared a breakfast for him as Joseph and Oscar moved the trunk and the box from the house and to the bed of the cart. Some of the neighbors were watching what was happening.

Joseph thanked Oscar and Freda for everything and said goodbye to the others in the house.

While leading the draught animal and cart out of town people waved and a few handed him some small bags of food.

When passing the barracks where James and Meta were staying their daughter Lucy watched and said, "Look, Joseph is leaving."

4

It was a pleasant morning as Joseph led his young ox, old cart, and all his possessions out of Ensenada. As Miguel had demonstrated, he walked along the left side of the draught animal holding a rawhide strap that would lead and coax the animal onward.

Before the town was out of sight, he turned and took a look at the place through which many foreign travelers would pass on the way to the interior of Texas and beyond. He realized that one could have reached the same destinations by traveling on land from Anchor Bay but there would have been more and larger rivers to cross. He hoped and prayed that life would get better for those not yet able to leave the crowded conditions at Ensenada.

The ox seemed content and obeyed instructions as they followed the path that previous immigrants had taken. They were moving in a northwesterly direction and that reconciled with the crude map he had prepared while in Ensenada. The wheels on the cart made a squeaky sound as they moved along.

Soon Joseph noticed deeper wagon ruts in the loose soil ahead of him. It was apparent that those before him had to struggle to get through low lying areas. He tried not to make the same mistakes, but choices were few as there were small bodies of water as far as he could see. He did not want to get stuck on the flat terrain as did the previous owner of his cart.

When the sun got to its highest, Joseph stopped for a rest and ate some fruit that had been given to him. He then jumped up on the bed of the cart and with his telescope searched the area for solid ground. Everything in every direction looked about the same.

He and the ox then followed the trail he believed would lead him to his destination. Suddenly he heard rattling just a few yards in front of him. It was a rattlesnake curled up near a small bush. Fortunately, the snake slithered away and off into some high weeds. Joseph was relieved, but it prompted him to open his box and pull out his pistol and handmade holster. He strapped it on and continued.

By the middle of the afternoon it got considerably warmer. It was time to start thinking about a place to stop for the night as Tex, needed some grazing time.

Not far ahead he noticed a dozen or so vultures hovering, circling downwards, and scanning the surface of the ground. Joseph wondered what kind of animal would provide carrion for their next feast. A little farther and off to the right he found signs of recent human activity as there were wagon tracts, footprints, and a small piece of clothing on a thorny bush. From there, he followed a trail that led to a freshly made grave.

It appeared that the grave had been hastily made or the person making it did not have the tool or the strength to make it deep enough. Some of the dirt had fallen away and left a hand exposed to the elements. Joseph got down on his knees and said a prayer. He then returned to the cart to get his spade.

It was getting dark as he finished digging a deeper grave. He tied a bandana over his face and then transferred the body into it. It was a man dressed in German looking clothes, boots, and a hat by his side. He refilled the hole.

Joseph then washed up in a nearby shallow body of water. The water felt refreshing but was salty in taste. Sad and exhausted he threw the old tent on the ground and fell asleep on it.

The following day he woke up just as the sun started to rise. After building a small fire he drank a cup of coffee and ate the jerky and bread that he had been given. While doing so he spotted a tall, thin mesquite tree. He removed his axe from his storage box and cut it down and trimmed off all the branches leaving him with a pole that was about twice as tall as he was. The top half of the pole was just the right thickness for a sturdy walking staff. He cut the lower half in two equal parts that he could use to support his cart at night to create a level and safer sleeping surface.

He then selected the two biggest branches as material for a cross. He tied them together with rawhide, erected it on the grave, and bowed his head.

Then with a pistol by his side, a hiking stick in his left hand, and a halter leading to an ox in his right hand, Joseph started out again in a northwesterly direction.

After a few hours he stopped at a creek. Not knowing the depth, he tied the ox to a nearby bush until he could find the best way to get to the other side. He walked upstream and with his new staff poked around in the water looking for a shallow and firm place to cross. He did not want his trunk or box to get wet or float away.

This soon paid off. He found the right spot. The brute strength of the ox and the large wheels on the cart made it easy to reach the opposite bank without incident. Joseph muttered to Tex, "You are turning out to be a pretty good investment. Keep it up."

By the middle of the afternoon the trail had improved some. It was packed harder and Joseph now expected to make better progress.

Ahead of him he suddenly noticed two riders coming his way. As they got closer, Joseph became concerned because of their rough looking appearance and that they were looking closely at the load on his cart. He was glad he had his pistol by his side.

"What are you doing?" asked the first rider.

"I'm just moving along and looking for a place to settle down," Joseph shouted.

"We're out looking for some work, but we aren't having much luck. We heard the military is doing some recruiting. We want to see what they are paying these days."

"I don't know much about that because I just came from Germany, but I wish you luck in finding work."

"Where did you get that ox? It sure would be some good eating."

"That's Tex and I can assure you that no one is going to eat him. He is a working animal," Joseph announced.

"We don't see any brand on him."

"He doesn't need a brand because he's got me to protect him. Now I will be on my way."

The two riders looked at each other and decided it might be best to keep on going. They headed in the direction Joseph had just come from.

As Joseph resumed his trek, he saw darkened clouds approaching from the west. Believing a storm was on the way he stopped and fastened the tattered tent around the trunk and box. A fast moving, hard rain was followed by some grape sized hail. He found cover under the cart but there was no protection for Tex. The storm quickly passed but Joseph stopped for the day because of the wet ground. He managed to capture enough rainwater to fill his water container.

There was good grazing for Tex and he had his fill of fresh water from the crevices in the ground. As planned, Joseph propped up the front part of the cart with the supports he had made so he could sleep on it. To make room for himself he placed the trunk on top of the box.

Joseph was awakened the next morning by sounds of howling coyotes. At first, they sounded like they were far away but coming from different directions. Soon they sounded closer but then quickly faded away. He assumed that they had closed in on a deer or other wild animal.

The rain had soaked in, but the mosquitoes were a real nuisance. It seemed that they multiplied with every step he made on the damp grass and weeds. In addition, the wheels were squeaking louder as they turned. Joseph wished the squeaking wheels would scare the mosquitoes away.

When making a slight turn on the trail, Joseph noticed something light colored in the brush a good distance away. After a closer look he found human bones. He assumed the person had died of disease or starvation until he saw a hole in the skull. He then speculated that the hole came from a gunshot or arrow. He removed his hat and said a prayer.

Later in the day, as he was looking for a good stopping place for the night when he thought he heard a voice. As he went further, he heard a cry for help.

"Where are you?" Joseph shouted.

"I'm over here by these trees. I broke my leg and need help," someone replied.

"I'll be right there," Joseph hollered. He proceeded with caution should it be a trap.

It wasn't a trap, but a man lying on the ground with a broken leg and a shot gun not far away.

"What happened?" asked Joseph.

"I was in the oak tree when I shot a wild turkey, but I fell when I was coming down from that heavy limb. I am so glad to see you. My name is Andrew."

"My name is Joseph. I think we can get you fixed up. I'll work on the leg while you are thinking about how you will reward me with a Texas home cooked meal and a drink of whiskey," he said while quickly straightening out his leg. He could tell Andrew was in severe pain.

"Now don't' move. I'm going to make some splints and come right back to put them on," he said.

After the leg was wrapped up Joseph got the ox and cart and helped him get on it. He then asked, "Where is that turkey?"

"It should be over there in those bushes. It will be the best meal you ever had," Andrew said with a groan.

Joseph found and inspected the big bird and then put it on the cart.

Andrew said, "My place is about a mile from here. We'll go down a little way and then make a turn to the left. I can tell you when."

Donna was in the kitchen of their two-room house when she heard a squeaking noise. She looked out of the window and saw her husband on the cart. She ran outside and was followed by their two young children.

After Andrew described what happened and the introductions made, she and Joseph helped him into the house and onto the bed. She inspected her husband's leg and thanked Joseph for rescuing him.

Joseph said, "I believe I will go out and feather the turkey."

Donna replied, "I'm so glad. That will give me time to fix a little something for supper. I can prepare the turkey in the morning."

The children watched as Joseph struggled with the turkey. The feathers were harder to pull out then he expected. Anticipating that, Donna came out with a bucket of warm water and suggested he dip the turkey in it. The feathers, large and small, then were much easier to remove.

When supper was finished Donna said, "I know a good meadow where your ox can graze. Is he tame enough for me to take him there?"

"I think so. Tex is getting used to the routine and should cooperate. If not, I'll give him a good lecture," he answered.

"I've never met an ox with a name," she replied. "I think Tex and I will get along just fine."

The children followed their mother and the ox to the meadow. Their dog was not far behind.

Joseph pulled up a stool while Andrew remained on the bed with his leg extended.

Andrew said, "Joseph, thanks to Donna, I can provide that home cooked meal tomorrow, but we don't have any whiskey in the house. I will have to honor that request another time."

"I was just kidding about the whiskey. I only wanted to distract you when we set the leg. It worked and that part is over with," Joseph replied.

"I'll get well soon. I have a family to feed. Tomorrow Donna will take me to the village to find a doctor and maybe something for the pain. Soon things will get back to normal."

"You have a nice family."

"We're lucky and happy here. You know, we have seen a lot of strangers coming through these parts recently. They have created more conversations than anything since Goliad."

"What's Goliad?"

"I thought everyone knew about the Goliad Massacre!"

"When did it happen?"

"It was about a decade ago and not very far from here."

"I was young then and maybe the news didn't make it to my hometown in Germany."

"Maybe you had your own problems to worry about!"

"That could be. I do remember my parents talking about a place called the Alamo where many soldiers were killed."

"That's right. Almost two hundred defenders were greatly outnumbered at the Alamo and then wiped out by General Santa Anna's army. A couple of weeks later almost twice that many Texans, including volunteers, fought his forces but again were greatly outnumbered. They surrendered as prisoners of war and were taken to Goliad," he added.

"What happened then?"

"They locked them up in an old Spanish fort. About a week later, on Palm Sunday, they let them out but surprised and massacred them."

"What did that dictator do next?"

"He marched his armies eastward to San Jacinto where we, under Sam Houston, defeated them and captured him."

"That's good. Have you been to any of those places?"

"Yes, I was in the battle of San Jacinto."

"Those must have been difficult times."

"Yes, they were, but that's how I managed to get this land that we are on. Texas did not have much money, but it had lots of land. Many fighters were awarded land grants for helping in the cause."

"Thanks for the lesson. I'm sure I'll learn more about the history around here as time goes on."

"You will but also remember that the difficult times are far from over. Texas is still an untamed and rugged wilderness."

Andrew and Joseph then heard Donna and the children returning with Tex. Knowing Andrew was in pain and wanted some rest Joseph went outside. He fastened the beams of his cart to a large tree in the yard and got a good night's sleep.

Pleasant smells were coming from the house in the morning as Donna was preparing the wild turkey. Joseph stayed outside to mend his tent. The children enjoyed the ox and playing and jumping off the cart.

During the morning Andrew told Joseph where his axel grease was stored so he could cut the noise of the cart. In this land he knew it would be safer not to be heard.

For Joseph, it was now time for the big event. Sweet potatoes, squash, gravy, and cornbread were served with the tender turkey meat. Everybody got their fill and Donna presented Joseph with the leftovers as he prepared to leave. As he pulled out of the yard, they all expressed their desire to see each other again.

The ox, Joseph thought, would be content to settle down somewhere along the way but he would finish what he had started regardless of the hardships and dangers he encountered. He noticed that the squeaking noise of the wheels had diminished. To pass the time, he thought about counting the revolutions of the wheels to calculate the distance traveled but perhaps it was best to stay alert for snakes and other hazards.

The days were now getting warmer. Some clear stretches of land made it easier to make better time, but then high weeds or thick brush often slowed him down. Whatever the conditions were, it was important to keep on moving.

Joseph and Texs stopped when they came to a muddy creek. It was passable but he noticed that it was leading down to a larger body of water. He tied the halter to a tree limb and walked down to get a better look. The creek was draining into a river. The water tasted cool and fresh so he headed back to the cart to get his water container.

When he got back he was surprised to see two boys, about twelve and thirteen years old, on his cart trying to break into his trunk. He had no intention of using his pistol, but he kept it visible when he slipped up behind them and shouted, "What are you boys up to?"

"Nothing, we just have never seen such a nice trunk and just wanted to see it," the younger boy said.

"Already you have done two things wrong. First, you tried to steal what I have in my trunk and second, you lied about it. I watched you trying to break into it. Take me to your parents because we're going to have a good talk," Joseph replied.

"No," the older boy pleaded. "We will get punished. We won't do it again."

"What are your names?" asked Joseph.

"I'm Don and this is my brother Raymond," the older boy said.

"Don, my ox looks hungry. You go along that creek and pull as much of the tall grass as you can and bring it back and give it to him. Raymond, you stay here until he gets back," Joseph said.

"Raymond, now you take my water container down to the river but above the muddy creek. Fill it with fresh water and bring it back and load it on my cart. I suggest you don't run off with my container because your brother is going to stay here where I can watch him," Joseph ordered.

When Raymond finished the task Joseph said, "Now, both of you show me your hands."

With a worried look the boys raised and showed Joseph their hands. Joseph looked at them and said, "Those hands just now did something useful. They are meant for work, play, and eating. They are not meant to take something that doesn't belong to you."

"Now," he added. "I'm leaving but I want both of you to stand right here until you both make up your minds that you won't steal again."

Joseph took off on the trail ahead and did not look back. He was glad that his possessions were still all accounted for.

He went a little farther and found a good spot to stop for the night. It started to drizzle so he draped the tent over the spindles of the cart and went to sleep.

Joseph woke up to the pleasant sounds of cooing doves in the trees around him. It seemed they were communicating with each other and maybe it was about his presence in their habitat. He curled back the side of the makeshift tent so see that the drizzle had stopped. He watched a cottontail rabbit dart across the small clearing in front of him. He looked up and saw a bird of prey soaring overhead apparently looking for an unsuspecting rodent.

Joseph had exhausted his rations and leftovers and looked for something to eat while Tex was grazing nearby. Tex, he thought, was fortunate to have fresh spring-time growth all around him when he, the owner, could find little for nourishment. He found some wild grapes, but they were wrapped up in itchy ivy and thistles.

The squirrels too were making quiet a fuss while digging under some dry leaves...he could have shot one for food but did not want to waste ammunition on such a small animal.

Back on the trail, he soon came across another grave. Weeds were sprouting on top of it. Since he knew of no settlements in the area, he suspected that another German immigrant was buried there. He removed his hat and prayed.

A little later, he saw something out of place on the trail ahead. He came to an abrupt stop as he spotted a large curled up rattlesnake. Joseph slowly withdrew his pistol and shot it. When it stopped squirming, he recalled that Andrew had mentioned that rattlers were safe to eat and tasted good. He picked it up gingerly and put it on the bed of his cart.

After finding a good stopping place for the night, Joseph started a campfire from some of the dead limbs scattered about. After examining the rattles of the snake he skinned and cleaned it. After he added some seasoning, he put it on his skewer and cooked it for a long time. "It wasn't bad," he said to himself. It satisfied his hunger and he decided he could eat rattlesnake again.

Slowly and surely Joseph and his trusted animal continued the journey. By now the altitude had increased some and the countryside was not as flat as when he had started. Larger trees were more abundant and there was some higher ground enabling him to see farther.

He stopped when he saw something in the distance. Through his telescope he could see that it was a covered wagon. As he got closer, he saw a man examining one of his two draught animals. The man saw Joseph and waited for him. There was a woman on the seat of the wagon.

"It looks like you've got trouble," Joseph said.

"This ox has been slowing down and can't seem to pull anymore," the man answered.

"My name is Joseph. Let me look at it. I spent my life on the farm," he said.

"I appreciate it. My name is Max. I'm a pharmacist and don't have a lot of experience with cattle. What do you think?" he asked.

Joseph felt around the animal's left front leg and then tried to get the ox to move forward. The animal tried but the strain of pulling the heavy load prevented it from going very far.

"He's gone lame and can't handle his share of the load. It is odd because just the other day I helped a man that broke his leg, but I don't know how to fix this," Joseph said.

Max looked up at his wife on the wagon seat and said, "This is my wife, Sarah. My daughter, Jenell, is lying down in the bed of the wagon. Both are having respiratory problems, especially my daughter. We had problems on the ship, at the bay, and now in this wilderness."

Sarah forced a smile and he heard Jenell say, "I'm sorry. I just can't see anybody now. I feel too bad." Joseph saw her raise her hand as if to greet him.

After a pause Joseph said, "To me it looks like you folks need a rest and time to get well. I have an idea."

"I would like to hear it," replied Max.

The map I made for myself shows a small town ahead. Why don't we have Tex, my ox, replace your lame ox so you can go there. In town you should be able to find a place to stay for a while until everybody gets well. While there, you should be able to find another ox to buy," Joseph suggested.

"If your ox has a name it must be a good one, but we can't leave you alone out here," Sarah said.

"Don't worry about me. Max can return Tex to me tomorrow and then I can give him a ride back on my cart," Joseph answered.

"That's a good idea. Thanks for helping us out and I will be back tomorrow for sure. What should we do with the lame ox?" Max asked.

"Leave it here and you can decide that tomorrow," Joseph said.

"That is so generous of you to offer us your transportation to someone you just met. How can we repay you?" asked Sarah.

"I know there is no risk in loaning you my animal. I'm going to do a little fishing while you are gone but if I don't catch anything, I could handle a sausage or some jerky," Joseph said with a grin.

"We will find something for you. For now, we can give you some potatoes and carrots that we bought from a settler," Sarah said.

Joseph and Max made the ox switch. The third ox patiently waited. As they left with Tex, Max said, "One good thing about our choice of draft animals is that they haven't stampeded on us."

Joseph laughed and waved them on.

After Joseph found some grass for the injured ox he went fishing in the nearby river. He took his staff should he see another rattler and to use it for a fishing pole. He saw a water moccasin in the water near the bank of the river, but it quickly ducked out of sight.

He tied a string with a weight and a hook to the end of his staff, baited the hook with a grasshopper, and dropped the line beneath an overhanging tree.

After what seemed like a long time there was a sharp tug on the line. He pulled it up and found that he lost his bait, so he looked around and captured another grasshopper. Almost instantly the line stretched out and he hooked something. It was a nice size catfish.

That evening, under the stars of Texas, Joseph enjoyed a feast of fresh catfish, potatoes, and carrots. After he had his fill, he watched the many stars above and tried to identify the many wild sounds of the night.

While zipping on a cup of coffee the next morning, Joseph reviewed the map he had made and checked his compass as he had done so many times. He felt that he was traveling too much in a northerly direction when his destination was northwest of where he was.

After considerable and agonizing thought he decided he would abandon the trail he had been following and search for a more direct route.

That meant that he would have to cross the river. Not knowing what time Max would return with his ox he decided to make good use of his time to find the best place to cross the river. He left Max a note saying he would be back soon.

With his wooden staff he went upstream in hopes of finding a shallow place but couldn't find such a place. He gave some thought to building a raft for his trunk and storage box.

But first he decided to backtrack and follow the river downstream. Going in the opposite direction didn't seem very productive to him, but he eventually came to a spot that had a gentle slope down to the water and it appeared shallow enough to walk across. With his wooden staff he felt his way to the other side and was convinced that his rig could make it.

Shortly after he returned to the cart, he heard someone coming his way. It was Max on horseback returning his ox.

"Joseph, we finally had some good luck," Max said before he unsaddled. He then tied Tex to the limb of a tree.

"Where did you get that horse?" asked Joseph.

"It's not mine. I just borrowed it to deliver your ox and some food to you. Sarah sent some sausage, jerky and bread," he said.

"That sounds good. What happened?"

"We actually never made it to the town you mentioned. Before we got there, we ran into a rancher looking for a stray calf. We told him about our situation, and he said we could recuperate in his bunkhouse as his hands had left for a cattle drive."

"That's good. Tell me more."

"He said I should try to bring the lame ox back and if it didn't heal, he could locate another one for us. The best part is that Sarah and Jenell will have a place and some time to get well."

"Your news could not be better than that."

"Joseph, we have to thank you for getting us out of a jam. We will never forget it."

"I'm glad that I was able to help. Now, let me tell you what I have decided to do."

"What's that?"

"I think I can shorten my trip by a few days by going a different way. I'm going to cross the river below here and take a more direct route to the land grant. I'm anxious to get there."

"Are you sure you want to do that? No telling who or what you might run into."

"I thought about it a lot. I'm going to do it."

Max paused and said, "Good luck. It will take us much longer to get to the interior, but we will get there. It is a very large state, but if we're lucky, we will cross paths again."

"I hope so. It's nice to know you and give my best wishes to your wife and daughter," Joseph said as they shook hands and parted.

Joseph watched Max leave on horseback leading the ailing ox behind him. He thought the animal was walking quite well after the rest and not having to pull a heavy load.

When they were out of sight, he thought about the people he had met along the way but did not know if he would ever see them again. Would he meet or recognize anybody else from his native land? Would he receive any mail from his family in Germany considering the many obstacles and hardships he had already witnessed?

As he sampled the jerky, he saw large, dark clouds coming from the west.

He tied the trunk, box, water, and tent securely to the corners and spindles of the cart so that they would not slide or be washed away when crossing the river. He made a trial run first by carrying his rifle, pistol, and food to the other side.

Soaking wet he untied Tex and stepped into the river. Tex was hesitant but followed his master. For Joseph, the water was knee deep and getting deeper. Tex was having problems with his footing but struggled forward.

In the middle of the river the water reached the frame of the cart. The force of the current against it caused it to swing downstream putting more pressure on Tex. Fortunately, Joseph then stepped on higher ground and yanked on the yoke prompting Tex to lunge and splash ahead. Joseph and his possessions finally made it to the opposite bank. Everything was wet and muddy but still intact.

Joseph found a level place to stop and stretched the tent over the spindles of the cart and tied it down. With heavy rain pounding on the tent he enjoyed his sausage and bread. Although he had not covered much ground that day, he felt he made progress by having crossed the river and was starting a shorter route.

The problem with the shorter route was that there wasn't a visible trail to follow. Joseph now would have to use his compass, the sun, and his judgment to locate the society's headquarters at the land grant. Additionally, he anticipated that the telescope Captain Harris had given him would come in handy to study the landscape.

He pressed onward but soon found that he couldn't always travel in a straight line. Frequently he had to alter his course to avoid creeks, draws, thick brush and mesquite trees with very sharp thorns. He, however, welcomed many small meadows that were surrounded by majestic oak trees and beautiful wildflowers of many colors.

His thoughts were interrupted by a brownish hawk that suddenly lifted from the branch of a dead tree and snatched a small snake off the ground.

It had been a warm day and he was pleased to see the sun setting in the west. He spotted a shade tree and stopped for the night. Just then he heard a buzzing sound high above. He looked up and saw massive bee activity coming from a hole in a tree. He went a little farther and found another shade tree. There were no bees there but later in the night he was awakened by the repeated sounds of an owl hooting in the night.

With aching feet on a foggy morning, Joseph struck out again in the direction he had chosen. Suddenly something running through a wooded area got his attention. It was a deer, a yearling, being chased by a large shaggy coyote. They quickly disappeared out of sight. He recalled Andrew saying that some people call them "prairie wolves" and that a pack of them could chase and wear out a large animal and then corner and devour it. He hoped the yearling had escaped the sharp jaws of the predators.

Later in the day Joseph noticed that the land he was approaching looked different. There was not as much underbrush and some of the cedar and mesquite trees had been cut and burned. He saw cattle tracks and droppings indicating a good spring calf crop for someone.

He watched for sheds or pens but was surprised when a man and a boy on horseback abruptly pulled out in front of him.

"Hey, you," the man said, "Don't you know this is private property?"

"No, I didn't, but I did notice the land looked like it's been improved for grazing. Is it too late to ask if I can just pass through? I won't hurt anything," Joseph answered.

"At least you weren't trying to sneak through," the boy said. "We could hear the squeaky wheels for a long time."

"Oh yes. I greased the wheels a few days ago but I guess the rain and the river washed some of it away."

"Next time you can apply some cactus leaves...there's plenty of them around here. By the way my name is Gerald Baker," the man said in a softer tone.

"I'm Joseph Schmidt and I'm from Germany to start a new life in Texas. I'm on the way to a land grant," he replied.

"Well, you've got a goodways to go. My name is Skip Baker," the boy said. "You do not look very dangerous so why don't you rest a bit."

"Thanks, do you mind if I water Tex by your creek over there?" Joseph asked.

Gerald laughed and said, "Any ox that has such a distinguished name can drink all the water it wants. Also, it wouldn't hurt our feelings if you took a bath down there. Then you can let Tex graze and you can join us on the porch at the house. It's just around the corner."

Joseph felt refreshed after a swim in the creek and he was surprised that he was invited to the house. On his arrival, Gerald introduced him to his wife, Fran, and another son named Arthur.

Fran said, "Skip is sixteen years old and Arthur is thirteen. They are both a big help on the ranch. Now I know you are hungry so I'm going in to fix a big pot of stew."

"Joseph, we don't have visitors out here very often. I'm going to have a little whiskey. Would you like some?" Gerald asked.

Joseph was surprised when he answered by saying, "Yes, it's been a long time since I've had some."

Gerald poured two small cups while Skip and Arthur watched. He then said, "I'm sorry if I was a little rude to you today but out here you sometimes don't know who you can trust. It might be a cattle rustler, a horse thief, or someone just looking for trouble."

"That's okay and I understand."

"It may be worse where you are going because that area hasn't been settled yet."

"I'll be careful. I want to develop my land so I can raise crops and animals. My father said the land is the basis for a healthy and vigorous society. I can see you are providing red meat for those living in urban areas."

"We're trying. It's hard to do in these open ranges. Branding the cattle helps but it doesn't stop some from stealing them for meat or hides. Have you thought about branding your ox?"

"No. I don't have a brand, but I will have one soon."

"Why don't we brand your ox Tex? He wouldn't like it, but he would prefer it over being slaughtered."

"That makes sense."

"Good. Why don't you help Skip and me round up stray cows in the morning... you can use Arthur's horse because he has a chore to do. When we get back, we can shape some metal good enough to brand your herd of one. Then we can put some grease of the wheels on your cart."

"I can't think of anything I'd rather do. I'll be ready at the break of day," Joseph replied.

The next day developed as planned. Most of all, Joseph enjoyed riding the horse around the ranch as they were checking on the cattle and calves. They were in good shape due to the abundant vegetation from the recent rains, but some had strayed too far. When Gerald was satisfied that they were safe and accounted for they returned to the barnyard.

Greasing the cart wheels was much easier than producing a brand design for Tex and then burning it on him. Fortunately, the agony for the ox did not take long. Gerald said, "It was about as much fun for the ox as a human having a tooth pulled."

As they returned to the house Arthur was moving stacked firewood from one place to another to avoid a huge and growing ant nest. He didn't look happy while doing it, and according to Skip it was punishment for having told his parents a fib.

As the riders were unsaddling their horses Fran came out and invited Joseph to stay on their place another night since it was late in the day and she had prepared enough food to include him.

After the meal Gerald, Fran, and Joseph gathered on the porch as the sun was setting. They were ignored by a black and white woodpecker that had located some insects in their tall oak tree. Skip and Arthur went for a swim in the creek.

"Joseph, you are pretty good on that horse. Thanks for helping us out today," Gerald said.

"I like horses and enjoyed it because I've been traveling so slowly with my ox. I should be the one to thank you for the meals and the help with the cart and the branding," he answered.

"We've enjoyed having you here and wish you well as you finish your journey," Fran said.

"This has been a nice change for me. Even Tex, with his new brand, has less chance of being stolen. Talking about changes, I've been in this country for a short while and already there has been a change of government flags," Joseph said.

"There were other flags as well," she said. "The natives here watched the Spanish and French flags go up many years ago. The Mexico flag went up much more recently.

"What happened after that?"

"A brutal man named Lopez de Santa Anna, with the help of his corrupt followers, eventually took over the government. The settlers in Texas refused to live under a dictatorship and declared its independence from Mexico. We became the Republic of Texas in March of eighteen thirty-six."

"What then?"

"Santa Anna brought his big army up here and tried to get Texas back. He failed but we lost a lot of lives."

"I heard about that. A few days ago, I met a man named Andrew who told me about the loss of life at the Alamo and at Goliad."

"Many of those that got killed came from around here. My brother was a volunteer and was one of them," she said

"I'm sorry to hear that. As I continue my trek tomorrow I will think and pray for him. I didn't know him, but I have freedom because of his courage."

Noticing that Fran was on the verge of crying Gerald said, "Now, since Texas just recently joined the United States, we can fly that flag, but we haven't seen one yet around here. Have you?"

"Yes, I saw some back at Ensenada because the military was coming through there on the way to the Mexico border to settle a boundary dispute. The flag is red, white, and blue and has stars and stripes on it," he answered.

"It looks like we have another war on our hands. At least this time we should be better organized and equipped to handle it," Gerald said.

"I hope so. It sure would be nice to live in peace and always have leaders that would not get absorbed by money and power," Joseph said.

After the boys returned from their swim in the creek, the gathering broke up and everyone turned in.

Before departure the next morning, Joseph checked the ox's burn from the branding iron and found that it had started to heal. He made sure the leather strap would not rub against its wound.

Last evening's conversation with Mr. and Mrs. Baker was still on his mind as the wheels of the cart turned and turned. He thought about all those that had died for freedom's sake and prayed for Fran's brother as he had promised.

His forward progress was slowed down by more wet and dry creeks. Some of them had a lot of vegetation along them making it difficult and time consuming to find a large enough opening for Tex and cart to go through. Joseph slipped and fell in a boggy creek but, he quickly recovered.

When he reached the opposite bank, he spotted a pile of belongings that looked like they had been discarded by someone having to lighten their load. A big kettle was mixed in with some pieces of furniture. From there he came to a high point where he pulled out his telescope to study the view, but he did not see anything but more hills and another creek bed. He traveled a little farther and put Tex out to graze.

By noon the next day traveling seemed a little easier. As he continued down a gentle slope, a river bend came into view, so he went down for a look. Since the sun was shining brightly and the water was cool and clear he decided to stop for the day. While Tex grazed, Joseph swam and washed his clothes in the river and hung it out to dry. Then he unpacked his spade and dug up some worms in a wet area near the bank so he could do some fishing. After catching four perch about the size of his hand he cooked and had a good meal.

When he finished eating, he watched the slowly moving stream and listened to the many birds coming in for a drink. When darkness fell, he was startled when he heard a shot that sounded like it came from downstream. He doused his fire and hoped the smell of it and the fish would not attract someone downwind who might have seen him or his possessions. After bringing Tex closer to his campsite, he decided to stand watch for the night. With his pistol and his rifle by his side he sat on a log at the foot of a tall tree.

Joseph was tired and hungry at the break of day but relieved that the only sounds of the night were made by raccoons and other critters. The river was no longer visible as he continued walking on his sore legs and blistered feet.

Soon after seeing tracts made by domestic animals he found and followed a road that had been carved out by the carts and wagons. He got up on the bed of the cart, and through his telescope, he could see a settlement in the distance.

5

The sight of the settlement made Joseph forget how weary he was from the sleepless night and the weeks of trudging along. As he got closer he noticed a sign on a tree that welcomed him to the town of Schattendorf. This was not his destination, but he should be able to get some rest for himself and Tex.

The town, he thought, did not resemble the many villages in Germany that had been there for hundreds of years. There weren't any tall church steeples or mansions. Schattendorf was a settlement with few finished houses and buildings. There was, however, considerable activity in town with younger children playing in the yards and older children and adults working in their gardens. Joseph was pleased to see chickens and farm animals.

It apparently was not uncommon for people to see an ox or cart in town but one with a big brand like Tex got some attention. A small girl hollered "Hello Tex" and ran and into a small house to report it to whoever was inside.

When he came to a treed area by a flowing stream, he found a good spot to spend the night and catch up on his sleep. Also, there was good grazing for his hungry ox.

The town roosters made sure Joseph didn't oversleep the next morning. He tried to wake up and wondered where he could get a cup of coffee without having to make his own.

He was checking on the ox when he noticed a little girl and man coming his way. As they got closer, he recognized her to be the same girl that greeted Tex the day before.

"I want to show my Father your ox named Tex," the girl said.

"You are both welcome to look at him as much as you want," he replied.

"Hello Joseph," the man said.

Surprised, Joseph said, "Franz, I didn't recognize you with that beard. I'm so glad to see somebody from back home."

"It's good to see you too," Franz answered. "Why don't you come to our place and we can talk, and you can meet my wife, Carolina."

The little girl looked up and said, "My name is Anna and I'm already seven years old."

"Anna, I'm glad to know you. Since you are a big girl you can ride back on my cart. Does your Mother know how to make coffee?"

"Yes, my Mama can cook anything."

"Good. Let's get on our way."

They soon arrived at the one room house that had one entrance, two small windows, and a dirt floor. Carolina too was glad to see someone from the Baumberg area. She made coffee outside over a fire and they all sat down on some benches.

Franz said, "This house was vacated by another family who left to get closer to the land grant. We haven't decided when we're going there ourselves. We've had some sickness and we're not sure about the conditions in those hills. I don't think the Comanche Indians are happy about others settling on the land that they have occupied for such a long time."

"I sure hope that they don't give us any problems. There seems to be enough land here for everyone. As for myself, I plan on heading out of here in a few days. Have you seen anyone else here from the Baumberg area?" Joseph asked.

"Yes. Philip, Marie, and their two children left here with a large group not long ago. You might see them where you are going," Franz said.

"I think I know who you're talking about. I did hear they were heading to Texas and I hope to run into them. What's happening around here?" he asked.

"I'm making a little money by helping a prominent family build a house not far from here. I've got blisters on my hands and a sore back from cutting down trees and squaring them off. It will be a nice sturdy house when it is finished," Franz said.

"I want to see what you've done but today I'm going to take it easy and walk around town a little bit and see what's happening. Do you mind if I leave Tex and my cart here?" he asked.

"Of course, you can. Since you are staying here a few days we can stack your things inside the house. Anna will enjoy watching Tex," Franz answered.

"Have you heard about the celebration we're having this weekend?" Carolina asked.

"No. What celebration?"

"On Saturday evening, we will have music, dancing, food, and beer for everyone. You will probably see the preparations for it when you go downtown. It's about time we stopped and had some fun," she said.

"I couldn't agree with you more and I'll see you all there. Franz, if I can get your help in bringing in my trunk and box I'll be on my way," Joseph said.

There was very little extra room in the house but a corner was cleared and Joseph's possessions were placed on top of each other.

It felt unusual for Joseph to be walking without his staff or cart. The newcomers in Schattendorf were busy tending to their gardens, talking to their neighbors, and improving their modest living quarters.

Downtown there were few business establishments or recognizable public buildings. There was a shaded area that had been cleared of brush and groomed. From a volunteer worker there he learned that this is where the Saturday celebration would be and that someday a recreational hall would be built on it.

Near there and around the corner was another cleared area with a large oak tree. A sign on the tree said there would be a church service there on Sunday morning. Joseph was delighted to see it and planned to attend. The tree was large and had long, thick limbs. The lower branches were almost parallel to the ground.

At a general store Joseph bought coffee, salt, and pepper. At a feed store he bought work gloves and axle grease. The proprietors were friendly and talked about the weather.

As he left the feed store a man sitting on a bench asked Joseph, "Hey, aren't you the one with that ox named Tex?"

"Yes, I am. He and I started out at Ensenada and soon we'll be working our land on the land grant. Who are you?" Joseph asked.

"My name is Augustus and I'm going there myself if things ever get better for me and my family."

"What do you mean?"

"We had to wait for transportation when we were at Ensenada and again here at Schattendorf. I hear that our sponsor is having some serious financial problems."

"I think you are right. We even talked about that at Ensenada. I think they probably underestimated the costs involved and the number of people wanting to come here. Basically, I'm providing my own transportation."

"Young man, I admire you for that. I can't do that because my wife is sick and too weak to travel."

"It'll work out for you. You've come this far. My name is Joseph."

"Thanks Joseph. I enjoyed talking to you and take good care of your ox because he deserves it. I wish it had some relatives around here."

Joseph laughed and left.

The next morning Joseph started getting ready for the trip. Again, he greased the axel and inspected the spokes of the wheels. He tightened some of the wooden joints on the cart as they had shrunk and or had expanded from the wet and sometimes dry conditions on the way.

When Joseph was satisfied he went to see if Franz had returned from his job. He had not so Carolina gave Joseph directions to where he was.

The job site was just a short distance away. Franz was pleased to see him and show him what he and the other workers had done on the house.

The foundation was in place giving a good indication of what the house would look like when it was finished. It would have two large rectangular rooms that were separated in the middle by an open porch. The roof would cover all three parts.

A fireplace was planned for each room. One room would be a bedroom and contain furniture and heirlooms that had been shipped from Germany by the owner. The other room would be the kitchen and dining area.

Because the two rooms were separated, heat coming from the kitchen in the summer months would not have an adverse effect on the other room. The open area in the middle would likely become a hangout for a dog that would welcome or warn anybody coming to the house.

Fallen oak trees and their shavings and dust were all around. Franz said an outhouse would be built on the back end of the lot.

Next he showed Joseph the saws they used to cut down the trees and cut up the fallen ones. He held up a long two handled saw and said, "Joseph, the type of saw and its teeth are important but so are the sawyers on each end. If you were on the other end of this saw, we could finish this job much sooner."

"Thanks, but my schedule doesn't give me time. Would you show me how you cut those ends, so they'll fit when they meet at the corners?"

"I sure will," Franz said

After Franz showed him his techniques Joseph said, "I may not have another worker at the other end of the saw when I start in. I should find the right kind of saw when I get there because the society agreed to furnish equipment for us. I do have a good broad axe."

"You seem to have everything planned and I'll look you up if we ever get there."

"Thanks for the building hints. Now I'm going swimming. I'll see you tonight at the celebration."

It was still daylight when Joseph arrived for the celebration. Noticing that almost everyone else brought a dish or drinks he put a donation into a small bucket that was there for that purpose. There was a variety of chairs and benches around an area that would serve as the dance floor. Jovial band members were busy testing their instruments.

He was pleased to see Augustus and his wife and Franz with his family already there. He also recognized a few others he had seen since his arrival in town. It was good to see people of all ages out for a night of fun.

They got in line to eat before the hot food would get cold and the cold food would get warm. They were also worried that they might run out of food.

The beer was available for adults and the music started shortly. The small children were the first to swing back and forth or hop up and down with the music. The parents followed and at times picked up their little ones and danced around in a large circle.

Joseph watched the fun, drank beer, and enjoyed listening to the music that he had heard so often while growing up in his hometown of Baumberg. Suddenly, he was pulled out of his chair to dance by Augustus's wife, Carolina. Anna, and other women that were much older or younger than he was. He could find no one near his age who was not married to dance with him. He heard no one complain about his dancing but little Anna was the only one to ask him to dance the second time.

The music got louder and faster as the evening progressed. Between tunes, the band members shouted out jokes of which most had been heard before, but they were still funny, and everyone laughed. Those too old to continue dancing sang and swayed with the music well into the night.

Eventually everything started slowing down and people started leaving. Joseph decided he would have one more beer and then return to his cart. In the darkness and after too much beer it took him a while.

On Sunday morning there were no roosters to wake him up. When he finally did, he jumped up, got ready, and headed to where the church service was taking place.

He was disappointed and felt guilty when he found that the service was finishing. He waited until it was over and the crowd had mingled and left. After the alter table was taken away and the priest was packing his religious items Joseph walked up to him and introduced himself.

"I'm Father Fontaine," the priest answered. "I will be finished very soon. You may wait for me by the tree."

Joseph went to the long, low hanging limb of the old tree. Father Fontaine soon joined him and they had a long conversation. The priest blessed Joseph and then they shook hands, smiled, and parted.

Joseph felt better as he headed back to his cart. He led Tex to the outskirts of town to graze. While waiting, he realized his blisters were healing and his legs were not as sore. He then decided to visit Franz and his family.

Franz, Carolina, and Anna were sitting in the shade when he arrived. They were talking about the fun they had had at the town's celebration. Little Anna decided she would like to go for a walk.

"That's a good idea," said Carolina. "That will give us a chance to see how your work on the Hofmann house is coming along."

The four immigrants slowly took off on their Sunday afternoon walk. They stopped to greet others on the way but were often urged by Anna to go faster.

When they got to the Hofmann construction site, Mr. Hofmann was there looking at the workmanship. After introductions, they all walked around to verify that the foundation was sturdy and level. The timbers for the walls scattered around the foundation had been selected to be as straight as possible to protect its occupants from the elements and insects...a filler would be applied later as a seal.

Noticing that Joseph was interested in the construction, Mr. Hofmann asked Joseph, "Are you interested in helping on this job? I can pay you and my family could move in sooner."

"It's hard for me to turn you down because I have worked as a carpenter. But I am anxious to move on and build my own house. I know Franz is doing a good job for you. I do thank you for asking," Joseph answered.

"That's all right. Good luck and I am sure you will reach your goal. I hope we meet again," he said.

On their return to the house they admired the many blue, red, and yellow wildflowers along the way. Anna, with objections, was put to bed early as Carolina would resume her schooling the next morning. A little later Franz and Joseph loaded the trunk and the box on the cart so Joseph could get an early start the next morning.

The dirt streets of Schattendorf were quiet the next morning as Joseph started out. The trail that he was following had been etched in by immigrants before him. But soon the topography started to change. The hills were taller and the countryside more rugged. Draws had long since been carved deep into the earth exposing colorful rocks and formations.

The uncertainty of what was ahead made Joseph think about the job offer he had turned down in Schattendorf. Should he have accepted it and made some more money? Should he have waited to join a group of immigrants that might offer greater protection from desperadoes? What if he got sick like so many others on their way to the interior of Texas?

He erased those thoughts when he came to a large pool of water with a small waterfall pouring into it. He stopped to water Tex and take advantage of the lush grass. Joseph then sat down under a tree to enjoy fruit that he had been given.

In a thick cedar bush nearby, he noticed a cardinal. Then another cardinal joined it and brought food. The dark green bush behind them made them more visible and their red color even brighter.

Joseph wanted to stay longer but knew he must keep moving. The draw made a turn to the right and then to a large open area with very few trees. As he traveled through it, the sun was intense. Not having anyone to talk to he told Tex, "I now know why these Texans have such wide brim hats; it is because they throw more shade over your neck and shoulders. I think the sailors on the ship wore small hats so they wouldn't blow away. I guess I'm not in style anymore."

Tex did not dispute his master's theory.

Near the end of the day, Joseph moved through a small valley with hills on both sides. Since there were some water holes, he decided to stop for the night. He propped up the cart and led Tex to an area where he could graze and tied the halter to a tree branch.

Curious about his surroundings he hiked to the top of the tallest hill to study them with his telescope. It was steep so he took his staff for support and his rifle and pistol should he need them. It was a brushy hill and had lots of gravel and rocks on it. He had to watch his step as a misstep could cause him to slip and fall.

At the top he could see in every direction. Thinking he saw movement, he focused on the trail up ahead. It was a man on horseback coming in his direction.

Knowing he didn't have time to get down in enough time to secure his property he hid behind some mesquite brush.

The man reigned in his horse and looked all around. The man had seen the cart but was more interested in the ox. The man looked around again, jumped off his horse, and ran toward Tex.

Joseph was ready with his rifle and pistol and decided to fire the pistol into the air. The shot scared the man, so he quickly turned around, mounted his horse and raced away.

Joseph reloaded his pistol and slowly came down the hill. Tex was safe and the cattle rustler kept on riding. It took Joseph some time to get over the incident, but he was happy about the outcome. He felt that it was safe to stay where he was for the night.

While Tex grazed in the small valley Joseph spotted some dewberries near the creek bed. He gathered enough to eat and take along. It was a shame, he thought, that there was no way to make a dewberry pie.

The next morning, he was pleased that the eggs he brought from Shattendorf had survived the trip. He enjoyed his breakfast of coffee, scrambled eggs, and bread. The dewberries would come in handy later in the day.

There seemed to be no end to the up and down hills and obstacles of rocks and brush. Going uphill Joseph tried to help the struggling ox by attaching his lariat to the cart and pulling. There were times when it was better to push from the back side. Going downhill was a relief but if the grade was too steep, he tied the lariat to the rear of the cart to keep the cart from overwhelming Tex. When at a slant, he tied onto the upper side to keep it from turning over. During those times, going forward was slow.

Joseph was tired and hungry when got to a plateau overlooking a large valley. He could see for miles and a peaceful looking river far below looked inviting until he noticed some smoke rising. He unpacked his telescope to get a closer look.

There was some movement around a small fire. He could count four or five people mingling around. They looked like the Indians he had heard about. Their camp was near the trail he was on. There were more horses then men.

He checked his compass and map. He had already witnessed many incidents in just a few days so he decided not to continue on this trail. Since the breeze was coming from the southeast, he planned to go upstream and follow the western fringes of the trail where there was less chance of being seen. He then, as quietly as he could, applied more grease to the wheels of the cart to reduce the squeaking.

He turned to the west for a mile or so and could judge the distance to the river by the foliage and types of trees there. He then turned right and downhill toward the river hoping it would provide a good and safe place to cross.

When he reached the bottom, he came to a sizable pool of water. It seemed too deep to cross, but he could see shallows both up and down the river. He chose the shallows above the pool as it would be a greater distance from the Indian camp. There the water looked knee deep, but he would have to move some rocks to cover a hole in the middle to prevent injury to the ox or damage to his cargo.

He knew that crossing the stream with his possessions would stir up the sand and mud. Worried that the Indians might detect a change in the color of the water as it moved downstream, he waited until darkness to cross.

As he waited for nightfall a flock of wild turkeys came down to the riverbed to search for food. His mouth watered as he watched them, but he knew the sound of a shot would put him in even more danger.

When it was almost dark Joseph led Tex and the cart slowly across the river. Tex stopped for a drink and then pulled the cargo to the opposite bank. Then Joseph led the ox and its load up the bank and stopped in a grassy area under some tall trees. There was no moonlight for traveling so the night was spent there.

It was an uneasy night for the German immigrant. He did not know the intentions of the Indians that were camped not far away. He hoped the sounds of the night came from critters and not from Indians imitating them.

He was glad to see the first light of day so he could move on. He would have to travel further before he could risk looking for something to eat. By the afternoon, Joseph felt he had avoided trouble and could now concentrate more on what was ahead. He was getting weak from hunger and the grueling walk through the rugged hills.

Quiet unexpectedly Joseph came to a trail that resembled the trail he had previously been on. Just for a moment he thought about taking it up again when he saw a mound of dirt and rocks under a small oak tree. There were no inscriptions on it, but he assumed that another German immigrant had not made it to it's destination.

He knelt at the grave for a few minutes and then got up. He decided not to take the trail but try to stay on the eastern fringes of it. Although he made more progress on the level land it did not usually last long before he would have to go uphill or downhill again or negotiate a rocky draw.

He then came across a trail to the right that headed up to a small house and shed on a hill. It appeared that no one was there but he suddenly saw a large barking dog headed straight for him. When Joseph confronted the dog with his wooden staff the dog lost confidence, stopped, and backed off. Joseph expected someone to come out from the house, but no one did so he kept going.

It was now late in the day, so Joseph stopped near a small brook. He was confident that he could find some berries and small game. After tending to Tex, he walked upstream and sat down and waited behind some thorny bushes.

He waited for some time and was about to give up when he heard squealing and grunting. The sounds got louder as a bunch of small feral hogs scampered into a muddy clearing near the brook. Two larger hogs remained partially hidden behind some brush.

Without hesitation, Joseph raised his pistol and shot one of the small hogs. All the other hogs quickly scattered and disappeared. After the unlucky hog stopped moving Joseph picked it up by the hind legs and headed back to the cart.

He cleaned and hung the hog on the branch of a tree. Then he gathered some dry wood and started a fire. As it started to die down, he added some more wood since he wanted enough coals to roast his catch. The added fuel lightened up the camp site but then he was badly shaken when a man walked his horse into his camp.

"Don't worry," the man said. "I'm just passing through just like you are."

"How did you know that?" asked Joseph with a suspicious look.

"I saw you earlier today and you don't look like you are looking for trouble. My name is Woody Johnson. What's yours?"

"My name is Joseph Schmidt. Where did you see me?"

"I was on my way to see my sister and her family when I saw their dog try to scare you. They weren't home so I later followed your tracks and saw the fire. It looks like I'm just in time for supper."

"First tell me something about yourself that will make me believe you are not here to steal my things."

Woody hesitated and said, "I guess I can start by telling you I came all the way from Tennessee a long time ago to help people like you from the wrath of Santa Anna. Also, I brought some beans and stuff to make us some biscuits."

Joseph settled down and said, "I can't eat that hog by myself anyhow. It'll take some time to cook so take a seat."

When Woody sat down, Joseph noticed that he walked with a limp.

"Where are you headed?" asked Woody.

"I'm on my way to the land grant. I've got some land coming to me and will do some farming and ranching. I can't wait to get there."

"I've got some land up that way too, but it is not as far as where you are going."

"What are you raising?" asked Joseph.

"I have not done anything with it. I can't do much of that with my bad leg and I'm too restless to stay in any one place."

"Was that land expensive?"

"In a way it was but it didn't cost me any money. I got it for fighting at the Battle of San Jacinto."

"Did you know a fella named Andrew? I met him on the way up here and he got some nice land for volunteering."

"No. I didn't go there on a social visit. Santa Anna's army killed my wife and son and burned down our house when he tried to eradicate everyone who resisted him. The price I paid was much more than money."

"I'm sorry to hear that."

"I'd like to change the subject. Where did you get that ox?"

"A friend of mine, Miguel, helped me. I paid eighteen dollars for it but Tex has paid off because he just keeps on going.

"It looks like a tough animal," Woody replied. "I was a ranger here in Texas. I can't do that anymore because of my bad leg."

"How did you hurt it.?"

"Another ranger and I were chasing Indians who had stolen some horses. My horse fell on me while going over a rocky hill. My partner rescued me," Woody said.

"I saw some Indians coming up this way and it seemed they had more horses then they could use. I saw them through my telescope, and I managed to avoid them.

"You did the right thing...they may have been up to no good," Woody said.

Finally, the pork and biscuits were ready and the immigrant and his guest enjoyed a well-deserved meal. Not long after that Joseph turned in for the night on his cart and Woody on his bed roll with his head on his saddle.

The coffee was already made when Joseph woke up at the break of day. Woody was the first to speak.

"I know you are going northwest and I'm going the opposite way. My legs don't travel much but my horse does. I'll probably see you somewhere and someday up in your country."

"I'm looking forward to it. Then we'll have a beer," Joseph answered.

"That sounds good. In the meantime, be careful. I know Tex is dependable, but he won't help you make a fast get-a-way. You might run into a Mexican bandit that wants your money, a Comanche Indian that wants your scalp, or an outlaw that wants the ox for meat."

"I'll follow your advice. I also intend to find a good horse when I get there," Joseph said.

After they doused the fire they left in separate directions. Joseph had enjoyed the visit but was disappointed at himself as Woody had managed to come into his camp with a horse and without him detecting it. From now on, he would not let himself be distracted by his hunger or for any other reason.

He thought some more about what Woody had said about the many dangers on the trail. Already he had witnessed sickness and death on the ship, at Ensenada, and on his trek. He hoped and prayed that things would get better for everyone looking for freedom, opportunity, and peace in this vast wilderness.

He was amused by the many types of wildlife he was seeing but was aware that they too can cause pain and death. That, however, was not the case when he was startled by a covey of quail that exploded out from under some thickets. They scampered and flew off.

After a few more days Joseph arrived at another creek. He and Tex were hot and weary so Joseph stopped earlier than usual so both could cool off and rest.

Comfortable with his surroundings, he put his fishing line on the end of his wooden staff. After capturing a small frog, he dropped his hook in the water near some tall weeds at the edge of the bank. The line was motionless for a long time so he decided to leave it there so he could go and tend to his ox.

When he returned to the creek his staff and line were gone. He looked downstream and saw nothing but water. Then he looked upstream and spotted the staff floating in the shallows. He waded out and retrieved his pole, line, and a large black bass. It would be his next meal and he also found a good place to cross the next morning.

Tex didn't have any problem pulling the load across the creek the following morning, but the bank on the other side was steeper and more wooded than expected. Tex had to stand and wait while Joseph cut a large enough openings for the ox and cart to pass through.

Finally, following a lot of sweat and scratches, Joseph found passage up to an open area on top of the hill. While catching his breath he pulled out his telescope. He was surprised to see some structures in a large river valley.

6

Joseph couldn't help but admire the large river valley. There were large wooded areas, open prairies, and hills for as far as he could see. Spotting the settlement was a great relief.

Going down the hill would not be easy as it was rocky, and very steep. He managed to find a small flat where he left Tex and the load. That enabled him to look for the most desirable way to get down the hill. He located a trail that had probably been made by wild animals. He decided it was the safest route. Suddenly he noticed something unusual beside the trail. It was an arrowhead. He picked it up and put it in his pocket.

The trail bordered a draw and looked like it might lead to the grassy clearing far below. Tex moved slowly downhill and as he had done before, so Joseph fastened his lariat to the rear of the cart and pulled on it as much as he could on the steepest parts of the downward trail. Twice he found it necessary to wrap the lariat around the foot of a sapling and then slowly release it as the rig moved forward. Even Tex seemed relieved when they made it to the foot of the hill without a mishap.

The going was easier on the grassy prairie, but Joseph was still hours away from the settlement. It was hot and humid and looked like it might rain. With worn out boots and tattered clothing he came to a creek that looked like it was flowing into the river he had seen from the top of the hill.

Since there was water and grass for the ox at the creek, Joseph stopped for the day. The threat of rain had passed so Joseph went for a cool swim. He felt he would have a restless night but after watching the stars appear and disappear behind the drifting clouds, he finally fell asleep.

Joseph woke up at daybreak knowing that the day, June 1, 1846, would be a memorable day for him. He realized that the land grant was still a few days away, but he should be able to get some food, rest, and information at the settlement.

After crossing the creek Joseph followed the river westward and was surprised and pleased when he came to a shallow place where other carts and or wagons had crossed. When he reached the other side, he anxiously followed the wagon tracts to the settlement.

To his surprise, he saw a mule driven cart coming his way. It was led by a man with German looking attire...several grieving individuals were following him.

Joseph waved at them, but his greeting was not returned. Joseph soon discovered that the cart was carrying a small wrapped up body and a long shovel. Without a word, Joseph removed his hat and stopped as they slowly passed him by.

Sadly, Joseph continued traveling down the road. The next person he saw was an elderly gentleman with a long beard wearing a small hat. The man looked at Joseph and his rig and said, "My name is Otto. What's yours?"

"My name is Joseph. It's nice to know you," he answered.

"Joseph, you are the first immigrant I've seen come here by himself. I suppose you're glad you finally got here."

"I sure am but I won't be here long because I'm going on to the land grant. I can't wait to see my very own land."

"Maybe you've been out of circulation too long. Haven't you heard that we can't go there yet?"

"Why can't I? I've got papers for large acreage and I want to start clearing it so I can farm and raise livestock."

"We're all disappointed. We know that the Comanche Indians will resist settlers on the land that they have hunted and lived on for many years. Our tracts of land have not even been surveyed and we are told that it is too risky for the crews to go up there to complete them."

Joseph was astounded and sat down on the end of his cart to collect himself. Otto understood as he and the others had had the same experience.

"What is the Society doing about it?" Joseph asked.

"I don't know, and their agent here doesn't have many answers. If he's not hiding you might find him at the warehouse down the road," Otto said.

Joseph went on but had a difficult time digesting what he had heard. He thought about the warnings he had had from family members and friends, but he did not expect any problems in obtaining the land.

The settlement was not as thriving as he expected. There were some small houses and buildings that had been completed and a few more that were under construction. He spotted the warehouse Otto had mentioned. Makeshift tents and other shelters, using trees for support, were visible in many areas. Tree limbs and smaller branches were neatly stacked indicating that they would have another use.

Joseph decided it was best to learn more about the state of things before seeing the Society's agent. He inquired about the other emigrants from Baumberg, Philip and Marie, and found them under some trees near the river. Their two small children were there playing in the dirt.

Since they did not know each other well, Joseph introduced himself again. They did recognize Joseph and were thrilled to see someone from their hometown. Marie introduced their two children, Thomas and Klara. To Joseph, all four looked tired, weak, and undernourished.

Philip and Marie stopped what they were doing and got a pail of fresh water from the river below. They sat down on some logs where the children were playing.

Joseph started the conversation by saying, "I ran into a fine gentleman named Otto on the way in but I'm a little shaken up by what he said. Is it true that it's too dangerous to go to the land grant?"

"It's true. That's why we are all here. Even if it wasn't dangerous there still would be no reason to go there now because you couldn't find or work your tract of land without a survey," Philip said.

"It could be worse," Marie said. "At least the Society arranged for this beautiful piece of land here in this river valley. We received this lot we are on and it will be our home until things get straightened out."

"It is nice," Joseph said. "The river and the soil look good but there is only enough space for a garden. I'm interested in farming and ranching to make a living."

"So are we, but with the children, we have to make the best of what we have. As you see we are building a simple house so we can all survive the winter. We heard that it can get very cold up in these hills," Philip said.

"You two sure seem to have a good handle on things," Joseph said. "Thomas and Klara look like they are enjoying Texas. I know you have things to do so I'll go now and look around."

"Thanks for looking us up and we hope to see you again soon" Marie said.

Although Joseph and Tex had been walking for many days and weeks, he was still interested in knowing more about his new surroundings. He made a half-circle around the settlement and wandered if it had a name. He thought about writing home but did not yet know when he would have an opportunity to send a letter.

He eventually ended up back at the river. There was a nice clearing, so he decided to stay there for the night.

Tex had his fill but Joseph was hungry and thought his best chance for a meal was to catch a fish. He dug up some earth worms and baited his hook.

He found a large tree close to the water's edge that the river had washed away the dirt around its large roots and left them exposed. Believing it was a good spot to catch a catfish he dropped the hook into the water. It did not take long before he noticed the line moving around very slowly in the water.

Since there was no hard pull on the line, he lifted it and felt a strong tug. He discovered he had caught a large softshell turtle that was splashing frantically in the water. Fortunately, the pole and line were strong enabling Joseph to sling it onto the riverbank. With his sharp knife he found that much of the usable meat was on its legs.

He then built a fire in the clearing and waited until the coals got good and hot. He seasoned and cooked the meat to his liking. He felt, no matter what, that it was very good for the time and place.

Joseph had a hard time getting started the next morning.

It would have been easier to walk through the settlement, but he did not want to risk his possessions after all the time and trouble he had gone through to keep them secure.

He was surprised when he arrived near a meadow that had been converted into a large garden. It looked like it had been planted recently and several people, young and old, were working in it.

The nearest worker, an older woman wearing a bonnet, stopped hoeing as Joseph passed. She told him that a few of the families had chosen to share the work and harvest of a larger garden rather than have a private one.

As he continued, he noticed that the houses being built were mostly small and very plain. He assumed they were in a hurry to get protection from the elements, that they still intended to settle on the land grant, or would eventually build a larger home.

After arriving at the warehouse, Joseph fastened Tex's halter to a tree and went inside. The building was dark, crudely made, but serviceable for its purpose. It contained provisions for the settlers including food, tools, and grain. Joseph looked around and found a man working in the back.

"Hello, I'm looking for Heinrich. Do you know where I can find him?" Joseph asked.

"I'm the one here getting blamed for everything. I'm Heinrich. I saw you yesterday and heard you name is Joseph. What can I do for you?"

"I've traveled thousands of miles on the sea and land to learn that the tract I was promised is not available. Please tell me I was given the wrong information!"

"I'm sure they were correct because I've talked to most of them. I'm paid to help you as much as I can, but I can't undo the mistakes that may have been made. For now, and after I see your papers, I can award you a lot at this settlement. For you, the selection is good but soon there will be many more immigrants like you coming. Someday you may get what you came for, but now the biggest problems are the people's health and well-being. The cemetery here is getting bigger almost every day."

Joseph, with his head down, paused for a moment and asked, "Do you know Philip and Marie Braun?"

"Yes, I do."

"Is the lot next and west of them available?"

"Yes, it is."

"Good. It's a level lot and goes down to the river. I'd like to have that one."

"That's fine. Let's do the paperwork now," Heinrich answered.

After it was completed Joseph asked, "When and where can I mail a letter home?"

"We're expecting more immigrants very soon. Their guides will pick up any mail we have here."

"Good, I'll have a letter ready for them to take along."

Joseph returned to his lot to get a better feel of it. As he was stepping it off, he heard Philip call him and ask, "What are you doing?"

"I'm happy to be walking on my own land but I wished it would take me more time to do it and that I couldn't see from one end to the other," he replied with a snicker.

"That's great for us. It will be nice to have a neighbor from our hometown. What are your plans?" asked Philip.

"It looks like I'll have enough trees to build a one room house...if not, there are plenty more around here. I need a safe place to keep my things and get out of the weather when winter comes."

"We'll be finished before you. You're welcome to store your trunk and box with us, so you won't be tied down."

"I just might do that. In the meantime, I'll help you handle the logs on your house. Shelter for your family is more important than mine."

"Marie will be happy to hear that."

Joseph said "It looks like you're going to be short some logs. Tex can help us bring some in from the forest so he doesn't get lazy. He and I will see you early in the morning."

On the next day, as daylight was approaching in the river valley, Philip came over and found Joseph already busy...he was preparing a rig from thick rope to be used to pull more logs to Philip and Marie's lot.

Joseph was elated to see that Philip brought him a long sausage, bread, and grapes. He was also carrying a long two-handled saw that he had obtained at the warehouse.

Joseph and Philip weren't the only ones out looking for trees for their homes. Two men who had just started chopping down a tree looked with envy at Tex.

Philip chose a tree that closely matched the ones that he had already used. Together they sawed it down and then trimmed off the larger branches with their axes. Joseph and Tex then pulled the log back to the job site while Philip stayed to chop down another tree. When Joseph and the ox returned to the forest, they tied another log to the rig.

Tex took a few steps to stretch out the rope but then stopped. He refused to follow Philip's lead. Philip pulled and pulled on the halter, but the ox would not budge.

Joseph was amused.

Then Phillip said, "My brother always told me that I was stubborn, but I sure don't think I am as stubborn as this ox!"

Laughing Joseph joined Philip and then Tex started moving forward. After about a hundred steps Joseph turned loose and then Philip and Tex left with the log.

Joseph then started to chop down another tree Philip had selected. While he was working his way around the base of the tree, he noticed two Indians coming his way. They looked peaceful.

He concluded that they were peaceful when they offered him a piece of buffalo hide. They also indicated that they wanted something in return. He motioned that he had nothing to offer, so they looked at each other and then continued toward the settlement.

The harvesting of the logs went on for several more days until Philip thought they had enough to finish their one room house. Knowing that it was not large enough for a family of four, his plans included doors in front and back to simplify adding another room at another time. The logs were now on the lot, but hand hewing logs from hardwood trees was strenuous work and time consuming.

At mid-week Marie returned from the warehouse and announced that she had read a notice that everyone was invited to a town meeting on Saturday morning. It had been arranged by Bernhard Brandt and others to discuss local affairs and it would take place under the big shade tree near the warehouse.

The turnout was much bigger than expected and Mr. Brandt led the discussion by reciting his prepared text.

"Thank you for coming this morning. We could talk about our problems and grievances all day long, but I thought it would be best for all of us to think and talk more about what we can and should do to make life better here for all of us. We hope that the problems with the Indians and the land grant get resolved but now we need to make this settlement a good and safe place to hang out hats. Are there any questions or suggestions?"

"Yes," a woman answered. "My name is Veronika. Most of us are trying to survive and build houses for ourselves but we should also consider designating a central place for a town square. We will need a place for meetings, social events, and music. Let's be selective in cutting the trees there so we will have shade during the hot summers."

A man named Waldemar got up and said, "I agree. If we have a town square, I can visualize businesses and churches going up around it. We also need to come up with a good name for our town."

"I have an idea for a name," said Otto, standing up. "Since we are all starting over in a new land, we can begin again. Let's call this town in Texas Anfang, meaning beginning, and carve out a community that will always be here for work, safety, and enjoyment."

For a while there was complete silence. Then a young blind girl, named Katherine, stood up and started clapping. Everyone else then joined in by shouting, "Anfang, Anfang, Anfang."

Mr. Brandt had a big smile on his face and said, "That is a good suggestion. I'll see to it that the sign Anfang will go up and greet the next bunch of immigrants who find us in this wilderness."

The gathering did not break up when the meeting ended. After all the hardships they had experienced and the toil of building a shelter for their families, it was a relief for them to stop and visit with the friends they had made along the way. To everyone's surprise, Heinrich had provided a hearty soup for everyone that contained ingredients that the area gardeners had produced.

The rest, nourishment, and companionship lifted everyone's spirits. People of different faiths planned religious services for wherever they could find a suitable place. Volunteers or individuals were selected to lead the services until a member of the clergy would take it over. They expected people from all walks of life and religious preferences to show up in their little town of Anfang someday.

On Monday morning Joseph arrived at Philip's lot a with his broad axe in hand. After they greeted each other and finished discussing the town meeting Philip said, "Joseph, thanks for helping me cut and haul all these logs but now I think you should get started on you own house. I can square off my timbers while you start cutting yours down. I'll holler when I need help lifting a log up and I can do the same for you when you reach that stage."

"I will if you insist. I'll hammer in my corner stakes and get started now. My house probably won't look much different from yours. Call me when you need help and I'll do the same."

Joseph started by cutting trees on his lot since some of them were of the right size. The center of the lot would be cleared to make room for the house and garden and the most desirable trees on the perimeter would be kept for shade. He trimmed off the branches and stacked them to cure so they could be used for firewood and kindling during the coming winter.

During this time Marie, and her two children, Thomas and Klara, made friends with Tex. On occasion, they led the ox to the outskirts of Anfang to graze as the grass and weeds in their area had been depleted. Because of her growing children, Marie wished that Tex was a milk cow and named Texana.

It was a hot summer day when Anfang residents were working on their shelters and houses when they heard that another group of immigrants had come into town. When Joseph heard about it, he headed to the warehouse area to help greet them and see if he knew any of them.

He was elated to find that the group included many of his acquaintances from the ocean voyage. James, Alfred, Anton, and their families were delighted to recognize him. Joseph went among them and greeted Konrad, Gertrude, Martin, and their families.

He spotted Katharina and asked, "I have not seen Bruno yet. How is he doing since Petra passed away?"

Katharina paused and said, "You haven't heard!"

"Heard what?"

"He died before we ever got to Shattendorf."

"What from?"

"He was found dead in a creek with a whole lot of bee stings. He had gone for a walk and was probably still grieving over the loss of Petra and their unborn child. There was not much we could do for him. We gave him a nice burial and prayed for them."

"That is so sad. Nobody in their family survived the trip. I would think they had relatives in Germany!"

"Yes, they did. I found out where his siblings live and mailed them a letter from Shattendorf," she answered.

"That was thoughtful of you. That reminds me...I need to write home."

"Give it to Walter. He's handling all the mail."

"I'm going to write a letter home now. After you and your group get fed, Heinrich will tell you what the current situation is here. It may not look like it, but the town of Anfang will soon be on the map of Texas."

Joseph found Walter who told him he was returning to Shattendorf the next day. Joseph left to complete the letter.

July 14, 1846

Dear Mother and Father,

I am in a new town called Anfang. The trunk and box with everything in it got here safely on a Mexican cart that had been abandoned in a marsh. A friend helped me find an ox that hauled them up here. I have named the ox "Tex" and his disposition has improved since I bought him.

We have learned that we do not have access to the land grant which is about a two days ride on horseback. We are told that the surveys have not been completed due to the resistance from a nomadic Indian tribe.

I am fine but it was a difficult voyage for many, and some didn't survive. The Society is trying to overcome some of the mistakes that were made. I was given a small lot that slopes down to a beautiful river on which I am building a small log house. Philip Braun and his family from Baumberg are building a house on the lot next to me.

I believe I will receive your mail if you send it to me at Anfang, Texas, United States of America. Please share this letter with Jacob and his family. I think of all of you every day.

Love,

Joseph

Early the next day, Joseph delivered the letter to Walter. After seeing the worried look on Joseph's face, Walter assured him that his and the other mail would be handled properly.

By the time Joseph determined that he had enough logs, Philip had finished erecting the four walls of his house. Then Philip found and cut long poles that were fastened at a slant on top of the walls. After borrowing Joseph's ox and cart, he gathered long pieces of grass and other wild plants that were tied to the poles for roof covering.

Joseph kept busy hand hewing his logs. He assembled a few to see that he had chosen the right spot for the house. While placing a log on the third level he noticed a horse, rider, and pack horse arriving at his site.

It was late afternoon when the rider said, "Is dinner ready?"

"Woody, what brings you here?" Joseph asked.

"You might recall that I've got some land up here that I haven't seen in a long time. I brought along another horse thinking you might want to ride along."

"That sounds good and I'm ready for a change. Come and pull up a log. If you want something to eat, we'll have to catch it, shoot it, or pick if off a bush," Joseph said with a laugh.

"I figured that and that is why I brought along a big sausage like you Germans like to eat. I've got some fresh squash too."

Joseph started a fire in what would later become the garden area. After they sat down Woody said, "Don't let the Bend River fool you. All these creeks and rivers here can go on a rise very quickly when it rains hard upstream. It's good you selected high ground for your house."

"What's this about the Bend River?" Joseph asked.

"That's what they call this river because it meanders all through these hills. Sometimes, after a gully washer, the water will come out of its banks and you don't want to be in its way when it does. I've seen a wall of water come down even when it hadn't rained a drop where I was," Woody said.

"Thanks for warning me because I intend to spend a lot of time outdoors. You seem to really know your way around."

"I've been all over Texas with the rangers...the work took me to wherever there was trouble. I can't keep up with them anymore because of my bad leg. Right now, a lot of my buddies are engaged in the Mexican American War and my guess is that they are leading the way. I wish I was there."

"I'm sure you have a lot of stories to tell. I have a few about Germany and my long trip over here," Joseph said.

"I'm anxious to hear them," Woody replied.

"Now, I'm anxious to see your place. When do you want to go?" Joseph asked.

"Let's head out after morning coffee."

"Perfect. I'll tell my neighbors to watch my things."

Joseph could not believe he was saddling a horse after the many weeks of leading an ox through the wilderness. It felt good to sit up high and admire the scenic beauty along the way. The many hills no longer felt like mountains.

While passing through some thick mesquite brush, they startled some jackrabbits. There were three of them and were so alarmed they ran around in circles before they disappeared into the thickets. Joseph marveled at their long ears.

"Why didn't you catch one of them?" Woody asked with a robust laugh. "It would have made a good pet for you at your new house."

"I was thinking about running after one and grabbing it by those long ears but I'm still a little sore from cutting down trees. I'll do that another time and you can start thinking about a name for it," Joseph answered with a laugh.

It was the hottest part of the day when Woody and Joseph got to the top of a hill where they could see a long way. To the left and miles away, Woody pointed out another settler's house and some smaller structures. To the right he pointed to a creek that wound its way through the landscape.

"That's my land way down there," Woody said. "It goes from that rock formation on top of the hill down to the creek. I can't do much with it, but it is a good get-a-way for me...you may remember I have it because of my part in the Battle of San Jacinto. I can't believe that more than ten years have passed since we whipped Santa Anna."

"I'm glad you did but I'm sorry you had to pay such a high price. Your land looks great. Let's get go down for a closer look," Joseph said.

They went down to the marker where Woody's land started. From there, he pointed in the direction of the other three corners of the property.

Woody headed into the center of the property where there was a smaller hill that had a cliff parallel to the creek below. Joseph followed Woody alongside the rocky cliff until they came to a section with a large flat boulder.

Woody stopped, got off his horse, and said, "This is our spot for tonight, and we should get a nice breeze. We can cook our meal here."

With a surprised look on his face Joseph asked, "What are we cooking?"

"I don't know yet. I'm going hunting. You might just look around or go swimming in the creek. When you hear a shot, you can start a fire."

Woody left on his horse. The swim sounded good to Joseph, so he walked down to the creek to have a look. The water was clear and had a good steady flow over pebbles and rocks. There were some pools of water large enough for a swim.

Not long after as he was walking back to the campsite, he heard a shot. He quickly started the fire in the clearing by the cliff, confident that it would be needed.

Soon Woody rode into camp and slowly got off his horse. "I thought there was a turkey roost up the creek. This one is small so it should be tender and good with pinto beans."

The two men kept the fire going as it lit up the camp area and the open space under the boulder. Joseph asked about the cliff's indention.

Woody said, "I think that hole has been there a long time. Maybe dirt and rocks were washed out over time and maybe some Indians dug it out. I'm glad it is there because it is big enough to get some protection from the cold wind and hail. For me, that would be a luxury because as a ranger I spent many nights on the open prairie in all kinds of weather just waiting for daylight."

"I can see why you like to come up here. I can't wait to get on my land grant and work my land," Joseph stated.

"I don't want to discourage you but that might take a while. I think there now is more concern about the war with Mexico in the south then with the Comanche Indians in the north."

"I guess I just have to muster up some patience."

"You also might want to check around some more. Texas has a lot of land and wants to tame and keep it. I am always on the go and know that many people have settled on vacant land and improved it. I think that's what the government wants now."

"I believe I'll do that. I've got one foot on the ground because of that lot but I think I'm destined to raise crops and animals to feed people," Joseph said.

"I believe you'll be good at it. It's a coincidence that you mentioned the word destiny because some people, not all, are saying the United States is destined to march all the way to the Pacific Ocean. I'm content to stay right here in Texas but right now I'm destined to put my head on the saddle and go to sleep. I hope I wake up to the smell of coffee in the morning," Woody mumbled as he dozed off.

Joseph did manage to wake up early and make a pot of coffee. Woody took a long time to get up, stretch, and straighten out his leg.

Joseph asked, "What are our plans for the day?"

Yawning Woody said, "I know you need to get back to building your house but first I want to ride around and get another good look at my land. Then we can head on back."

While they were riding around the perimeter of the land, Joseph asked, "How did you find this nice piece of land way out here?"

"I caught up with a bank robber not far from here. When I was bringing him back, we cut through this area. I knew it was a bit rocky, but I liked it," Woody said as they left.

"I'm sure glad you have it. I'm going to pay more attention to the lay of the land should I come back here some time. What are your plans?" asked Joseph.

"I remember us saying we were going to drink a beer the next time we ran into each other. I didn't see anything in Anfang that looked like it had any suds floating on top," Woody said.

"I haven't either, but I bet somebody in Anfang will find some or make some by the next time you stop by," Joseph said.

"In that case I'm heading back to my sister's place. She and her husband are trying to eke out a living and sometimes I stay there to help them. The Indian threat there is not as bad as it once was but there are some low-class characters that come through," Woody said as he was leaving with his horse and pack horse.

"Thanks for showing me your place and I hope you get back up this way again soon," Joseph said.

Joseph worked long days in the summer heat so he could finish the Schmidt house. Philip had started developing his garden, but was still was available to help Joseph raise the higher logs. When the logs were in place Joseph fastened poles on top of them to support the roof.

On a September morning he put his scythe on the bed of the cart and led Tex out to locate something long and stout enough to use for covering the roof. He found tall grass, weeds, and cane on the riverbed, and stacked it on the cart as high as he could and then tied it down.

When he finished, he told Tex, "Don't you even look at my load. It's not for you. It's for my new roof and it'll be out of your reach."

On his return to the house, he fastened the material to the poles as tightly as he could so rainwater would drain down the back of the house. Although Joseph had not yet filled in the small spaces between the wall logs, he felt he had a safe place to store his trunk and box, so he made a platform to set them on. He then built a larger platform for him to sleep on. The floor would have to wait until a later time.

Now that the main phase of the house was finished Joseph walked around it several times to admire it. He then took off for the Braun house next door to get his things but after taking about a dozen steps he stopped, turned around, and confirmed that the house was still there. He almost couldn't beleive it.

He then had Philip help carry his things to his new house, the newest one in Anfang, said goodnight, and put his bedrool down and fell asleep from exhaustion.

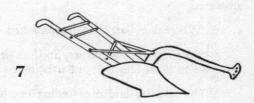

7

It took a while for Joseph to get started the next morning. He walked down to the riverbank with his tin cup of coffee and sat down on a log near a large pecan tree. After watching the clear water flow on by and listening to the birds sing, he decided to see what else was going on in town.

Activity near the new town square was steadily increasing. There were people he had not seen before, more homes under construction, and more domestic animals on the outskirts of town.

His friends from the voyage, Oscar and Freda, were happy to see Joseph coming toward them.

"It's so good to see you," Freda said.

"I missed you on the day you arrived here. How are you?" asked Joseph.

"We're fine now but have had some medical problems. We're getting better," Oscar replied. "We've been staying in this temporary shelter while our house is being built. It will be finished soon."

"Good, it looks like things are picking up in Anfang," Joseph said as he continued on this way.

He then recognized Otto sitting on a bench under an oak tree on the town square.

"Otto, I like that name you selected for our new town. Anfang is very fitting for what is happening here," Joseph said.

"The name just came to me while I was listening to Mr. Brandt and everybody seemed to like it. As you see, they've already started putting up some businesses. Who knows, maybe we'll be able to get some wood shingles for our houses someday," Otto said.

Joseph sat down by him and replied, "I hope so too. Then our roofs would not leak so much."

"That would be nice," Otto replied. "Oh; by the way, I heard that Bart, one of our late arrivals, has a large piece of land northwest of here."

"What is he going to do with it," Joseph asked.

"I ran into him the other day. I think he wants to sell it, or part of it," Otto answered.

"Where does Bart live?" Joseph asked.

"I don't know, but you may find him sitting on the bench near the warehouse. I suppose he is the only Bart or Bartholomew in town."

The next day, and after feeding Tex, he headed to the warehouse as he was curious about Otto's remarks.

He found a man sitting by himself near the warehouse. He walked up to him and said, "My name is Joseph Schmidt and I live here in Anfang. Is your name Bart?"

"Yes, it is young man. What can I do for you?"

"My friend Otto told me that you might have a piece of land for sale."

"That's right. I have six hundred and forty acres northwest of here, but my situation has changed. My wife Ingrid died from cholera right after we got here. I know she likes wildflowers that I take to the cemetry every day. Our son, Arnold and him family in Germany, may not have received my letters yet and may not know that she has passed away."

"I am so sorry to hear that," Joseph replied.

"That has changed everything. I don't know if I will stay here in Anfang or return to Germany to the only remaining family I have. That is the reason I would sell half of my land."

Joseph replied, "I am entitled to three hundred and twenty acres of land way north of here, but it will be a long time before I can develop it due to the conditions there."

"I am familiar with the problems up there. I have seen you and your famous ox, and I know that you are anxious to work the land. I am in a predicament, but I may have a solution for both of us."

"What do you mean?" Joseph asked.

"I could sell you half of my land at a fair price and you could pay me when you start producing livestock and food. That would leave both of us with three hundred and twenty acres of good land, and, I would ask that you keep a close eye on my half," Bart said.

"That sounds good, but where is the land?" Joseph asked.

"Have you ever heard of a ranger named Woody Johnson? It is on this side of his land."

"I sure have. I have been on his land and that means I have crossed yours. What you are saying sounds almost too good to be true!"

"It is good for me too. It makes my decision to stay here in Anfang or go back to Germany much easier, as I would have you to watch my property. I don't want any squatters to make themselves at home there. Should we get the paperwork started?"

"My answer is yes, and thank you for trusting me," Joseph replied.

"Thank you for making me feel better."

They then shook hands and parted.

Joseph was so excited he could not wait to spread the word, but he first stopped at the general store. A little later, he stepped outside wearing a Texas style hat to give him more protection from the sun and rain.

From there, he headed to Otto's house to tell him the good news.

"Thank you for the tip," Joseph announced as he got there. "Bart and I made a deal and I soon will be the owner of three hundred and twenty acres of land between Bart and Woody Johnson's land."

"Congratulations. When are you going up there? It looks like you need to break in your new hat."

"I don't have a horse and I believe Tex would disagree if I tried to saddle him," Joseph answered.

"I have an idea. I have a pretty good horse I bought from one of those guides that came here. You know that I am a trader of sorts and that is how I ended up with the horse. I've seen the house that you built, and I think you did a fine job. Would you and Tex help me finish my house? If so, you can have the horse and saddle and I'll be ready for when the first cold front comes in."

Joseph took a look at the one room house under construction and said, "I'll be gone a few days to inspect the land. When I get back my horse will have an important name and then I'll be here to finish your mansion."

They shook hands and Joseph returned to his house. There he saw Philip and Marie in their yard and told them what he had done and where he was going. Everyone noticed that Joseph had a new hat.

By noon the next day, Joseph stopped on the hill overlooking the creek and land he was now buying. Rather than going directly to his tract he rode along the rim to study the land below and the potential for it. He did the same on top of two more hills where he could see his land from different angles. He made mental notes of the groves of trees, open areas, and rock formations.

Since his tract had not been surveyed, he rode around the perimeter to visually estimate where his side boundaries would be. He already knew his northwest boundary bordered Woody's land and the creek was the northeast borderline. Not having any measuring devices, he decided to step off the width of Woody's six hundred and forty acres and then divide it in half for the tract of land he was buying.

At the creek, he watered the horse, and tied its bridle to the trunk of a small shade tree.

First, he stepped off the distance along the creek. It was not easy as the creek weaved back and forth like a twisted snake and the rocky creek bed was slippery. The upper boundary was even more challenging as he had to circle thickets and allow for the increased distances of the up and down slopes in the hilly areas.

When he finished measuring, he ripped his red handkerchief in four pieces and marked the upper and lower locations. He felt confident that all boundaries were accurate enough to start planning for improvements near the center of the property. He was also happy that the creek had several nice pools of water between the two creek boundaries.

At the crack of dawn the next morning Joseph ate bread and salted beef and then washed it down with cool, clear, creek water. He then anxiously hiked to an area he thought would be the best for his house.

He selected the open area that sloped down from the hills above the creek. In about the middle of that area was a mound that would make a good home site. The mound was high enough to avoid flooding in the house as the water could be diverted around either side of it.

Joseph stood in the middle of the mound and looked all around. On the hills above were jagged rock crevices and rugged looking trees and brush. Below and nestled between groves of larger trees, was a large open area where he visualized farm buildings, pens, and plenty of space for crops. He knew he would have a daunting task ahead as the field was full of rocks.

On Joseph's return to Anfang, he went directly to Otto's place to discuss the completion of his house.

Otto was pleased to see him and after Joseph got off his horse he asked, "How was your trip and did you come up with a name for your horse?"

"The trip was good, and I found an ideal place for my house and the improvements. Say hello to my horse, Roam.

"You mean Rome as the Rome in Italy?"

"No."

"You mean Roam like you're going to roam around and look for a pretty young lady?"

"No, but that wasn't a bad idea. I mean Roam like I'll be roaming around a lot going to and from my new place on the creek and here. If the land grant ever gets settled, I'll roam up that way too. The horse isn't fast, but it is solid and dependable."

"I knew you'd like it and I'm sure Roam likes his name. I've picked out the trees I need to finish the house. When can you start?"

"Tomorrow morning. We can use Tex to do some hauling," Joseph answered.

The next day it was back to the forest for Joseph and his ox. The trees that were flagged were cut, trimmed, and hauled to Otto's place. There Joseph hewed the logs to Otto's liking.

As the days passed an occasional brisk of cooler air came through and encouraged Joseph to work faster. When the higher logs were ready to be put in place Otto had Anton, the blacksmith, help Joseph lift and position them.

Next Joseph selected, cut, and fastened the roof supports. Then the cart was used to bring in an assortment of grassy material to cover the roof. Otto handed it to Joseph in bundles so he could fasten it securely to the supports and upper walls of the house.

Otto and Joseph were in good spirits when the door and windows were being installed. When Joseph hammered in the final nail Otto said, "You really earned that horse and saddle. I hope Roam takes you wherever you want to go. He and the saddle are all yours."

"Thank you. It really helps me out. Now I hope you can find something that will fill in the cracks before it gets too cold."

"I believe I will. I'm going to go and see your friend, Alfred, as he is having a kiln dug. There is plenty of limestone in these hills," he said.

"I didn't know Alfred was doing that. I guess I've been too busy and away too much. I'll go and see him myself because I need some too," he replied.

Autumn was in the air as Joseph saddled Roam and slowly headed to the warehouse for supplies. He rode around the town square to check the progress of the buildings that were being built. Just then he heard someone call his name...it was Alfred supervising some workers constructing a new building.

"What are you doing?" Joseph asked.

"I'm using some money I made in Germany to get started here in Anfang. It'll be another store and Maxine will help me run it. As time goes on, it will be good experience for our children. What are you up to?" asked Alfred.

"I just finished helping Otto build his house. I still have some work left on my own house and then I'm going to make some improvements on some land that I'm getting way up in the country," Joseph answered.

"That might take some money to develop. Do you need a little work?"

"I'm a little short. What do you have in mind?"

"Konrad has finished digging a kiln for me not far from here. I, and a lot of others, need something to fill in the spaces between the logs and rocks of our houses. It will take a lot of limestone rock chunks and firewood to cook and produce the lime. You could gather some with your cart and bring it to him. When he finishes making some, I'll pay you and throw in the mortar you need to fill in the voids of your house," Alfred promised.

"I can help you for a while. When do I start?"

"You can go see Konrad now and start tomorrow. He will be glad to see you and he'll tell you what he'll need. Don't overload your cart because I know it means a lot to you," Alfred said.

Alfred was right. Konrad was glad to see Joseph that day but even more since he arrived with his ox and cart.

"Joseph, we haven't worked together since we helped Captain Harris fix up the ship after that bad storm. People here are already finding out that mud doesn't hold for long in those cracks. I need a long, hot fire to cook the limestone," Konrad said.

"I'm not known for cooking, but I can help you with the wood and rock gathering," Joseph replied with a laugh. "Tex is ready too."

"Good. That's what I need help on. With some hardwood and chunks of limestone rocks we should be able to produce some good filler for those houses and buildings. The first freeze will be here before we know it," Konrad said.

Having already spent considerable time in the wooded area near Anfang, Joseph knew where to locate wood as fuel for the kiln. He then cut and trimmed logs and limbs to manageable sizes and delivered them to the kiln site.

There was no shortage of limestone rocks in the foothills nearby. After the first load he found it necessary to grease the wheels again and again as they were squeaking louder and louder. He also went to the warehouse to get more work gloves.

When delivering a load of rocks the next day, he was surprised when he found James at the kiln feeding the fire.

"Hello James. Good to see you," Joseph said.

"It's nice to see you too. It looks like we're both working for Alfred now. Konrad said the fire will be burning day and night for some time and he needs some rest now and then. I'm happy to earn a little money until I find something permanent," James said.

The work at the kiln continued and the finished product was now ready for use. Alfred received payment from those that had the money and gave credit to those who could pay later, and gave it to some that were ill or could not pay anything.

As Joseph delivered wood and rocks for those who still needed lime, his thoughts were often about his land on which no work was being done.

Meanwhile, peaceful Indians came into Anfang from time to time to trade or admire the possessions that the German immigrants had. Two of them watched Joseph spread mortar into the empty spaces on the front of his house. They walked around the house where the filler had already hardened. Joseph could tell that they were fascinated at what he had done.

At the end of a long day in the middle of November, more German immigrants arrived. While Joseph was in the warehouse getting supplies, Walter, the guide, approached him and handed him some mail.

Joseph had finally received a letter from home as he recognized his mother's handwriting. He held it, stared at it, looked around, and went outside and sat down on the bench. His hands were shaking as he unsealed the letter.

September 14, 1846

Dear Joseph,

We have received your letters mailed from Ensenada and Anfang. We have read them over and over and told all our relatives and friends about your adventure. You know who is writing this letter, but I have a lot of coaching from the others here on the farm.

We are so relieved that you have survived all the hardships that you have endured. We have prayed and still think about those who did not get there, and those that are still suffering.

We are all doing fine on the farm. Your father is pleased because the harvest was a little better than expected. Jacob is working hard and wants me to announce that you now have a niece named, Franziska. Dorothy is busy with the little ones and helping in the house and the garden. Guido talks about your ox and tries to help his little sister. Franziska is healthy, cute, and a bundle of joy.

We miss and love you more than we can describe. We admire you for what you have done and what you will still do. As we seal this letter on your 24th birthday, we believe you are enjoying this special day with friends in Texas and thinking about your family in Germany.

Love,

Mother and Father

Joseph read and reread his first letter from home. He was pleased that all was well on the farm but couldn't believe he had overlooked his own birthday. He then returned to his house and opened his trunk. He placed the letter carefully inside with his other documents.

Joseph rode back to the town square where Alfred was working on his new building. His oldest son, John, was helping him.

"I know why you are here," Alfred said. "You know the demand for lime has dropped off a little and you want to go to your land."

"You guessed it. My house here is secure and I need to get something going on my new one," Joseph replied.

"That's fine. I was expecting it. Go to the house and Maxine will pay you. When you get back, I will have more work for you if you want it. Also, there is a lot happening on the other side of the square. With your energy and skill, you could earn some more money over there."

"That's good to know. I'm sure that a lot of citizens can't wait till you open your store!" Joseph said.

"I hope you are right. Getting the supplies here won't be easy but we'll make it somehow," Alfred answered as he resumed his work.

Joseph collected his wages from Maxine and prepared for a longer stay on his land. Later he picked up a sturdy wheelbarrow at the warehouse.

Traveling with a loaded ox driven cart was much slower, especially over several rugged hills. After his arrival at the land and while Tex and Roam grazed, Joseph built a small fire near the mound where he would build the house. He ate and made plans for the next day.

After morning coffee, he cut four stakes from a cedar tree. After careful measuring, he hammered them into the ground as corner markers for the house. He stood in the middle and looked in every direction. He felt he had made a good choice for its location.

He then saddled Roam and road around to locate trees to cut as logs. He discovered that they generally were not as tall and straight as the ones at Anfang.

For the next several days he cut and trimmed a dozen of the best trees he could find and hauled them to the home site. There he performed the strenuous task of squaring them off with his broad axe. He then placed them in a rectangle on the mound and left spaces for doors in the front and back.

After another night under the stars, Joseph woke up early on Sunday morning. He started the day by sipping coffee from his tin cup as he strolled down to the creek. He sat down on a boulder and said some prayers he had learned while growing up. The longer he sat, the more beautiful seemed the sounds from the birds and the trickling of the clear water over the stones in the creek below.

Later in the day he cut a long pole from a thin mesquite tree and for the first time went fishing. After catching three small catfish he cooked them right away as the sky was graying and it looked like rain. It soon started getting windy and much colder, so he gathered his bedding and the two animals and headed for the small cave on Woody's place. There it was still cold, but the cliff provided a barrier from the howling wind. He could only imagine who and when someone else might have been there before him to escape from the weather or an enemy.

By morning the wind had died down, but it was still chilly. Joseph found, and moved rocks from nearby and piled them up near the home site to be used later for the fireplace.

When he had enough, he turned his attention to the open area below the house where he would eventually do some planting. The soil looked rich, but it has a lot of rocks on the surface. It had to be cleared before he would be able to do any serious plowing and planting. He intended to move and stack them neatly in a straight line on the edges of the field so they might someday serve as a fence to help control livestock. It would be grueling work.

The days and nights were getting colder as it was now the middle of

December. He had had his fill of beans, biscuits, and pecans and craved meat. Having seen a lot of wildlife he, with rifle in hand, hiked into the hills. He sat down on the back side of one facing the breeze and overlooking a large clearing below.

After a long wait, he was surprised when a doe ran across the clearing. Seconds later a large buck followed. Joseph was ready and dropped it in its tracks. It was dark by the time Joseph had a hearty meal of liver, onions, and beans. He decided to return to Anfang the next day to make venison sausage.

It was almost dark when Joseph got back to Anfang. Knowing Anton had some hogs, he went to his blacksmith shop to see if he was still there.

He came out to look at the deer.

Anton said, "I've got the hog and a smokehouse, and you have a big deer!"

Joseph replied, "Let's make sausage together and we'll split it up. We'll have cooking sausage right away and smoked sausage by Christmas. I have a sausage stuffer."

"I'll see you here at daybreak. Maybe I should have opened a meat market," Anton said with his robust laugh.

The conditions for making sausage were perfect as it was a cold and dry. They set up a table behind the shop where the deer and hog was trimmed, ground, and seasoned. After they had run the mixture through the stuffer into the casings, they tied them into rings so they could be hung.

The sausage was split into two groups and hung on poles suspended from the ceiling in the smoke house. Some would be cooked and eaten soon, but most would be smoked and dried so they would last for a longer time. Anton would maintain a small fire in the smokehouse until they were ready.

A few days before Christmas, Joseph was busy chopping some firewood on his lot when Alfred rode up on his horse.

"How are you, Joseph?"

"I'm fine and just getting some firewood together. What brings you here?"

"One of my workers is sick and another hasn't shown up since I paid him. I could use some help to finish building my store."

"I suppose I could use some money for things I will need on my land. I can help you for a couple of weeks. When should I start?"

"Tomorrow, if you can. I want to open as soon as possible. Things are picking up around here. Some shops are ready to open. Konrad is busy again at the kiln... many people are trying to keep that cold air from coming into their houses. Also, I ran into Katherina yesterday and she said there was a doctor moving into town."

"That's good news. Too many people are suffering. Too many people are dying. I hope he hires Katherina because she knows who is sick," Joseph said.

"I hope so too. She is the most courageous and giving person I know. I'll see you in the morning," Alfred said as he left.

Joseph was the first to report to the jobsite and saw that the walls were in the early stages of construction. Alfred showed up next accompanied by two young brothers named Klaus and Rupert he had just hired.

The work was hard as the logs were bigger and the spans longer. The brothers were inexperienced, but they were strong and happy to have a job. On their third day, Alfred stopped them early as it was Christmas Eve and gave each a small bonus.

That evening Joseph was invited to the Braun house next door for dinner. They ate the sausage he had given them. It was delicious.

On Christmas morning, Joseph rode to the town square to attend a religious service. This would be the second Christmas in a row without his family.

Bernhard Brant recited some readings from a prayer book and Meta led the Christmas carols. After that, everyone mingled for as long as they could tolerate the cold and sleet. Martin and Beth invited Gertrude, Otto, and Joseph to their late Christmas dinner.

Otto was the first to arrive with a bottle of wine he had been hoarding. Joseph brought his wooden nativity set to display along with some smoked sausage for their cupboard. Gertrude brought her measuring tape as she would sew a dress for their daughter, Louise, who was now six years old.

All six enjoyed their Christmas meal of turkey, gravy, sweet potatoes, squash, and pecan pie. After the meal they discussed the Christmas's of the past. When Joseph returned to his house, he rewrapped the nativity set and gently placed it back in his trunk.

The next day the heavy work on the general store continued. The brothers, Klaus and Rupert, worked hard and were eager to learn more about the trade from Alfred and Joseph. Logs were still needed and were drug in from the forest by mules.

On a day when the day's work had been completed, Martin stopped by to view their progress. While he and Joseph were engaged in conversation, Martin motioned for Joseph to look at Gertrude and Otto taking a walk together.

Joseph said, "All of a sudden they look much younger then when we saw them at your Christmas dinner."

"They didn't know each other until they came to our house. I hope she remembers to sew that dress for Louise," Martin said with a laugh.

"I don't think she'll ever forget that Christmas day," Joseph sa id. "She's never been married. I'm sure you know Otto is a widower."

Martin then said, "Yes I do. He's a good man. Not to change the subject I wish you would build a bank here. Then I could get a permanent job."

"That will come along before you know it. Woody Johnson said the town will not be complete until it has a tavern. What worries me is that I am a farmer but I'm spending too much time building things. I can't wait to put some seeds in the ground."

When not interrupted by winter weather, work on the general store progressed at a steady pace. After the rafters were cut and fastened, Joseph verified that they were evenly placed.

Shortly after, Alfred arrived and said, "Joseph, the rafters look good to me. You and the brothers did a good job...you showed good leadership."

"Thanks, I learned a lot from my father and older brother. When can we expect the wood shingles?" Joseph asked.

"They were hard to find and will be delayed. If you wish, you can go back to work on your land. Rupert and Klaus can finish up here."

"I believe I'll do that. I've got a lot to do up there."

"I'll have Maxine get your pay ready. You can also borrow one of my mules if it would help you out."

"I'll take you up on that," he said.

Joseph was weary from the heavy cutting and lifting and spent the next day just preparing for his trip. Philip and Marie were happy to tend to the ox so they could take their children for rides and gather firewood. Roam and the pack mule were ready to carry the things Joseph needed for a longer stay on his land.

When Joseph arrived at the site, he was relieved to see that the logs he had collected, and the equipment he had hidden, were there and undisturbed. As nightfall came, he sat by the fire and thought about all the things that had to be accomplished before he could take anything to the market.

He was anxious to build a corral and barn and improve the fields, but thought it best to have shelter for the frequent changes in the weather. He decided to design and build a small house first. He could add to it at another time.

The building started when Joseph connected the dozen logs he cut and hewed. Since it would be his permanent residence, he felt it would be time well spent to locate the best of the many trees on the property. When he located one, he chopped it down, trimmed it, and had the mule haul it to the home site where he squared it off. It was hard work, but it would have been more difficult during the heat of the summer. Joseph felt a sense of accomplishment with each log that was put in its place.

He was surprised at the fluctuation of the weather. Initially it was very cold and then there were a few days of more pleasant weather. That was followed with bitter cold winds that prompted Joseph to seek shelter in Woody's cave. There were days of rain and a light snow that made the already beautiful countryside sparkle.

Placing the higher logs took a lot of rope and determination but they too were soon fitted into position. Cutting and placing the roof poles was easier but locating tall grass and other suitable foliage for the roof was a bit harder during the winter. The rectangular rocks that had been gathered for the fireplace would remain on the ground until he would expand the size of the house.

While installing a window, Joseph suddenly noticed movement in the hills above him. He removed his telescope from his saddlebag and watched two riders who looked like they were coming his way. He made sure his pistol was handy and stood up his rifle in plain sight.

One rider with a beard looked all around as they got closer. He stopped, looked around, and then hollered, "We're missing a horse. Have you seen one?"

"The only horse I've seen for some time is the one that belongs so me. Other than that, all I've seen is the mule over there and lots of wild animals. Who are you?"

"I'm Reinhold and live in that house just south of here. This is my son, Timm, but he doesn't talk very much."

"I'm Joseph. I've seen your house from a distance. If I see the horse, I'll bring it to you."

"I'm thinking the Comanche's got it and it's already headed north by now. We're going to keep on looking," Reinhold said as they turned toward the creek to water their horses.

During March of 1847, Joseph finished installing the windows and doors. The floor, filling in the voids, and a more permanent roof would have to wait for another time. Before leaving to go back to Anfang, he stored his tools inside his new country house.

On the way back, Joseph saw that two more houses were being built in the remote countryside. He saw no one, but assumed some of his fellow countrymen were moving to the outlying areas because of the inability to settle on the land grant. It reminded him that he should have his property surveyed soon to prevent encroachment from others.

Before dark and near the end of the ride back to Anfang, Joseph stopped in the middle of a flowing creek so Roam and the mule could have a drink. While waiting and watching he heard a noise in the dry leaves. He then got a glimpse of a rabbit being chased by a mature bobcat. The rabbit was no match for the big cat that quickly disappeared into the thickets with its catch.

Early the next morning he opened the box that had made it successfully over the sea from Germany to Texas. He withdrew his assortment of seeds his father had selected and packaged for him.

He decided that carrots, tomatoes, cucumbers, and peas would do well in his garden. After he returned the mule to Alfred, he went to the warehouse to see about a plow.

Heinrich told him they were currently being used by other residents but that his friend, James, should soon be finished with one. He went to his house and found James plowing his plot with the help of Alfred's other mule. Meta came from the house and greeted Joseph.

While James was finishing the breaking up of the soil, Joseph asked Meta, "Where is Lucy?"

"She hasn't felt good. We went to see Dr. Wald yesterday and he said she'd be fine in a few days," Meta answered.

"I'm glad she is getting better. I know she likes to run and play. By the way, who is Dr. Wald?" he asked.

"You haven't heard! We finally have a doctor in town. Everyone is relieved. He's located near the square," she answered.

"I'm anxious to meet him. I'll look him up," Joseph said.

When James finished plowing, he helped Joseph carry the plow to his place.

When they got there Joseph said to Tex, "You're going to save me a lot of blisters today. I'm going to finish fitting you to this plow and we're going to go up and down this garden area for a while. You should be thankful we're not plowing on our big place. If you get bored, I'll sing you a song."

Thomas and Klara, the Braun children from next door, enjoyed watching the ox and Joseph plow to loosen and lift the rich soil. When the work was done, Joseph went down to the creek to wash up.

After the ox had a rest and some water, Philip plowed a section of their lot. When he finished, they loaded the plow on the cart so it could be returned to the warehouse. Thomas and Klara enjoyed riding in the cart with the plow...they waved to everyone they saw on the way. Marie stayed behind to prepare an evening meal for all of them, enjoying the quietness.

The following day, Joseph remembered that he would need a handle for the hoe he had brought from Germany. On the way to the wearhouses he decided to stop and meet the new doctor. Not seeing any signs, he stepped inside a small building thinking it was the doctor's office.

He saw a counter, some shelving, and a beautiful young lady cleaning out a dusty cabinet.

They looked at each other, both speechless for a while. She broke the silence and said, "I know who you are. You are Joseph and you have an ox named Tex."

"How did you know that? I don't remember ever seeing you before."

"Yes, you have. You saw me wave at you from the inside of a covered wagon when I was sick. My name is Jenell."

"Jenell! You must be Max's daughter! Your mother is named Sarah."

"That's right. You rescued us when we needed help. I was too sick to get up and greet you," she said.

"You sure made a nice recovery. What are you doing here?"

"My Father is opening a drug store in here. He is away trying to locate some medicine and supplies."

"Please tell your parents hello for me. I'm spending my time here in Anfang and up on some land in the country. I sure hope to see again soon," Joseph said as he left.

Jenell looked out of the window to watch him leave. Joseph jumped up on the saddleless horse but slid off the opposite side and fell into the dirt. He got up quickly and hoped he had not been seen. Of course Jenell saw him fall but managed to keep from laughing out loud.

8

Joseph dusted off his clothes before he entered the warehouse. He found the hoe handle that he needed and returned to his garden to finish preparing his plot for planting.

As he placed the seeds carefully in the Texas soil, he thought about his father who had packed them for him. He hoped they would burst out of the ground so he could watch them grow.

As he finished, Philip came over and said, "I think those seeds will thrive here. I'll help you keep the varmints out."

"Thanks, I'll do the same for you," Joseph replied.

Philip said, "Now your garden and ours remind me of the name of our town. We are beginning again with our gardens, in a faraway place called Anfang."

Loud thunder and bright lightening awoke Joseph early the next morning. A hard rain soon followed that confirmed what Joseph already knew...his roof was not waterproof. There were many leaks and one of them was right over his bed.

It was the middle of the morning before the sky cleared. The rain was a blessing for the gardens in Anfang, but the river had risen a couple of feet and would be impassable for a day or two. The river water had turned brown and was flowing much faster than usual.

Before leaving for the warehouse to get some supplies to take with him to his new land, Joseph asked Marie, "Do you need anything from the new drug store in town? I'll be passing right by it on the way to the warehouse."

Marie said, "No, we are all feeling fine and nobody got hurt today. Thank you for asking."

On a warm day in May, Joseph arrived at his country home and viewed the meadows and creek below. He tried to visualize fields of grain replacing the countless rocks lying around. He realized it would take a long time to tame it, but a good start would be to develop a smaller section now and expand it over the years to come.

He admired the area where he had removed some of the rocks and stacked them in a straight line. Day after day, with his wheelbarrow, he loaded and hauled rocks to the edge of the field.

The clear water creek below the field made the exhaustive work more tolerable. It was a place to swim and cool off at the end of a hot day.

"Joseph, you look a little sunburned. Did you come all the way up here to play in the sun?" Woody asked jokingly as he arrived unexpectedly.

"No, but if you need some more rocks on your place, I've got plenty I'd like to sell you," Joseph replied.

"If you run across any gold or silver, I'd like to talk about it. I'm on my way to check out my place. When the sun goes down tomorrow, I'll be here for something to eat and I'll bring the whiskey."

"Good, I can't recall the last time I've had any. We'll eat if the fish are biting. I'll see you then."

The routine of hauling rocks off the field was not different from days past with the exception that Joseph stopped earlier on this day to do some fishing. By his favorite spot he caught two bass and three big perch. He was starting a fire near the house when Woody showed up with whiskey. When the coals were good and hot, Joseph started grilling the fish and heating the beans.

"It sure does smell good and I'm hungry," Woody said.

After finishing the meal, Joseph asked, "I have heard some talk about a peace treaty with the Comanche Indians. Do you know anything about that?"

"Not much. We'll have to wait and see how it works out. History is not on our side," Woody answered.

"Maybe the land grant will be opened up," Joseph said. "There are a lot of people anxious to settle up there."

"It won't happen overnight. The surveyors can't do their work if it's not safe. If it's not safe for them, it surely would be risky for the settlers," Woody said.

After Joseph took a sip of whiskey he said, "I agree but I have a question. Have you ever wished you were a little bit sick so you could go and buy some medicine?"

"Joseph, you've been in the sun too long or that whiskey is disrupting your thinking. You'll have to explain that."

"She is the most beautiful girl I have ever seen. Her smile is so radiant I had trouble getting on my horse."

"Where did you see this girl? In your dreams?"

"No. Her name is Jenell. She is working in her father's drug store in Anfang. I need a good reason to go there again."

"Nobody wants to be sick. You found your way from Baumberg, Germany to Anfang, Texas. It seems you could just walk into the drug store and say hello...I don't think she is going to bite you. What is her last name?"

"I don't know but I'll find out. You're right, I need to get my feet back on the ground," Joseph answered.

"While you're doing that I'm heading back. It's a nice still night," Woody said as he started to leave.

"I'm tired and sore all over and I'm turning in myself. I'm going back to Anfang in the morning. I'll see you the next time you come back," Joseph said.

In Anfang, Joseph slowly looked over his garden and smiled because everything was sprouting. Philip, Marie, and their children came over to see him.

"The garden looks good. I can tell that it had some expert help from my thoughtful neighbors. Feel free to take what you can use because I won't be able to eat it all," Joseph said.

Marie said, "Our garden is taking off too. Help yourself to the potatoes and squash any time."

"I sure will. It looks like we, and the other people here, are looking forward to some better meals," Joseph replied as he dismounted. "Maybe times are getting better."

Having been away from town for some time, Joseph became aware of the changes taking place as he rode into town the following day. Even more immigrants had arrived and there were more carts, wagons, and draught animals on its streets.

Suddenly, he heard someone call his name. It was Martin who was watching a construction project.

"Guess what!" Martin said. "They are building a new bank here. When it's finished, I'll have a job here as a teller."

"That is great. Be sure to put in a good word for me when I come into your bank to borrow money for livestock and equipment."

"I hope to be that loan officer by then and that will make it easier," Martin said. "I know you would take care of your obligations."

A man with a gray mustache walked up and asked, "Martin, who is your friend here?"

"This is Joseph Schmidt. We came to Texas on the same ship. Joseph, this will be my new boss at the bank, Mr. Kuhn."

"Joseph, what kind of work do you do?" Mr. Kuhn asked.

"I'm a farmer, but here I've been mostly working as a carpenter."

"I could use another good hand to get the bank up and running before somebody else builds one. I've heard about you and I'll pay you for six days for every five days you work until the building is finished."

"I'll be the first one here on Monday morning."

"Good, I'll see you then," Mr. Kuhn said as he departed.

"Joseph, you're lucky to have a second line of work. You got a job just by stopping by here," Martin said.

"I stopped thanks to you and then just got lucky," Joseph replied.

"There will be more building here. There is a livery stable going up on the edge of town. Also, two, and maybe three new churches are in the works," Martin said. "This Sunday a Father Matthew is saying Mass on some property not far from here."

"That's good news. I've been waiting for that. I should be on my way now," Joseph said as he left, leading his horse behind him.

He next stopped in front of the new drug store. There now was a small sign next to the door.

He went inside and was greeted by Max who was busy talking to an elderly couple about some medicine that might help them. While they were talking, Joseph looked around the room and waited. From a certificate on the wall he learned that Max's surname was Miller.

Max gave Joseph a hearty welcome after the couple left.

"Joseph, Jenell told me she ran into you while I was gone. It's so good to see you," Max said.

"It's good to see you too Mr. Miller," Joseph answered.

"You don't have to call me Mister. Please call me Max like everyone else. Sarah and I, and Jenell, will never forget how you helped us when we needed it. We stayed at the rancher's bunkhouse for a while and then in Schattendorf for a long time. When we got here, we took over a house vacated by a family that moved further out of town. Sarah and Jenell are fully recovered and now I want to help the people here as much as I can. What have you been doing?" Max asked.

"I built a small house here and have been doing some carpenter work here and there. I've got a large place up in the country that I'm going to develop into a working farm and ranch since there is so much uncertainty about the land grant. It is hard work, but I enjoy doing it," he said.

"I'm sure you will do well."

"I plan to. Please tell Jenell and Sarah hello for me."

"I will. Goodbye Joseph."

On the way to his house, he felt good about having landed a job and seeing Jenell's father again. But his joy turned into sadness when he saw a man leading the familiar mule and cart coming his way.

He stopped off to the side, got off his horse, and removed his hat. On the cart was a body wrapped in blankets. The mourners, some of them children, were crying as they slowly made their way toward the cemetery.

At home he checked his garden for weeds and insects. When he finished, he got back on his horse to go pick dewberries. It did not take him long to fill his bucket among the low-lying brambles. When he was finished, he sat down on a stump and ate a few. Then he watched an armadillo foraging for food coming directly toward him. When only a few feet away the animal jumped up and scampered back into the low thickets.

It was an overcast morning when some Anfang residents converged on a vacant piece of property not far from the town square to attend a Sunday morning church service. Most of them were wearing the best clothing that they had for the very first time since removing them from their trunks. The garments were mostly heavy for the time of year, but they were proud to have an opportunity to wear them.

Lucy, the daughter of James and Meta, showed off her new dress Gertrude had made for her. It was a little snug since she had grown an inch or so since the measurements were taken.

Father Matthew greeted everyone as they arrived. Since there were few benches, the ladies sat on them. and the men and older children stood behind them.

They listened intently as the priest celebrated the Mass and gave an eloquent and assuring homily. At the conclusion of the service, Father Matthew promised he would return to Anfang as soon as he could.

Just then the sun broke through the clouds, and the men started removing their coats. They all drifted toward the shade trees and gathered in groups. Getting a permanent priest and building a church were the major topics of discussion.

Planned or not, Joseph and the Miller family came together under one of the trees. Sarah was the first to speak.

"Joseph," she said, "My husband and daughter have already expressed their appreciation for your helping us out back on the trail. Thank you so much for loaning Tex so we could find some shelter. Jenell and I were sick and exhausted at the time and it gave us time to recover."

"I'm so glad you are well. Now I hope people here get better. Many are sick and many have passed away," he said.

Then Max said, "Joseph, I know you are healthy, but I've noticed you scratching yourself."

"I picked some dewberries the day before yesterday. I may have brushed against some poison oak or something. It'll go away," he answered.

"If not, come by the drug store," Max said. "Maybe I can help you."

Wanting to be part of the conversation Jenell asked Joseph, "How is Tex doing?"

Joseph said. "He has been very dependable but I'm going to start lightening his load because he's slowing down a bit. This afternoon my neighbors, the Braun's, are going to take him on a picnic. Their kids enjoy the ride in the cart and Tex likes the fresh grazing."

"That's nice," Jenell said. "Not every ox gets to go on a Sunday afternoon picnic."

Everyone laughed. The crowd then started to dwindle as the faithful starting returning to their homes.

Joseph was the first to arrive at the bank construction job on Monday morning. He took the opportunity to see what had been done and what hadn't. The bank foundation was rectangular but there was a small triangular space on the corner that would become the bank entrance. It would allow easy access from both streets. Porches and hitching posts were planned for those two sides.

Viktor, a carpenter, was the next to arrive. Mr. Kuhn came next to describe the work he wanted done for the week. He expressed a desire to have the bank half-finished by the end of the week. He said a wagon load of lumber should arrive later in the day.

Martin arrived later in the morning. He would not be on the payroll until the bank opened but for that reason, he was willing to help some by running errands or by moving the barricades.

At noon they took a short break. Surprisingly, Jenell showed up while Joseph was sitting on some logs in the shade.

"Hi Joseph, I've got some ointment for you. My father said it might help you get over the itching," she said.

Joseph was bewildered for a moment, took off his hat, and said, "Well, thank you very much. I'm going to use it right away. I didn't bring any money."

"No, my Father said to give it to you, but I was thinking."

"Thinking about what?"

"I haven't been on a picnic in a long time."

"You know, I haven't either. I'm tied up here until Saturday, but we can go on Sunday. My garden is doing well, and I'll prepare the food," Joseph said.

"I'll bring the lemonade. Can you come and get me?" she asked. "From here it is just down the street."

"I could find you wherever you are. I'll be there in the middle of the afternoon," Joseph said as she left to go back to the drug store.

The load of lumber arrived as expected. Mr. Kuhn showed the teamster where he wanted it.

Joseph and Martin helped unload and stack it when Martin said, "Joseph, since Jenell came by it seems like your rash has healed and the blazing sun isn't so hot as it was before. Be careful with your hammer so you don't have blue thumbs at the end of the day."

"We're just friends," Joseph said. "She's from a good family. We met on the trail coming up here."

Martin snickered and Joseph smiled as they finished stacking the lumber.

The work on the bank aroused a lot of curiosity among the settlers who were walking or riding by. The barricades were there for safety and security purposes but also to minimize the time spent answering questions about the structure.

On Wednesday, Oscar and Freda noticed Joseph working and came inside the partial building. Mr. Kuhn did not object, viewing them as future customers of the bank.

Freda said, "Joseph, we don't want to keep you from your work, but we just wanted to tell you what we are doing."

"Please tell me," he said.

Oscar answered by saying, "We have a lot of mustang grapes growing on our property. They are ripening and we're going to make some wine just like we did in the old country."

"That's good to know. When it's ready I'd like to taste it," Joseph said.

"Yes, and we will give you some. We would like to tell you more, but we have to go because we have so much to do," Freda said as they went around the barricade.

On Friday morning Joseph was up on a ladder framing some partitions of the building. He stopped when he noticed Jenell walking by with Katherine, the young blind girl. Jenell waved as they passed on by. Joseph smiled, waved back, but kept on working.

A little later he heard Viktor and Martin laughing.

Joseph asked, "What's so funny?"

"Just a few days ago you said Jenell was just a friend. Look at what you've done!" Martin said while pointing at the ladder.

Joseph realized the ladder could no longer be moved, as a board used for bracing had been threaded through the ladder between the upper rungs. The board had been fastened from a fixed wall on one end and then rested on the rung of the ladder to hold it up to allow time to fasten the other end. The ladder, however, was not removed before nailing the board to the newer wall.

Joseph turned red as he grabbed his hammer and quickly pulled out the nails and removed the ladder. He said jokingly, "I just wanted to demonstrate how a ladder could be secured so it wouldn't be stolen."

On Saturday afternoon, Mr. Kuhn came to the job site and paid Viktor and Joseph their wages for the week. He was pleased with their work and confirmed that they met their goal of being half finished by this day.

On Sunday Joseph gathered the ingredients for the stew he would take for the picnic. After loading it and the equipment he wanted, he led the ox and cart to the Miller residence, a two-room house with a wood shingle roof.

Max and Sarah welcomed Joseph. Jenell chose to walk with Joseph rather than ride in the cart.

They moved slowly along the Bend River until they came to a nice shaded clearing near the riverbank. After finding a good grazing spot for Tex, Joseph started a fire and surrounded it with rocks. Soon he hung the pot of stew over the hot coals. He placed the thick log that he had brought along, on the ground so they would have a place to sit. There was a soft breeze coming from the south over the river that cooled them off after their long walk.

For a while very little was said. Joseph and Jenell seemed content with the moment...together for the first time on a beautiful Sunday afternoon.

Joseph got up to stir the stew, but his eyes were fixed on Jenell's flowing dark hair, sparkling blue eyes, and gentle smile as she was looking around the countryside.

She broke the silence by saying, "It's starting to smell good. Where did you learn to cook?"

"That's really stretching it," Joseph answered. "I was always outside somewhere but my Mother showed me how to make the stew and she is the best cook in Germany. Since my garden is producing now, and I have you as a good reason, this is the first time I've ever made it by myself. Most of my cooking has been over a campfire and pretty simple."

"I like to cook and bake. After we enjoy the stew you can try my apple pie," she said.

"I could smell it on the way. You are lucky it's still here."

She laughed and said, "Look over there. Tex must have had his fill. He's lying down under the tree."

Joseph said, "Tex has done everything I've asked of him, but I don't want to wear him out. I will really need some horses or mules and a wagon to go back and forth to the land to do the heavy work. The dirt out there has never seen a plow."

"Do I have to worry about what's going to happen to Tex?"

"No, you don't. He can still do light duty for someone in Anfang. I'll make sure he'll be taken care of."

"What kind of work are you doing up there?" she asked.

"I've already built a small house but I'm going to make it bigger. I will also build a barn, corral, and plow and plant the field."

"It sounds exciting!"

"It is. It's time consuming but it is a pretty place above a good sized creek. There are others settling in the area as well. What are your interests?"

128

"I'm helping my Mother at home a lot. There is much to do as we're still settling in. I'm also helping my father get the drug store up and going. When I have time, I do some reading for Katherine, our neighbor, because she can't see, and her parents are having a hard time. I think I would like to be a schoolteacher."

"I think you would make an excellent teacher. I know Katherine...she has a lot of spirit. Right about now my mother's special stew looks ready. Are you?" Joseph asked.

"Yes, I'm very hungry."

The young immigrants enjoyed the stew, lemonade, and apple pie but on this occasion any meal would have been well received. When the sun began to set, they loaded everything up on the cart so they could be back in Anfang before dark.

On the way back Joseph held the halter leading to the ox in his right hand, and Jenell's right hand in his left hand. They both wished the walk would have taken longer.

On Monday morning, Joseph was the first to arrive at the bank job site. Mr. Kuhn was the next and said, "Joseph, you are early. That's good and I appreciate it because we want to open as soon as we can."

"I noticed that the supplies came in and know what needs to be done, so I got started. I would like to take off a little earlier this afternoon because I have something important to do. Is that okay?"

"Of course, it is. I know you'll get in a day's work."

After work Joseph wrote home.

July 5, 1847

Dear Mother,

I have addressed this to you to fulfill a promise I made before I left for Texas. Yesterday I made your special stew by myself. I obtained the beef from a friend, but some of the other ingredients came from my garden which came from the seeds Father selected and packaged for me.

The occasion was for someone special. Her name is Jenell and she lives with her parents here in Anfang. We went on a picnic. She sat on a log and watched me as I stirred your pot of stew. She is kind and thoughtful, but I cannot describe how beautiful she is. She said the meal was the best she ever had.

I've been very busy here. In fact, I overlooked my birthday until I got your letter. Please give my niece, Franziska, a big hug from her Uncle Joseph. Also give my congratulations to Jacob, Dorothy, and Guido.

Father, I've been very busy. I have the small house here, but now I plan on settling on a large tract of land northwest of here. Here, I'm making some money doing carpenter work which I will use to improve the land. The work gives me a lot of time to think about my strong roots in Germany.

Love,

Joseph

The work on the bank building continued with Viktor and Joseph doing most of the labor. When the work on the walls and the roof were completed, Mr. Kuhn unexpectedly asked them if they needed a few days off before starting the more tedious finishing work inside.

Both were very much in favor of it. Viktor took the time to spend with his large family and working on his own house. Joseph asked Mr. Kuhn if he knew of any surveyors in the area. He was referred to Gary, an accomplished surveyor, who had completed some work for him. They arranged to leave early on the day after next. That gave Joseph a day to prepare for the trip and a chance to see Jenell. He had seen her going into the drug store, so he went in.

They greeted each other with big smiles. Joseph said, "I'll be going to my place for a few days to help a surveyor mark the corners. I just felt like seeing you and telling you about it."

"I'm so glad you did because I was going to ask you to the house for supper tomorrow," she said.

"I wouldn't miss it for anything. I'll be there," he promised.

The next day Joseph prepared for the trip. After tending to the ox and garden, he sharpened his axe. When he finished, he saddled Roam and rode over to Otto's house.

"What brings you here?" Otto asked.

"I've got something I want to talk about. I know you do some trading," Joseph said.

"What's on your mind?"

"I need to step up. Tex and the cart can't handle the jobs I will have on my big place. I'll be hauling lumber and equipment up there and farm products back here so I will need a solid wagon and a couple of good horses or mules. Can you keep your eyes open for me? I'll be splitting my time between here and there for a while."

"I know you'll be back here. I've seen you and Jenell together," he said with a grin.

"You know!" Joseph answered, "I've seen you and Gertrude walking around a lot. Don't wear out too many shoes."

Otto laughed. "We're just good friends and we both like to talk. I'll save some time to find you a wagon and draught animals. In return, I will ask for is a big deer quartered and delivered here this winter. I can make some sausage that will feed me for a long time.

"Let's do it," Joseph said.

Later in the afternoon, Philip was working in his garden when Joseph stepped out of his house and then saddled his horse.

"Joseph, you look like you are going to church. I have never seen you look that clean and dressed up during the week," he said.

"This is the new me. I'm going to the Miller house for supper. I was personally invited by the nicest and prettiest young lady in the world and I don't want to disappoint her," Joseph said as he pretended to brush some dust from his shoulder.

"We can't wait to meet her," Philip said as Joseph rode away.

Joseph shook his boots off before entering the house as he noticed they had a real floor. Sarah gave Joseph a warm greeting and told him he looked handsome. Max shook his hand and invited him to have a seat.

After a brief discussion about the summer heat, Jenell entered, "Hello Joseph," she said with a smile.

Joseph stood up, taken in at her in a long yellow dress. After he found the words he said, "Hello Jenell, it's so nice to see you again."

They all chatted a bit before sitting down at the table. They then joined hands and gave thanks. Mrs. Miller served pork schnitzel, sauerkraut, roasted potatoes, and fresh bread.

The conversations continued well after the delicious meal. They talked about their relatives and places they had left behind and might never see again. But they were also enthusiastic about the new traditions that they were creating in their new world.

Sarah mentioned that the varmints were tearing up the garden and she didn't know what do about it. Max said he was having a hard time stocking his drug store because his sources were limited. Jenell and Joseph were happy to be together and still happier when Sarah served pecan pie.

Gary, the surveyor, arrived at Joseph's house early the next morning. He was on horseback and leading a pack mule. He noticed that Joseph had an axe strapped to the top of his bedroll.

"What's the axe for? Are you planning on helping me clear the way for my instruments?" Gary asked.

"I can do that. But also, I'm interested in finding the best way to get to my land with a loaded wagon. On horseback it is no problem but with the ox and the cart it wasn't so easy. Maybe you can help me find the best way around some of those hills." Joseph said.

"I am familiar with the lay of the land up there. I can put up a few markers on the way to your place. I'm sure you don't want to pay me while I'm watching you work...you can cut the trees or limbs down anytime," Gary said.

"That's what I wanted to hear. I'll work my way back," Joseph said.

When Gary and Joseph approached the taller and more rugged hills, they left the established trail and rode through some small valleys. Gary hung brightly colored cloth markers on trees as they rode along. Some trees and brush would have to be eliminated on the upper side of a wash to make it easier for the wagons to come through.

When they came to Joseph's land, he led Gary to the upper corner of the land where he had tied a part of his red handkerchief. There they got off their horses to view the countryside.

Then Joseph pointed to the other estimated property lines and his house.

"How did you measure it?" asked Gary.

"I stepped it off."

"I'll want some help later but now I'm going to look over the whole property. If this marker is less than thirty steps away from the permanent marker that I'll put in, I'll buy you a beer" Gary said.

"I'll buy you one if it's not. Now I'm going down to the house to do some measuring because I still want to install a floor, shingle roof, and a cooking stove when I have time. Let me know when I can help you," Joseph answered.

After Joseph finished the house measuring and removing more rocks from the field, Gary summoned him for help.

For days, Joseph helped the surveyor with the handling of the equipment and the cutting of the brush to improve the visibility between the markers. When the exact location of the first corner marker was determined, Joseph stepped off the distance to his temporary marker.

Gary asked, "How many steps were there?"

"I counted thirty-one steps. You won the beer," Joseph answered.

"You would have won if you had shorter legs," Gary said with a big grin on his face.

Joseph laughed and said, "I'll buy you that beer when I get the chance. I'm happy that I lost the bet because my land is wider than I expected. Are you ready to call it a day?"

"Yes, I'm ready to jump into that nice creek of yours," he answered.

After the swim, and while the horses and mule were grazing, they made a meal of chili and cornbread.

When they finished, Joseph asked, "I plan on digging a well out here. What are my chances of finding water?"

"That's something you won't find out until you try it. My guess is that you will but it's going to be some tough digging," Gary answered.

"I'm going to try. How about the land grant? Have you done any surveying up there?" Joseph asked.

"No, I haven't and I'm not too excited about working up there yet. I know there was a peace treaty signed, and I'd like to believe that both sides will abide by it, but I suspect the problems between the Comanches and the settlers are not over. Even here, I would keep my eyes open," Gary replied.

"I will be careful," Joseph promised. "We should be turning in now. I'll start the coffee in the morning."

"Good, and if the weather holds out, we should be able to finish the field work tomorrow," Gary said.

In the middle of the next day the field work was finished when Gary hammered in the last metal rod down by the creek. It was located just thirty-four of Joseph's steps from the red handkerchief Joseph had hung in a tree.

"Joseph, you did a pretty good job in estimating the boundary lines," Gary said. "I'll do the paperwork and look you up in Anfang and then we'll finalize the survey."

"I'm well pleased. Now I'm going to work my way back to town by cutting down a few of those small trees that are in the way. Thanks again for putting up those road markers for me."

"That was easy, but it'll help you go back and forth to your place. Don't forget about the beer you owe me," he said as he packed his tools and left.

Shortly after that Joseph locked up the house and followed the new route around the nearby hills. He cut small trees near the surface of the ground so carts and wagons could travel through more easily.

There were more obstacles then he remembered so it was necessary to stop at nightfall along the trail and continue the next morning. He knew the road would not be perfect but that it would improve with use over time.

Again, Joseph was he first to arrive at the bank but couldn't get started as the doors were locked. After a short wait, Mr. Kuhn showed up with the keys.

He said, "Nice to see you Joseph because we have a lot to do. The vault was installed while you were gone so the work is cut out for you and Viktor. How were your days off?"

"Good, I got my country place surveyed and did a little road work," he answered.

"That's a sign of progress," he said. "The bank will be here for people like you."

"I think I'll be here for a bank like yours," Joseph responded as Viktor showed up for work.

Mr. Kuhn said, "You men know what needs to be done. I'll be busy myself trying to get everything ready for opening day."

"We'll do our best," Viktor said.

Viktor and Joseph worked well together, and since they were now working indoors, they were not concerned about the weather. Mr. Kuhn was in and out frequently to plan and arrange for the furniture and supplies they would need. Martin still stopped by daily to see if he could do anything to speed up the process so he could get to work as a teller.

On an afternoon when they were all there, Otto burst into the building, walked past Mr. Kuhn, and went to where Joseph was working.

"Joseph, I just came from the general store. There is a young man with a family who asked me where he could sell his wagon and horses. He said they came from Schattendorf yesterday and don't need them anymore. They look like they could use the money," Otto said.

Joseph looked at Mr. Kuhn who heard what was said. He said, "You can go and see what you can do. Remember you have some pay coming and you could be our first bank customer. If you need more money, Martin can handle the paperwork."

Otto and Joseph hurried to Alfred's General Store. Before they got there, they heard a child shout, "Look, its Joseph."

"Anna, you've grown! How old are you now?" Joseph asked.

"I'm already eight years old," she said as she ran to Joseph and hugged him.

Otto watched in amazement as Franz, Carolina, and Joseph greeted each other.

"What going on Franz?" Joseph asked.

Franz said, "I did some more work for Mr. Hofmann at his new store in

Schattendorf and he asked me if I wanted this wagon and horses for the wages. Carolina and I decided it's our chance to come up here before our next child arrives. We found a vacant house here, but we need other things more than the wagon and horses."

"Otto has been on the lookout for a rig for me for my new place in the country. The two horses and the wagon look very good. I've been working and I can buy it from you. I can pay half now and the other half when the new bank opens. Also, I won't need Tex and the cart anymore, so you are welcome to have it if you keep in mind that Otto likes to borrow the rig now and then."

The transaction made all parties happy and they decided to make the exchange the next day. Otto left and said with a smile, "It's so nice meeting you folks and, Joseph, don't forget the venison you promised me this winter."

That night Joseph had difficulty sleeping. He thought about having given up his ox that had done so much for him. He knew, however, that Franz and his family would find him useful and take care of him. He also felt excited about the horses and wagon that would be useful in developing his picturesque land.

The exchange took place the next morning outside the bank building. When it was complete, Franz led the ox and cart, with Carolina and Anna, to the general store to shop for food and clothing.

Joseph left his purchase under a shade tree and was anxious to show it to Jenell. He also realized he now had three horses and no ox.

At the end of the workday, Joseph got in his wagon and headed to the drug store to see if Jenell might be there. Jenell and Max were in the process of closing.

Jenell lit up when Joseph entered and said, "It's nice to see you and what brings you here?"

"Fortunately, I don't need any medicine today. I just bought a wagon and two horses, and I just wanted to show them to you."

Max said, "That's great. Let's have a look," as all three went out on the porch.

Max continued and said, "They look very strong and reliable to me."

Jenell said, "I'll give my opinion after I get a ride in it."

"You two go ahead. I'll lock up here and go home," Max said.

Joseph was all smiles when he helped Jenell get up in the wagon. He then asked, "Where do you want to go?"

"Let's go to your place. I haven't seen it," she answered.

"It looks nice," Jenell said as they arrived at Joseph's house.

"I'm not finished with it yet. I'm going to replace the roof with shingles, add a wooden floor, and install a stove for cooking and heating," he replied.

They got out of the wagon and toured the house and garden. "It's lovely," she said. "Let's walk down to the river."

"It's beautiful. I'd like to go fishing here sometime. Can we?" she asked.

"Yes, but I think we should first seal the plans with a kiss," he said.

Jenell and Joseph embraced, kissed, and slowly returned to the wagon.

When Joseph helped Jenell off the wagon at her parent's house he asked, "Did you like the wagon ride?"

She answered, "Yes I did. I also feel like I've been floating on a cloud ever since your first visit to our store."

9

On a hot and dry September day in the year 1847, the sounds of the saws and hammers were constant on the streets of Anfang. Joseph and Viktor had completed the interior of the bank and were now building the porches and covers for the two sides of the building facing the streets.

Nearby, Ralf, another immigrant, was putting the finishing touches on a tavern he was building. Not much farther away, Bernhard Brandt was managing the construction of a Catholic Church. Klaus and Rupert, the two brothers, were hammering away on a pavilion for the town square that had to be finished for an October celebration. A Mr. Bergner was spearheading the construction of another church. To accomplish their goals, many of the workers on these projects were working in a trade that was different from the ones they had had in the old country. When Joseph and Viktor finished erecting the hitching rails in front of the bank, their job there was done.

Time had seen the emergence of another method of building homes and businesses. It was slower and very labor intensive, but perhaps enhanced the longevity of the structures they needed. The abundance of rock, in this case mostly limestone, had created work for the stonemasons who came from Germany and those that were willing to learn the trade.

For Alfred, who owned the first kiln for producing lime in the area, and Konrad and James who were running it for him, it meant more business. For Viktor, it meant continued employment as he needed it for his family of seven. He had already spoken to a stonemason named Sebastian who had a job lined up for him.

Joseph wanted to finish his house in town. For the floor, he purchased the leftover lumber from Mr. Kuhn at a reduced price. Hauling it to his house was simple with the horses and wagon. The next day Joseph went back to the forest to cut more trees for the beams. Takinig his broad axe, he chipped away on the sides of the logs so he would have a flat surface for the boards.

When the floor was finished, he left in the wagon to get the shingles he needed to recover his roof. When he arrived back at his house, Gary was waiting for him with the completed land survey in his hand. He had another man with him.

"Joseph," Gary said. "My friend Jake rolled into town to join a surveying crew. I decided to go with them to the land grant to do some work. It's good money. We'll leave in a few days."

"I'm anxious to hear what the place looks like. Look me up when you get back. Then I'll buy you that beer I owe you," Joseph said.

Gary went over the survey while Jake looked on. Joseph was pleased and paid him for the work. After they left, he carefully placed it in his trunk.

Before Joseph could install the roof shingles, he had to remove the original roof material. After he stripped away the grass and cane, he removed the poles that had held it up. He made a better ladder for getting up on the roof from the poles.

The roof required another trip to the forest for logs that he could hew into beams to support the cross boards on which the shingles would be fastened. It all took a lot of effort, but it allowed him lots of time to think about his special friend, Jenell.

He was trimming the beams when, without notice, he heard a pleasant voice call his name. It was Jenell coming to see him. Katherine, the blind girl, was with her.

"Joseph," she said. We don't want to interfere with your work. We just want to go down and spend a little time by the river. I want to describe to Katherine everything there from the sounds she hears."

"That is a great idea. I've got plenty of log remnants, so I'll set up a bench for you," he answered.

Joseph then continued to work on the roof until he got thirsty. After a while, he prepared three cups of lemonade and took them to where his guests were sitting.

"How are things going?" he asked.

Katherine answered, "It's nice here. I heard you coming. Thank you for the lemonade."

Joseph said, "I knew you'd be thirsty."

Katherine then said, "There was a big frog that jumped in the water and made a loud splash. We heard five different kinds of birds and one sounded like a mockingbird. A rabbit came in real close to us to nibble on something...Jenell said its nose wiggled a lot while it was eating. The river sounds very peaceful as it flows over the rocks and pebbles. Where does it go from here?"

"From here it goes a long way until it turns into a larger river. The larger river flows all the way to the Gulf of Mexico," Joseph said.

"The Gulf of Mexico is too big for me. I like this river better," Katherine said.

Jenell was surprised when Joseph said, "Then let's all go wading."

With Joseph's lead, the three held hands and slowly walked in. The stones were slippery so they held on to each other until they came to a sandy spot where they could get a firm footing. There they formed a triangle and laughed, sang, and splashed water on each other to cool off.

Before returning to the riverbank Katherine said, "The water in the river makes such a beautiful sound out here. This is the first time I've ever been wading. Thank you so much for bringing me."

"You're welcome to wade here anytime. I enjoyed it as much as you did," Joseph said as Jenell and Katherine left to continue their walk.

By noon the next day, Joseph had finished his new shingle roof. All that he still needed was a source of heat for cooking and cold weather.

He hitched up his horses and left to attend the opening of Mr. Kuhn's bank and to locate a wood stove. At the bank, curious residents of the area came in and out to see the new facility. Perhaps the happiest of all, was Martin, who was on the payroll as a loan officer...he had been rewarded for his genuine help and interest in getting the bank started and he would hire someone to perform the duties of bank teller. Martin's wife Beth was all dressed up as was their daughter, Louise, who still managed to get into the dress Gertrude had made for her.

When Martin had a free moment Joseph said, "It won't be long before I'll be looking for a loan here. In the meantime, I hope you're practicing on your tuba for the Anfangfest in October. I sure am glad I live on the other side of town."

"You're interest rate just went up," said Martin jokingly.

Mr. Kuhn was the busiest of all as he wanted to welcome everyone who came in. After he thanked Joseph for the work he had done, Joseph saw Jenell and her mother come into the building.

Sarah, the first to speak, said, "The bank looks nice. It will help the town."

"I think you're right. It should also help me get started on my big place," Joseph said.

"I'd like to see your big place sometime," Jenell said.

"I'd like to show it to you. I'm taking some wood shingles up there on Saturday. You're all welcome to come along," Joseph said.

Sarah and Jenell looked at each other and Sarah said, "It sounds like fun. Max has been so busy with the new store. I believe a little change would be good for him. We'll bring something to eat."

"I'll see you early Saturday morning. I'll bring Roam and my wagon, so we'll all be comfortable," Joseph said.

Joseph's next stop was Alfred's General Store.

"Joseph, how are you doing?" Alfred asked.

"I'm just fine. I came in to see if you're getting a lot of compliments about the workmanship on this building!" Joseph said.

"Oh yes, we just had one the other day, but we later learned that the customer had forgotten his glasses," Alfred said.

They both laughed. Then Alfred showed him his stock of wood burning stoves. Joseph picked out one and the metal pipes to go with it.

"That's all I need today. Let it rain because it's very dry," Joseph said as he and Alfred walked out the door. John, Alfred's oldest son, had already loaded the stove and pipes on his wagon.

All three then stopped and took off their hats as another procession passed slowly by. The same man was leading the same ox and cart as so many times before, but this time the body was in a wooden casket. Alfred knew the man inside had died of a heart attack while harvesting logs in the forest for the house he was building.

As Joseph sadly left for his house, he passed by the site where his church was to be built. He found it in the early stages of construction but the workers had already left for the day.

With a wagon load of wooden roof shingles, Joseph arrived at the Miller house early on Saturday morning. They were anxious and ready to go to the country.

Max said, "I'm taking my horse because I haven't ridden in a while and it will lighten the load on the wagon. I'm looking forward to today because we haven't seen any of the country north and west of here."

The four of them rode through the middle of the town and on the outskirts met Franz and Carolina leading Tex and the cart. Anna was sitting on a stack of firewood. They all waved at each other as they passed.

Jenell said, "It's good to see Tex alive and well."

Sarah said, "I believe Tex is the most popular ox in Texas." Everyone chuckled.

Joseph and the Miller family enjoyed the ride into the countryside. The weather was still warm but there were visible signs that autumn was on the way.

Before getting to a small creek they had to stop to let a mule drawn wagon finish crossing. It was the Schuster family going to Anfang for supplies. They all got acquainted with each other and continued in opposite directions.

Traveling on the path Joseph had cleared, they soon arrived at Joseph's land. All four pitched in to transfer the wood shingles from the wagon into the house.

Joseph enjoyed showing Jenell and her parents the house and land. Since he did not yet have a table, they moved to the shade of a grove of pecan trees to have a picnic from the back of the wagon. Jenell walked around the wagon and among the trees to view the hills above and the creek below. Joseph reached into his saddlebag for his telescope. Max and Sara watched as Joseph showed her how to use it.

"This place is beautiful. I can see why you like coming up here," she said.

Joseph said, "It will look even better after I cultivate the field, enlarge the house, and build a barn.

"That will be a lot of work," Max said. "Don't you get tired?"

"Yes, I do but it's a good kind of tired," he answered.

"That will all take a lot of time," Sarah said.

"I have time but there will be a delay before I start here. I'm going to help build the church. I already have one house in Anfang and it seems that a house of God for everyone is more important than my house here. I'll be at the church site Monday morning along with anybody else who shows up," he said.

After more fun, and relaxation they decided to leave so they could be home by nightfall. Jenell talked her father into letting her ride his horse on the way back. Joseph found out she was a capable rider.

On the way back, Max thought about getting a larger brim hat like Joseph's had. Sarah wished Joseph's land was a little closer to Anfang. Jenell hoped that Joseph would ask her to accompany him to the Anfangfest. Joseph regretted that he had not listened to his mother when she offered to teach him how to dance.

On Monday, Mr. Brandt was glad when Joseph arrived at the church site as he had seen his work at the general store and bank building. Two other husky volunteers were already there.

Bernhard showed the three of them what had been done and what the plans were. He then said, "I've got somebody lined up to bring in some rocks and logs and you should see them soon. The lumber and the shingles we need will be harder to find. Do you have any questions?"

The three looked at each other and nodded that they didn't.

"That's good. I'll be in and out of here looking for material and workers. I'll bring plenty of water for everybody," Bernhard said.

The task at hand seemed massive to Joseph as the roof would be higher and the spans longer requiring a stronger foundation. Some stones were already in place and mortared but many more would be needed.

He was aware that local stonemasons had started a rock quarry not far from the church site. There they drilled holes through sections and slabs of rock to break them away to a smaller size so they could be handled, transported, and stacked more easily. Meanwhile, at the kiln, Viktor and James were busy cooking lime for the mortar to secure the rocks. They worked long hours due to the increasing demand for their product.

During the week volunteer workers for the building of the church came and went. Some could not stay long because of their age or health but most had other responsibilities. Although it was not yet needed, Anton built a tall ladder that could be used later to work on the roof. A cabinet maker named Leon was building an altar at his home. Gertrude and her friends had consulted Father Matthew and were busy making church vestments.

As usual, the construction of something new in Anfang created curiosity. Even the friendly Indians in the area were aware of the activity and seized the opportunity to do more bartering. Some brought bear fat or buffalo meat. Others brought hides, pumpkins, and honey. They left with money, food, clothing, or in some cases, things they had never seen before.

At the end of a long day Woody showed up at the work site. Joseph said, "The church isn't ready, but you can sign up while you're here."

"That's not what I had in mind just now. I noticed that Ralf's Tavern is open. This would be a good time for you to buy that beer you owe me!"

"Let me dust myself off and we'll find those suds you've been looking for," Joseph replied. Shortly after that, their horses were tied to the hitching rail at Ralf's Tavern.

There was only one customer and he asked them, "Do you boys want to play some Skat?"

Woody answered, "I can't play today because I'm here to collect a debt and catch up on the news around here. I'll be happy to join you another time."

Ralf welcomed them into his new establishment and served them two mugs of beer at a small table.

"Did you ever find out what Jenell's last name is?" Woody asked with a big grin.

"Her last name is Miller," Joseph answered.

"It must be getting serious if you know her last name."

"She is a nice girl and we've had some good times. What are you doing in town?"

"I'm going to spend some time on my land. How's the church coming along?"

"Good, but it is hard work, and everyone is hoping for cooler weather. A lot of people are helping when they can. Now, with all the limestone and granite rocks around here, carpenters are becoming stonemasons and the stonemasons are becoming carpenters."

They had another beer and talked until it was dark. Then they stepped outside and Joseph said, "You are welcome to camp on my place here, so you don't have to travel at night."

"Thanks, but I'm leaving now, I'll be on my place by midnight. As a Ranger, we didn't let the weather, or the time of day keep us from moving on. I'll see you again soon."

On an October morning the first noticeable cool front came through just as the rock foundation and floor of the church were nearing completion. The coolness lifted the spirits and production of the seven workers present at the time. One of them got a lot of hard looks as he whistled too loud and for long periods of time.

At noon, two men on horses arrived at the site. One was Mr. Brandt and the other Father Matthew. Bernhard introduced him to the workers who showed them the work that had been done. They were cautioned not to trip or fall over the construction debris scattered in and outside of the building site.

While Father Matthew and Bernhard were touring the property, Gary showed up unexpectedly. He was in a hurry and wanted to see Joseph.

Joseph said, "You look troubled. Is something wrong?"

"Yes, very wrong. Jake, the surveyor, was killed by the Comanches."

"No. That can't be. What happened?"

"We were working on separate hills. Some Indians were taking our horses we had tied to a tree near where he was. I think he tried to stop them because I heard a shot and a ruckus."

"How many were there?"

"I saw a cloud of dust, four or five Indians, and a bunch of horses. I found Jake but it was a gruesome sight. The rest of our crew buried him, and we came back. I

143

returned on a packhorse. I need to get word to his family in east Texas."

Everyone there heard what was said and gave their condolences to Gary as he had lost a good friend. He accepted the offer from Father Matthew to have prayer service for Jake.

Later that evening the workers, surveyors, and others from Anfang gathered by the church construction site. The priest took a bible from his saddlebag and presided over the service and the hymns that followed. Some of the grievers sat on the rocks that would support the walls of the church. Jenell and her parents were also there.

The work on the church resumed the next day as there was a lot of interest in finishing the exterior work before the arrival of cold and wet winter weather. The desire to do well helped overcome the lack of construction experience that some of the workers had. Logs came in from different directions and flat chunks of rock were accumulated to help fill the voids between the logs. There were enough experienced workers, like Joseph, to make sure that the finished structure would be sound.

Those working in the evenings could hear the musical instruments that were warming up for Saturday's Anfangfest.

At mid-week, before going to work, Joseph saddled Roam and rode to the Miller house. Sarah invited him in for a cup of coffee. He took off his hat and went in.

She said, "Max has already left for work. A lot of people are looking for relief from intestinal problems. I hear that Dr. Wald is very busy too and he has hired someone named Katharina to help him."

"I know Katharina," Joseph said. "She was on our ship and spent most of her time helping the many sick people on board. That's good news for her and our town. Is Jenell here?"

"Yes, she'll be here in a moment. Pardon me because I need to go out and feed the chickens," she said.

Just then, with her big smile, Jenell came in from the back room, poured herself a cup of coffee, and sat down at the table with Joseph.

Joseph said, "I've seen majestic mountains in Germany, birds of all colors by the seashore, pretty wildflowers in Texas, but I have never seen a more beautiful sight than I am seeing right now."

Jenell blushed and said, "Thank you Joseph. I think you are very kind and very handsome. Can I tell you two secrets?"

"Sure, you can."

"This is the first time I've ever had a cup of coffee and I don't like it, but it's still the best beverage I've ever had. Secondly, Mama already fed the chickens this morning. She probably thought we wanted a little privacy, or you had something important to say to me."

"I do have something important to ask. Jenell, will you accompany me to the Anfangfest on Saturday?"

"I'd love to go with you. I'll be ready when you come to pick me up."

The pavilion at the town square was not large enough to accommodate a large crowd but it was designed so it could be enlarged. On the north end, Klaus and Rupert had built a platform to serve as a stage for entertainment and other local functions.

On the south end were tables so the food and drinks could be served. Tables to eat on were few but there were various types of benches scattered about. Some were already occupied by the older citizens waiting for the music to start.

The band members and some others were dressed in unique German costumes. A variety of musical instruments that had survived the pounding and swaying of the tall ships, were tuned and ready on the stage. Meta and Martin were members of the band getting ready to start playing.

Adjacent to the pavilion there were a few tables and chairs for those who wanted to play cards or dominoes. Games for children were set up and ready.

Jenell was ready when Joseph got to the Miller house. Sarah and Max watched their daughter as she was being helped onto the wagon. Their plans were to join them a little later.

Joseph escorted Jenell to the town square where he paid a modest fee to help defray the expenses for the event. They mingled among the early arrivals and those coming in. Between the two of them, they knew and talked with many of them. It was the first time most of their acquaintances had seen them together.

While they were sipping on a stein of beer the music started. It thrilled the audience, of which many had not heard an entire band since they left the cities and villages of Germany. People started venturing on the dancing surface which consisted of smooth and solid dirt. Those not dancing sang when they could remember the lyrics and swayed with those beside them. A singing yodeler, wearing a small brimmed hat with a feather in it, was followed by a slower waltz and a faster polka. Children of all ages were skipping and dancing to the beat of the music.

Joseph found himself in a dilemma...he wanted to dance with his lovely girlfriend, but he didn't want her to discover his clumsiness. Fortunately, Jenell had noticed that he had been watching the feet of the better dancers and he had already given some excuses for not dancing.

When the band began playing a slow tune and many people were dancing, she grabbed his hand gently and pulled him into the midst of the dancers. She, with confidence and grace, softly directed his movements until he loosened up and felt more comfortable.

When the music stopped, she said, "Joseph, I enjoyed that. You are a good dancer."

"What do you mean? I bumped into you and stepped on your feet a couple of times."

"We have to keep in mind that we came from different parts of Germany. Songs, folk music, and the way people dance can vary between different sections of the country. If we practice a lot, we can eventually dance our way up to the stars."

Joseph was dumbfounded. After hesitating he said, "I guess you are right. Let's wait for the next tune that is a little faster and we can learn more."

"That's a good idea. Right now, I see my parents sitting over there. Let's join them," she said.

Jenell and Joseph were lucky in finding a place to sit by her parents. Joyful people near and passing by were greeting each other but heard only portions of what was said due to the noise from the band and the crowd. They shook hands with immigrants they had seen in town but hadn't met and hoped they would remember their names.

When Jenell and Sarah were discussing quilting techniques with other women, Max looked at Joseph and said, "Let's go and raise the level in our beer steins."

They then walked and talked while wandering around in the crowd. It was good to see everyone having fun and not thinking about the hardships they had endured and those that were still to come.

When they returned to their spots, Joseph asked Jenell to dance as the waltz they were playing was just right. They completed more circles and ran into fewer people than on their first dance. The pause before the next dance was brief so they resumed dancing. They, however, were interrupted by Max who wanted to dance with his daughter and Sarah who wanted to dance with Joseph. They and the others were careful not to bump into a small girl, about three years old, who was demonstrating her dancing skills to anyone who would give her attention.

The band members got more creative and louder as the evening progressed.

Too soon, however, they played a medley of popular German numbers announcing that the music of the Anfangfest would soon be over. But everyone clapped and shouted their appreciation so loudly that they played another tune. Then the crowd cheered, and they played another. After the third time the band started packing their instruments bringing an end to the festivities.

On the way back to the Miller house, Joseph looked at Jenell and said, "I am wondering if you, and your folks need some pecans for the winter. There are some nice pecan trees in the river bottom not far from my place. I'm going to pick some tomorrow afternoon and it would be much more pleasant if you came with me."

"Yes, and Yes. Mama will need some for baking and I am looking forward to going with you. I'll take Papa's horse and fill his saddlebags. I'll stop by your place and we can go on from there."

They arrived back at the house at the same time her parents did. He helped her down from the wagon, walked her to the door, and they gave each other a big hug.

Jenell arrived at Joseph's house on horseback on Sunday afternoon. Joseph saddled Roam and they slowly followed the river until they came to a gently sloping meadow filled with tall pecan trees. The pecans were larger than some they had seen and were plentiful on the ground and on open clusters hanging from the limbs.

Joseph cracked the shells of a few by squeezing two on them together. He peeled and gave a sample to Jenell. She then took two small bags from her saddlebags and gave one of them to Joseph. As they were picking pecans off the ground it got cloudy and breezy and looked like it might rain.

After all the saddlebags and the other bags were filled with pecans, they draped them over their horses. They led their horses to a large smooth boulder where they could sit and rest, admiring the winding river and listening to the leaves whispering in the wind.

Just then a rain shower drifted over the landscape. Jenell said, "Look, there's a rainbow. The arc and the colors are breathtaking."

"Yes, it is a beautiful sight and a good time to ask you an important question."

With a big smile and an excited look, she said, "What do you want to ask me?"

"I love you. Will you marry me?" Joseph asked.

Jenell waited a moment and then turned to Joseph. She gave Joseph a big hug and a kiss and said, "Yes. I love you too. I will marry you and be by your side forever."

Jenell could not wait to tell her parents about the betrothal. When they got to her home, she eased off the horse before Joseph could help her down, and ran into the house.

"Joseph asked me to marry him and I accepted," she said as Joseph came in.

"We're so excited for you. You two make a perfect couple," Sarah said.

Max said, "Joseph, we'll be so happy to have you as a son-in-law. When's the big day?"

"We talked about it on the way. We were thinking about the middle of January," he answered. All four agreed.

Then Sarah asked, "Did you find any pecans?"

Jenell said, "We almost forgot about them. Yes, they're very tasty."

"Good. I'll make some cookies for when you two are man and wife."

"That gives me even more to look forward to. Now I'm going to write a letter to my family and give them the good news," Joseph said.

The next morning after he had mailed the letter, Joseph showed up to help finish the exterior of the church before the arrival of severe weather and the Christmas season. He now had an additional motive for making good progress on the building. By the end of the week, the hewed timbers were in place and the supports for the roof shingles were fastened down.

Alfred and helpers Konrad and James were instrumental in furnishing the lime to seal in the chunks of rocks between the horizontal logs. When that was finished, they constructed a rock walkway for the congregation.

Joseph and Anton, the blacksmith, carefully erected the church steeple with lumber that had been furnished by an anonymous source. When the steeple was finished, they climbed back down and were joined by the others to take a look. They then congratulated each other for a job well done.

It was windy when they were installing the shingles on the roof. One by one, the shingles went from hand to hand, up the ladder, and onto the roof. The sounds of the constant hammering were heard downwind for a long time.

As the roof progressed, the need for workers decreased allowing some to leave. Joseph and Anton stayed to finish nailing down the last shingles until Anton was summoned to his blacksmith shop to shoe a customer's horse.

The wind was increasing as Joseph was installing the last few shingles. Behind him he suddenly heard a noise and turning his head he saw the ladder fall to the ground. He finished nailing in the last shingle believing someone would come along and stand it up again.

But there was no one in sight. "If I had the lariat from my horse," he said to himself, "I could tie it to the steeple and climb down." He then walked around the roof trying to come up with a solution but there was none other than taking the risk of jumping down.

A little later he spotted Martin coming his way...Joseph could see the sly look on his face and suspected that Martin would seize the moment.

Martin said, "Joseph, let me tell you that you have a problem. You are on the roof and your ladder is on the ground."

"It's not a problem. One of my best friends just came to stand the ladder back up again."

"I didn't know I was such a good friend. Not long ago you said you were glad that we lived on the opposite sides of town so you couldn't hear me practicing my tuba."

"I was just joking. I think you're a fine tuba player."

"I also heard that you said that you hoped the workers here wouldn't leave when we started the band practice for the Anfangfest. Is that true?"

"I might have said that in humor to perk everyone up. Actually, the band sounded very good and I'm sure you saw me gliding around in front of the bandstand with my wife to be."

"I did see you stumble around out there. I'm ready to make a deal. I'll stand up the ladder if you buy me a beer."

"I'm thirsty. Let's go."

Together the two friends entered Ralf's Tavern. There were three men sitting at a dimly lit table playing Skat. Joseph bought two mugs of beer.

Martin said, "Here's to you and Jenell. She's a good catch. I heard about your wedding plans."

"Thanks," Joseph said. "I'll be making some improvements on my land soon. I hope it will be easier to get a bank loan from you than it is to get off a tall roof."

After finishing the beer, Joseph and Martin thanked Ralf and said goodbye to the card players who did not respond. Apparently, the game was so intense the players did not hear them or did not want to be distracted and make a mistake that would lead to defeat.

At sunrise the next day, Joseph rode back to the church to inspect it again. Among others already there were Father Matthew and Mr. Brandt who were discussing the unfinished interior.

Since the two looked so busy, Joseph got back on his horse to find Jenell and tell her the priest was in town. He found her at the home of Katherine's parents outside sitting on a bench...she was verbally teaching Katherine how to multiply and divide numbers.

Joseph said, "Father Matthew is at the church now. Maybe we should see him about a wedding date."

"Yes, we should. Katherine and I can finish this lesson tomorrow," Jenell answered. With Joseph's help, she got on the horse and sat behind him. Katherine waved them on even though she couldn't see them leave.

Jenell and Joseph were not the only ones who wanted to see Father Matthew. While they were waiting for him Mr. Brandt said, "Joseph, you did a lot of good work on the church and I know you have a lot of other things to do including walking down the aisle with this nice young lady. We have enough men and women to finish the work here."

"You're right about that but if you need me again for anything let me know. I see Father Matthew is ready for us now, so we'll be spending some time with him," Joseph said.

After a long discussion with the priest, the young couple returned to the Miller house. It was lunchtime and Max was there as he had closed the store for the noon hour.

During the meal, Jenell told them that the wedding date had been set for January fifteenth and that Father Matthew would preside over the ceremony. She said that she and Joseph should provide the church with more information including Baptism Certificates. Joseph said that the church had been given the name of Saint Anne Church in honor of the mother of the Blessed Virgin Mary. Other wedding details were discussed well past the time that Max should have returned to his store.

Later in the day Jenell helped Joseph gather his things as he had planned to leave town to work on his land. After they hooked up his wagon, they purchased the boards that he would need for the roof and floor of the house. It was a heavy load.

Max was still at work when Joseph brought Jenell back. Jenell offered to take care of Roam while he was away. He then received a fresh pecan pie from Sarah and a warm embrace from Jenell.

For the next few days, on his rural land, he removed the grassy roof and poles and replaced it with wooden beams, boards, and shingles. The pecan pie took much less time.

When the roof was finished, he installed beams inside the house to support the boards for the floor. At night the draft coming through the spaces between the logs was a cold reminder that he would have to make another trip with a load of lime.

Joseph did not want to return to Anfang with an empty wagon. He had seen plenty of deer and deer tracts on his place and was indebted to Otto for finding the horses and wagon that were serving him so well.

On the evening before his departure, he hiked into the hills behind his house and sat on the side of a ridge overlooking a dry creek bed. The waiting paid off as some deer were nibbling their way down toward the creek. One of them had horns so he shot it. He admired the seven-point buck, threw it over his shoulder, and headed back to the house.

When he could see the house, he stopped to catch his breath and put the carcass on the ground. To his surprise a doe and a larger buck came running past him. He shot at the buck and it stumbled and dropped. With the help of one of his horses, both deer were hanging high in a tree near his house by the time it got dark. It was mostly a sleepless night for Joseph as it was very cold, and he was worried about wild animals interfering with his harvest.

In the morning Joseph started a campfire to get warm and to make some coffee. He then inspected the two deer and found that they had not been touched.

On his return to Anfang, Joseph's first stop was Otto's place. He was happy to see the two bucks in the back of the wagon.

"Which one do you want?" Joseph asked. "I'm here to pay off my debt."

"The ten pointer has more meat, but my old teeth would prefer the younger one," he answered.

Joseph hung it in a tree and skinned and quartered it for him. When he was finished Otto said, "We're even for now. I'm going to enjoy making some fresh sausage but I'm keeping the choice meat for venison steak and jerky.

"That is good use of the meat. As you can see the horses and wagon are working out for me. I'm glad you found them. Now I'm going to the blacksmith shop to see Anton," Joseph said.

Anton admired the buck and said, "That's the biggest buck I've seen around here. What's the plan?"

"I furnish the venison, you add some pork, and we'll split the work for some fresh sausage. When can we start?" Joseph asked.

"Let's just hang it up now and start at daylight. I've got just the right size hog to go with it," Anton said.

The sausage making took up the better part of the next day. On completion of the smoking process, Joseph planned on giving some of his to the families of Jenell, Katherine, and Phillip.

In the meantime, Jenell helped Joseph prepare for his next trip. She went with him to the bank to see Martin about his future credit requirements. Martin said that he had already talked to Mr. Kuhn about his intentions related to his land and that he said his reputation alone made him creditworthy.

Next, they went to the kiln to arrange for quicklime. James told them that it would be ready by the next day.

Then Joseph said, "Let's go to the general store to see Alfred. I want to buy a new coat."

Alfred was pleased to see them come in together. Jenell was surprised and lit up when Joseph said, "We're here to look for a warm coat for Jenell. This December seems colder than the last."

Alfred led them to the back of the store and showed her the three coats he had in her size. She tried all of them on time and again during which Joseph and Alfred talked about the climate, the war with Mexico, the economic crisis in Germany, and the mustang grape wine Oscar and Freda were making. When the purchase was completed, Jenwll thanked Joseph with a big hug.

When they got back in the wagon Joseph said, "You made a good choice and you look good in it and it will keep you warm when these cold fronts come in. What are you plans while I'm gone?"

"I've been thinking about that. You know my parents and you've told me a lot about your family. I want to write them a letter and tell them about myself, my parents, and you and me together."

"I think they would appreciate that more than anything," he answered.

"I'll do it while you are gone and then we can mail it together when you get back." The letter was finished the next day.

December 17, 1847

Dear Mr. and Mrs. Schmidt,

My name is Jenell Miller. I know your son Joseph has written you about me, but I want to introduce myself to you. Since there is such a large body of water between us, I know of no other way than to write this letter.

I am 21 years old and came to Texas from Germany with my parents, Max and Sarah Miller. Mama takes care of us, the house, and the garden while Papa is a pharmacist working long days in our shop here in Anfang. All of us enjoy the company of your son who helped us out on the trail when we needed it and now makes life more enjoyable for all of us. I like music, the outdoors, cooking and want to be a teacher someday. Most of all, I am in love with your son Joseph.

I recently accepted Joseph's marriage proposal and by the time you receive this letter my last name will be the same as yours. I will be so proud of it. With the help of Joseph and many others our new church, St Anne's, will be ready by Christmas day. That gives us two very important events to look forward to. Our wedding date will be on January 15th.

Please extend my love and best wishes to your son Jacob, his wife Dorothy, and their two children Guido and Franziska.

Love,

Jenell

10

Joseph had a lot on his mind as he was returning to his land with enough quicklime to finish the exterior of his one room house. On his agenda were getting married, increasing the size of his county house, and becoming productive on his land.

Before he got there, he met Reinhold on the road that had been formed by the pioneers who were settling in the area. Reinhold told him that he never recovered his missing horse and that his son, Timm, was back at his house not doing anything. He said he and his wife, Wilma, were having trouble motivating their son.

He also met Eric Schuster on the part of the road Joseph had cleared. Eric thanked him for it as it shortened his trip between Anfang and his ranch which was just north of Woody's place. He invited Joseph to stop by anytime to see the livestock he and his family were raising.

The moderate weather for the time of year was welcome since there was no stove in the house. Also, the mortar of which the quicklime was the most important ingredient, could harden better without the risk of a hard freeze. He took great care in smoothing out the filler between the square logs as this house was going to be their permanent home.

On the third day, while he was working on the side of the house, he noticed some movement in the distance on the other side of the creek. Through his telescope he saw three Indians on horseback moving away from him. He thought they looked like Comanche's, the dominant tribe in the area. He felt they must have seen him or his house but kept on going because of a peace treaty between them and the settlers.

On the night of the fifth day he had finished filling all four walls. The flicker of the lamp subsided and added just a little warmth to the cool and damp night air.

In the morning before leaving, he took a long look at his house. His plans were to add a larger room to the front of the house requiring three walls of rock and mortar. He already had enough rocks for the fireplace. He could take a few from his rock fence, and some would be gathered or cut from the hillside behind the house. In front of that, he planned a porch as shade from the morning sun and to have a place to view the flowing creek and the horizon.

Toward the end of his return trip to Anfang, Joseph stopped at a creek to water the horses. While waiting, a small flock of wild turkeys had decided to do the same. The one bringing up the rear was the biggest, so he pulled out his pistol and shot it.

Shortly after he arrived at his house in town his neighbor, Philip, came over to greet him.

Philip said, "I think Jenell misses you. She's been coming by here every day to check on things."

"I'm anxious to see her. After I clean up a bit, I'll go find her. I brought you a surprise for keeping an eye on my place here," Joseph replied.

Joseph reached into the back of his wagon and handed him the big gobbler.

"Thank you. It's a nice change. We'll all enjoy it. Marie makes very good gravy," he said.

Jenell was filled with joy when Joseph got to the Miller house. Sarah heated coffee and served dewberry jam on buttered bread. At length they, mostly Jenell and Sarah, discussed the apparel, ceremony, and reception for the upcoming wedding.

Jenell and Joseph then went to the drug store to see her father. They waited until Max finished filling a bottle with medicine for a waiting mother. When she left Max said that inadequate diets and living conditions were still having an adverse effect on the settlers, new arrivals, and the Indians of the surrounding area. Max asked Joseph about the progress on his land but could not wait for the answer as another pale and weak looking customer came in to see Mr. Miller.

They then went to the church where they would marry. Leon, and a companion of his named Simon, had just delivered the alter Leon had made. Bernhard, Gertrude, and others were there but not too busy to show the progress that had been made inside.

Bernhard said, "Leon has told me that the wooden cross was ready and that he and Simon would bring it here in the morning. Joseph, would you help Simon take it up on the roof and help him install it? Leon and I will be here to make sure that the ladder doesn't blow down. That can happen."

Joseph turned a little red and said, "I think you're right about that. It would be my pleasure to help. Is the bell here yet?"

"Yes," he answered. "It is here, and we want you to hang it when you are finished installing the cross. You can then thread the rope through the little hole and then drop it down to us."

Joseph said, "I think you should be the first to ring it because you took so much of your time to organize everything."

"I would rather the priest ring it first. I just want to stand back and listen to the bell inviting everyone to come," he said.

The next morning the Anfang citizens were at the church to watch the installation of the cross on top of the steeple and the bell. The onlookers cheered when Simon and Joseph came down the ladder.

After the ringing of the bell on Christmas day, Father Matthew blessed the packed church and its people. After the Mass he thanked the congregation for their accomplishments and said he would pray and recommend that they should be assigned a fulltime pastor as soon as possible. In closing, he said he would be available to visit the sick and disabled until his departure in about two weeks.

After Mass the attendees continued to mingle and admire the church. Jenell received complements on her new coat. Joseph was invited to Christmas dinner at the Miller house and arrived with the Nativity wood carvings Fritz had given him. It was a holy and joyous day that was replicated by many denominations and households in and around Anfang.

It was a cold and miserable day for the people and animals of the Texas hill country when the calendar changed from 1847 to 1848. The wind howled, the sleet peppered the ground, and snow accumulated against the houses and shelters of Anfang. Most thoughts of celebrating the New Year were erased by the need to stay warm.

Those that did not have heat were welcomed into houses that had stoves or fireplaces. Father Matthew had shelter with Oscar and Freda, but he spent most of his time away comforting those that were ill. James helped Joseph load and distribute firewood from his wagon for those that needed it. Max, Sarah, and Jenell housed a young family of three that had just arrived from Germany and were looking for another place to live.

By the third day of the year the cold front had passed on by and the snow and ice melted away. Outdoor activity resumed as the population assessed their food supplies and water. By the seventh day Father Matthew had held funeral services for five people.

On Saturday, January 15th, everyone was wearing their Sunday best to attend the Rite of Matrimony for Joseph Schmidt and Jenell Miller. Mixed in with the joy of this special day was the sadness that none of Joseph's relatives could be there for the occasion and many of Jenell's lifetime friends didn't know she was getting married because of the unpredictable overseas mail service.

There were, however, many good friends they had made while crossing the ocean, trekking the land, and building new homes. Some came to the church by wagon or cart, some on the back of a mule or horse, and some by foot. A few needed a walking cane but as they entered the church, it had the same soothing feeling as that of entering a large cathedral back in the old country.

Gertrude looked with pride at the vestments Father Matthew and the servers were wearing as she and her friends had spent many days sewing them. Even without an organ or piano, the singing led by Meta, was soft and beautiful as Jenell walked down the church aisle with her father. Everyone admired her in her long white dress her mother had made. Little Lucy, carrying the wedding ring on a small pillow, was all smiles in her new dress.

Joseph looked at his lovely bride with awe as she joined him in front of the witnesses. During the service they exchanged vows. Joseph slipped the wedding ring on her finger and was given permission to kiss the bride.

After the marriage covenant, Mr. and Mrs. Joseph Schmidt exited the church while the chorale group was singing and the congregation applauding. Joseph helped Jenell onto his wagon, but he did not have to take the reins. Max led the married couple and everyone there to the pavilion at the town square where the celebration continued. The weather was cool but acceptable.

Meta was the busiest of all as she had led the singing in church and was hustling to play her concertina in the band with Martin and other musicians. The music played but no one started dancing until the newlyweds had finished the first dance. After that the young and the old joined in with the men wanting to dance with the bride and the women with the groom.

The food people brought was set up on tables at the end of the pavilion. Next to it was a wedding cake and gifts for the bride and groom. Included was a bottle of mustang grape wine from Oscar and Freda. The drinks, including the beer Max had furnished, were already coating the vocal cords of those starting to sing German folk songs. Father Matthew joined in the fun and could be seen amongst the crowd being introduced, or introducing himself, to anyone he didn't already know.

Later when everything started winding down, Max led Joseph's horses and wagon to the pavilion. With everyone shouting their best wishes, Mr. Schmidt helped Mrs. Schmidt up on the wagon. Max and Sarah watched as their only child and son-in-law rode away.

Jenell prepared coffee the next morning. Joseph's watched her for a while and said, "I thought you did not like coffee!"

"It is a cold morning and I'd like to share some with my husband," she said. "I like the smell of it."

Later, Max and Sarah were delighted when Joseph and Janell came by. After the hugs, Sarah sliced some bread and laid out cheese and slices of ham. The modest wedding gifts were neatly stacked in the corner of the room.

After the meal, Joseph went over to the gifts and picked up the bottle of mustang grape wine, opened it, and sat it in the middle of the table. Sarah got up to get four wine glasses that survived the journey from Germany.

Jenell was the first to take a sip and said that it could be a little sweeter. Joseph said it was a little tart but much better than the wild grapes he had eaten on the trail. Sarah tactfully said the occasion made it taste very good. Max said it would taste better in two or three years.

Max said he would return the wine bottle to Oscar or Freda the next time they came to the drug store. Sarah then went to the cupboard and handed Joseph a big square bottle with a big lid full of molasses cookies. Each cookie had a half of a pecan baked on top. Joseph and Jenell loaded the wedding gifts in the wagon knowing they would not have to buy much food for a while.

As they were getting ready to climb up into the wagon, Max said, "We've got one more gift for you to take along."

"You may not want to take the wagon every time you go back and forth to your land," Sarah added.

"What is it?" the couple asked.

"A new saddle," Sarah replied.

"With a second saddle you can both ride your horses or take the wagon if you have a load," Max added.

The young couple then followed Max and Sarah to the back room of the house where the saddle was hidden. Joseph picked it up and carried it to the wagon, thanking them over and over.

"One more thing...we bought the saddle from a Mr. Graf who made it at his home. He wants to build a shop so he can expand his business. I promised to tell you about it," Max said.

"I'll go talk to him. It might be best to start the rock work on our house after it warms up a bit. A little extra money now might mean a smaller loan later."

"Thanks again for the saddle and for mentioning my name to Mr. Graf," Joseph replied.

After Joseph and Jenell settled in and became accustomed to their new routines, Joseph started thinking more about moving ahead with plans to further develop the house and improvements on the land. But first, he located Mr. Graf's house and found him behind his house working on a saddle Eric Schuster had ordered. Mr. Graf kept on working and said, "I talked to Martin at the bank yesterday and I will get some help in financing a shop to work in. Since you built much of the bank it seems you could build a good place to make and sell leather goods. Do you have time for it?"

"I can make time. My friend, Franz, needs some work too and together we could build you a good place to do business in this growing town. I've already seen your vacant lot," he answered.

"That's good," Mr. Graf said. "I've drawn a plan and want a couple of extra windows so I will have more light to work in. When can you start?"

"We'll be in the forest for some timber the first thing in the morning," Joseph promised.

While Joseph and Franz were preparing for and working on the shop, Jenell found herself busy as well.

She continued to help her father at the drug store whenever he needed it. She spent many hours with Katherine describing the environment and reading books she could not see to read. When running errands in town, Jenell had a zip in her walk, a smile on her face, and willing to show anyone her wedding ring.

It was now over two years since Joseph had left the fields in Germany where hearty meals were always waiting for him. Now it was his wife and not his mother making sure food was on the table cooked just right. Today the onions mixed in with venison backstrap smelled great.

As soon as they sat down to eat, they heard a noise and a knock on the door.

"It's Woody. I think I smell some onions cooking."

Joseph opened the door and welcomed him in. "Jenell, this is Woody Johnson, the ranger friend I've been telling you about."

"It's nice to meet you Mr. Johnson. Come on in," she said with her usual pleasant smile.

"You can call me Woody. Here is your wedding present. I'm sorry I could not make the ceremony, but my sister was sick, and I had to help her. Since you have two houses now, I figured you could use another lamp somewhere."

"Thank you, Woody. We do need it. Why don't you light it now so you can get a better look at the venison steak smothered in onions," she said.

Woody didn't need any more encouragement. They sat down and ate while Joseph and Jenell told him about the wedding and other local news. Woody told them that he had come from Ralf's Tavern and was on his way to his land next to theirs. When they finished, Jenell got and sat the big jar of molasses cookies on the table. He watched her unscrew the big lid.

Before Woody reached in to take a cookie he said, "That's a square jar with a round lid. I'm surprised you Germans haven't invented a square lid that will turn on top of that square jar."

They all laughed but then the discussion got more serious when Woody asked, "Have any of your people started coming back from the war with Mexico?"

Joseph said, "I have heard that a few have returned but I have not had a chance to talk to any of them. What is the latest on the war?"

"The fighting is over with," Woody said. "The treaty may be signed by now. If it is, you can go fishing in the Rio Grande River and you'll still be in Texas. Or if you prefer, you can ride all the way to the Pacific Ocean and then be in a territory owned by the United States. Over time, you will probably see more and more people and wagons coming through here and heading further west."

"We're carving out our lives right here, but I can sympathize with the people looking for adventure and more opportunity," Joseph said.

Jenell said, "I agree...for us, it seems like our days get better each day."

They invited Woody to stay for the night but he insisted on traveling in the moonlight to the land he had earned for fighting in the Battle of San Jacinto. He did say, however, that it would take at least five more molasses cookies to get there.

Meanwhile, after Joseph and Franz finished building the saddle shop for Mr. Graf, Joseph went to see Sebastian about the masonry work to be done on his house in the country. He found him and Viktor laying rock for a house on the outskirts of Anfang.

"What brings you here?" Sebastian asked.

"I could use some help on my house northwest of here. I'd like to talk to you and Victor about it," Joseph said.

"Just wait till we finish this little section and then we can talks," Sebastian said.

When they were ready, Joseph explained that he wanted help in building the addition to his country house. The discussion between the three resulted in a plan to have Viktor help Joseph and stay on the property on weekdays until the job was finished. Sebastian added that he could come and go as necessary as had already hired a returning soldier from the Mexican War to help him expand his business.

After the visit he went to see Martin at the bank about a loan.

Martin said, "We've already approved you for a loan and we can provide the money whenever you need it. Sebastian and Victor have demonstrated good work and fairness so the outcome will be good. I have only one suggestion for you."

"What's that?" Joseph asked.

"Use caution with ladders," he answered with a laugh.

Joseph thought about telling Martin that he would if he promised not to stumble over his tuba but held his tongue because he had already achieved his goal at the bank.

His next stop was the drug store where Jenell was on duty. He told her about the loan approval and the work that was planned.

"With all that help I know we can move out there sooner but I'm sure going to miss you during the week," she said.

"I'll be thinking about you all the time but before we know it, the house will be finished and we will always be together," Joseph promised.

The plan to build the rock addition was expected to work quite well as it would enable Joseph to see his bride on weekends. At the jobsite, Joseph's principle duty was to locate and gather the rocks needed. Workers drilled the holes in them, broke them apart, and chiseling them to the desired size. They were then nestled in place and surrounded by mortar.

Joseph excused himself a little earlier on the third day so he could ride to Reinhold and Wilma's place. He talked to Reinhold first as he was out feeding his cows. Then he went to their house and found Timm sitting on the front porch.

"What are you doing here?" Timm asked, "We don't get a lot of company."

"I'm looking for someone with a good grip and a strong back to do some work for me. I can pay a good wage," Joseph said.

"What kind of work is it?" Timm asked.

"I need a well dug near my house. The stonemasons and I will be busy at the same time putting up some rock walls for the house. It sure would be nice if my wife and I didn't have to go down to the creek for water all the time," Joseph said.

"Do you have the tools?" Timm asked.

"I've got the tools to start," Joseph answered.

"I'll talk to my folks about it," Timm promised.

"I think you're old enough to make that decision yourself," Joseph said.

Timm squirmed a bit and then said, "I'll see you in the morning."

When Joseph was back in the saddle Wilma stepped out on the porch to join Timm and wave goodbye. It was the first time he had seen her smile.

As promised, Timm did show up for work early the next morning. He seemed anxious to start and Joseph showed him where he wanted the hole dug. Joseph had a pick, shovel, crowbar, and a tall pole ladder propped up against a tree limb near the well site.

Joseph said, "You won't be alone out here, and you will get some help. When the hole gets deep enough, we will line it with rocks, so the walls won't cave in. I'll pay you at the end of each week."

"I've never been paid for my work. I'll do what I can to get you some water down there," Timm said.

"If not, we will try again. I'll be around here if you need anything," Joseph answered.

Viktor had brought his own tools and started preparing the foundation for the heavy rock walls. Joseph, with wheelbarrow and horse drawn wagon, gathered more rocks. The hard labor for all three continued for weeks and they helped each other out when necessary. Joseph provided most of the food from the weekly trips to Anfang and from hunting and fishing.

As the well hole deepened, Joseph helped Timm bring up the dirt and rocks from the bottom. He had obtained a shovel and scoop that was about twice as long, as he was tall, that helped bring the soil up. When the pole ladder became too short, Joseph made a rope ladder and tied it to the trunk of a nearby tree. A rope with a bucket tied to one end made many trips up and down the shaft.

As the height of the walls of the house went up the depth of the well went down. Joseph helped Viktor place some of the larger rocks on the walls and fireplace. The front door of the original log house would soon become an interior door allowing passage between the back room and larger front room.

At the end of a long day, after Timm had left and Viktor was resting, Joseph saddled Roam to visit Eric Schuster who had invited him to see his ranch. He found him and his wife Hilda sitting on the front porch. Eric was smoking a pipe and Hilda was doing some mending. When they recognized Joseph, Eric went inside to get another chair.

"I'm a little sore from digging a hole and working with rocks, but I think I can still get off of this horse," Joseph said.

"Come and have a seat," Eric said. "Our boys, David and Dominik, are still out working with the sheep,"

"I was a little surprised when I saw the sheep droppings. I thought you were just raising cattle," Joseph said.

"On this land you can do both. People up in the east like the wool and when you are finished shearing you still have the sheep. We couldn't do it all without the boys and the dogs," Eric answered.

"Jenell and I are going to mix a little farming and ranching. We might consider raising some sheep or goats someday," Joseph said.

"Do you have any dogs?" Hilda asked.

"Not yet," Joseph answered.

Hilda then looked at Eric and said, "It seems we have too many now."

Eric got the message and said, "Joseph, would you take a pup off our hands? Eventually he could help guard your house and herd your livestock."

"Yes, and Jenell would like a pet. I want to pay you," he answered.

"You already did when you cleared the road that shortened our trip to Anfang," Hilda said.

Hilda got the pup and handed it to Joseph when he was back on his horse. The young dog became a welcome distraction form the strenuous work. For much of the time it was kept in the bed of the wagon so it wouldn't fall into the well.

Timm continued working diligently on the well while Viktor concentrated on finishing the stonework on the house. Joseph helped the one who needed it the most.

On a warm muggy afternoon, Joseph was helping Viktor do the chimney work on the house when they saw Timm scrambling out of the well and running up to where they were working.

"I did it. I did it. I found the water table," he shouted.

Viktor said, "I've never seen anybody so happy for getting all wet and muddy."

"Congratulations, Timm. Your persistence paid off. It will make life easier for Jenell and me. I'll help you finish it and then we'll line the bottom with some gravel and sand from the creek. For now, let's call it a day and we'll see you in the morning," Joseph said.

Reinhold and Wilma followed Timm to his job site the next morning because they wanted to see what their son had done. Wilma was holding a potato cake and noticed that Joseph was paying Timm for the work he had done.

Viktor followed them to the well. Everybody looked into the dark hole, and Joseph asked everyone to be quite for a moment. He then picked up a small stone and dropped it into the hole. They all cheered when they heard a splash.

The potato cake went well with the coffee Joseph had made. Viktor turned to Timm and said, "I'm going to talk to my boss, Sebastian, about you. Over time there will be more houses to build and wells to be dug out this way. When that happens, he could use your help."

"Be sure and let me know. In the meantime, we have some catching up to do on our place," he said. His parents smiled.

On Friday Joseph enjoyed the trip back to Anfang as he was looking forward to spending more time with his wife. Since his last trip dazzling red, blue, and yellow wildflowers had decorated the countryside. He stopped to gather the most majestic ones.

Joseph was right. Jenell was elated to see her husband, the bouquet of flowers, and the dog playing in the bed of the wagon. She said, "That is a cute dog. In the Schmidt tradition we will have to come up with a good name for it."

Jenell arranged the flowers in a jar of water. She then stood back and looked at them again and again.

On Saturday, and after they had taken care of the horses and worked in the garden, the young couple took the wagon into town to buy supplies. Their first stop was Alfred's General Store. While they were looking at some well buckets, they heard the church bell.

When Jenell saw that Joseph looked puzzled she said, "That's Otto ringing the bell you helped install. He has offered and is ringing it every day at the noon hour."

"It has such a nice sound. It's the first time I've heard the bell from a distance," he said. "Otto is very reliable, and he'll always ring at the right time."

The next stop was to buy some boards and wood shingles. After it was loaded Jenell had to hold the dog due to the lack of space. They visited Max at the drug store, Sarah at her home, and Katherine at her parent's house. At all the stops, their dog received the most attention.

On Sunday afternoon Jenell packed a picnic basket so she, Joseph, and the dog could go for a walk. The basket was hand woven and a wedding gift that they were using for the first time. When they came to a fallen tree they stopped to rest, eat, and admire their primeval surroundings.

Jenell said, "I can't wait to see what you've done on the place. How long will it take to finish the house?"

"I can't wait to see both of us together in the house. If everything goes well this coming week, we can move real soon. It would be best to wait until we have a finished roof and floor before we move in," Joseph said.

"It's all so exciting. I'll start getting things ready here," she said.

When Joseph pulled up to the unfinished house the next morning, he jumped off the wagon and finished the task of tying the new bucket to the end of the rope. He slowly lowered it into the well and then pulled up a bucket of cool water using a turn handle he had made.

Viktor pulled up in his wagon shortly afterwards. Without hesitation they started doing the heavy work to finish the addition. Joseph left to cut and chop more beams for the floor, roof, and porch while Viktor located and cut the rocks still needed to finish the upper part of the walls.

On the third day the heavier work was finally finished. Joseph paid and thanked Viktor for his work. Before leaving, Joseph calculated and listed the material needed to finish the house.

When approaching his house in Anfang, Joseph saw Jenell and their dog come running to him as the sound of the horses and wagon must have alerted them. Joseph, although tired and weary, picked her up and whirled her around. The dog jumped up and down looking for attention.

Joseph asked, "Have you thought of a name for the dog?"

"No, I haven't. Have you?" she asked.

"That dog follows you here like a shadow. Maybe Shadow would be a good name for that little rascal!" Joseph said.

"I think it's a great name...Shadow it is. Let's go feed him and then we'll feed ourselves. Supper is almost ready," she said.

Since wood products were scarce on the frontier Joseph and Jenell left early in the morning to try to locate some. They were fortunate to find what they needed and were loading it up when Walter told Joseph there was a letter for him at the warehouse. They went to pick it up and he opened it.

April 4th, 1848

Dear Joseph

Warm greetings to you and Jenell but I have some sad news to report. Joseph, our dear Father passed away yesterday. I saw him returning from the fields when he grabbed his chest and fell near the barn. There was nothing that Dorothy or I could do for him.

As you can imagine our Mother is weeping and sitting in her chair with her rosary in hand. She asked that I send you her love and that she found comfort when Father Lange came to see us. Franziska and Guido are already missing their grandfather. We are receiving a lot of condolences and expect a large gathering for the burial.

If Gustav Schmidt was still here to talk to us, he would say we should keep on supporting and loving our families under the watchful eyes of God and not to worry about him.

Jenell, thank you for the letters you sent. It is an honor to have you in our family.

Love,

Jacob

Joseph handed the letter to Jenell and sat down on a bench and buried his face in his hands. When Jenell finished reading the letter she cried too but tried to console Joseph. After a while they stopped at the Miller house to relate the news to Max and Sarah.

To Joseph the sound of the church bell on Sunday morning was solemn. Father Matthew greeted everyone at the door and soon thereafter announced that the Mass intention was for Gustav Schmidt, a parent of a parishioner. After the service church members approached Joseph and Jenell to express their sorrow.

That afternoon Shadow couldn't find anybody to play with him until Thomas and Klara, the children next door, asked if they could. Jenell told them they could but they must not go down to the river by themselves.

Joseph looked at the load of building materials on their wagon and said, "Jenell, I'm not sure about going to the land just yet."

"I understand and I am grieving with you," she said. "I think your father would be proud to see what you're accomplishing. You can reminisce about him while you're building our home. In the morning I will pack your food while you are hitching up the horses."

"I suppose you're right. In a week we can pack our things and move into our new house. It will be nice to have you by my side," Joseph said.

"I'll be busy too getting things ready for our move but first I will write your family and let them know we received the letter and that we will always remember and pray for your father," she said.

"That's nice of you. In the morning I'll get an early start. The sooner I leave the sooner I'll be back."

The work was waiting for Joseph when he got there but he first wanted to verify that the well still had water. He pulled some up with ease and found that it was clear and had good taste. The work started with the installation of the windows that had been strategically planned for ventilation and security purposes. While working on them he hoped they would never see an enemy approaching.

On Wednesday he started positioning the rocks, beams, and boards for the porch. He installed them so the water from rains would drain down the front of the porch.

On Friday he installed the heavy entrance door. The hardware Anton had made for him worked well. In addition to the lock on the door, he mounted metal brackets on the inside of the door...should it become necessary, one could place a board on them to help prevent entry of an intruder.

It was a pleasant spring day when Joseph started back to Anfang with an empty wagon and a mind full of thoughts about his deceased father and grieving mother. He wished he could sit by her rocking chair and talk about old times.

On his return to the little house on the river, Jenell was a welcome sight as she came running toward him. Shadow failed to break into their warm embrace.

"I have to go in and check on the soup," Jenell said. "After you put up the horses and wagon, I've got a surprise for you."

"I can't wait to see, hear, or eat it. I'll be right in to find out what it is," he said.

After entering Joseph sat down at the table and said, "The soup sure does smell good. Is that a new recipe?"

"No, we've had it before," she said.

"Then what's the surprise?" Joseph asked.

"When we move tomorrow, we won't be alone," Jenell said, with a smile.

"Of course, we won't. We'll have a big load, but we'll still have room for the dog. It would be too long a walk for Shadow," he said.

"I'm not talking about Shadow."

Joseph looked at the twinkle in her eyes, hesitated, and then sputtered, "You mean. You mean. You mean I'm going to be a father!"

"Yes. There will be even more joy in our lives," she said.

"That's wonderful. It's good that we're moving to a bigger house. I'm going to watch you closely, so you don't fall or work too hard. Whenever you need something you must tell me," he said.

"Don't worry. I'll be fine and I'm so glad we have each other. Now the soup is ready, and it should be good nourishment for all three of us."

After his third helping Joseph said, "We can pack in the morning and see your parents at church. After that we'll be on our way."

While loading his trunk on the wagon, Joseph had recollections of the loading and unloading of his trunk and toolbox on the oxcart while hiking from Ensenada to Anfang. Other fixtures, kitchen goods, bedding, clothing, and a stove filled up the wagon. There was enough room left for Shadow but in the wagon was not where he wanted to be while his masters were attending the church service. The parishioners could hear Shadow whimpering when they came out of church.

After visiting with Jenell's parents, Joseph and Jenell left for their new home in the country.

Sometime later when it came into sight, Jenell said, "The house looks so inviting. I can't wait to go inside."

Joseph said, "It will be a good place to raise a family. When we need to do something in town, we can stay in our small house."

It did not take long for them to unload the wagon. While Joseph was installing the cooking stove Jenell started putting their things in place. Shadow looked unsure of himself as he was watching the antics of a horned toad prowling around an ant nest.

Near the end of the day they sat on the porch to rest and admire the view. As the sun was setting behind them, they watched the shadows of the evening extend across their fields, down to the meandering creek, and over the vast landscape beyond.

At the break of day Jenell went and slowly lowered the bucket into the well for the first time. She swung her long dark hair aside so she could get a better look. As she raised the bucket to the surface, she smiled and hummed her way back into the house with fresh water.

Joseph walked around the yard and surroundings to determine the best locations for the barn, corral, and crops. He asked himself, "Where do I start! Which is the most important? They are all dependent on each other."

Joseph looked at the open area where he had already cleared away rocks and built a rock fence. He carried a shovel with him and inspected the soil in different locations. He considered the slope of the land and tried to visualize the effects of whatever rain and runoff they might get. He also wished he could consult his father to help determine the most efficient and practical layout for their farm.

"What are you thinking?" asked Jenell when he returned to the house.

"We can't do everything at once. This year we'll have to concentrate on having enough nourishing food for the three of us. We'll start with a garden and get a few chickens and a milk cow. We're fortunate to have deer, turkey, and fish on our place. Saturday we can go into Anfang and pick up a plow."

"I'll help you work on the place when I can. I was raised in the city, but I love being out here in the country. The house will be warm and ready when the baby comes but we will need a crib," she said.

"Tell me what you want. I will build it and you can make it comfortable for our baby. Have you thought of a name?" he asked.

"Yes, if it's a boy I like the name Benjamin. If it's a girl Gretchen sounds nice. How about you?" she asked.

"If it's a girl I like Bernadette. If it's a boy I like Johann. Most of all I hope the baby is healthy," Joseph answered.

"I agree and my parents think I should see Dr. Wald. My father, as a pharmacist, has gotten to know him well. I think I could see him on Saturday," she said.

"That's a good idea. We'll leave early Saturday and take care of a few other things," he replied.

Max and Sarah were happy to see their daughter and son-in-law when they arrived. The week that had just passed, was the longest time they had not seen their daughter.

Max accompanied Joseph to see Otto who had accumulated a few old and rusty farm implements people had traded or did not need due to a death in the family. He showed him a sturdy plow that only needed minimal repair and Joseph agreed to buy it. Max insisted on paying for it.

Sarah took Jenell to see Dr. Wald who stayed open later than usual to see her. After the doctor's visit they went to the general store to buy food for an evening meal at their house.

After dinner, Sarah opened a bottle of Mustang Grape Wine. When they were all served Joseph said, "I want to take this opportunity to make an early toast to the expansion of our family."

Jenell said, "I can't have wine, but I have some more good news. You're going to have to make two cribs."

Joseph's eyes widened and for a moment he was speechless. He put his glass down and got up to give his wife a big hug. "Wow! That is a surprise...a very good surprise. Raising twins will be a lot of fun. We'll just have to come up with some more names."

Sarah said, "I'm excited too and I'll be here for both of you whenever and wherever you need it."

"Jenell and Joseph, by the end of this year your family will double in size. It's a blessing and I'm looking forward to having two grandchildren," Max said.

"I'm looking forward to it too but now I think I'll have Jenell's glass of wine," Joseph said.

The year 1848 was a busy and eventful year for Mr. and Mrs. Joseph Schmidt. Having kept the small house in Anfang was a wise decision as it provided a place for them to stay when they made weekend trips into town for business, recreation, and church services. They were also pleased that their Anfang neighbors, the Braun Family, had asked to use and maintain their garden there for a share of the harvest.

When Joseph completed the woodwork for the two cribs, he started cutting down cedar trees to provide posts for the corral. He stopped for a while when Timm stopped by to check on the performance of the well he had dug. He was pleased with it and said he was going to help Viktor build another house in the vicinity.

Another day Hilda Schuster the wife of Eric, brought by a fresh leg of mutton as a friendly gesture. Jenell thanked her and showed her the house. Later they cooked it outside on an open fire as it was already very warm in the house. The meat was tender and delicious.

It was a very cold day, however, when it came time to take Jenell to Anfang for medical care. Among those notified was Katharina who had delivered more babies than anyone else in the river valley.

On a December morning and with Joseph and Jenell's parents present, Katharina placed two infants in the welcome arms of their mother, a boy and a girl.

11

On a typical spring afternoon in the year 1856 Jenell was singing softly to herself while she was hanging wet clothes on the wash line. Joseph and their draught mule were pulling up decayed tree stumps around the edges of the fields with a heavy chain.

After Jenell hung up the last garment she quietly returned to the house so she would not awaken Benjamin and Bernadette who were taking a nap.

Their beds, however, were empty. Noticing that the hook on the back door was unhooked she rushed outside looking for them. She saw them a short distance away and was getting ready to scold them when she saw they were picking wildflowers.

Bernadette said, "Look Mommy, we are picking pretty flowers for you."

Benjamin said, "Yes, we found them yesterday. We wanted to surprise you."

"They are so beautiful, but I was worried about you. How did you unhook the door? It is too high for you to reach!" their Mother said.

"It was Benjamin's idea," Bernadette said.

"But you saw the broom standing in the corner," Benjamin replied to her.

"Okay, okay, that's enough," Jenell said. "Don't do it again and remember we always want to know where you are. Now it's time to go inside. We're going to learn to spell some more words but first we will put my flowers in water so we can all admire them."

After Joseph returned from the fields and the twins finished their lessons for the day Jenell said, "Let's take the kids for a ride. It's a perfect day for it."

"That sounds like fun and I'd like to stop by to see Woody. I'll get the wagon ready," he replied.

"We don't need it. Let's just take the horses," she suggested.

"Good, I'll saddle them up. We can take our time so the twins can ride bareback on our old horse. We can circle around and check the cattle on the way back," he said.

"While you're getting the horses ready, I'll feed Shadow, so he won't be tempted to follow us," she said.

Benjamin won the battle between himself and his sister to sit in front on the back of the old horse. When Joseph gave Benjamin a serious look about that, Benjamin told Bernadette, "You can take the reins on the way back."

The Schmidt family rode their horses up the creek, through a wooded area, and to a clearing where Woody's small square notched house was being built.

Woody was all smiles when he limped down to where they left their horses. Joseph helped Jenell dismount. The twins declined help from anyone as they were "big enough to get down by themselves." They slid off the saddleless horse and down to the ground with ease.

"Your house is shaping up. You must be getting soft because soon you'll have a roof over your head just like the rest of us," Joseph said.

"Maybe I'm just getting a little smarter or I'm a little tired of staying in the cave when the weather is bad. I do owe you and our other neighbors a lot for helping me build it. As you see I don't have chairs or benches yet, but we can circle some of those short logs and sit a spell."

Benjamin asked Woody, "Can we go and look at your cave again?"

"I don't mind but you should first ask your parents," he answered.

Joseph nodded his head in agreement and Jenell said "Watch for snakes and don't stay too long."

After the twins left Joseph said, "We like our farm and ranch here, but I'm still interested in seeing our other tract of land on the land grant. Would you care to go up there with me to see what it looks like?"

"You know I'm always ready to get on my horse and go somewhere. You just tell me when you're ready," he answered.

Jenell said, "While you're gone the kids and I will spend a few days in Anfang with my parents. I hope they don't spoil them too much."

"How are the twin's lessons coming along?" Woody asked. "I hear you're teaching them daily."

173

"They're both good students but Bernadette can listen for a longer time. I hope we have a school out here someday," she said.

"In a few years there should be enough children to have a school. It's just too far to travel all the way to Anfang every day. When the time comes, I can spare a few acres for your schoolhouse," Woody promised.

"That is so generous of you and will give everyone out here something to look forward to," she said as she got up off the log and gave Woody a big hug.

On the way back to their house they circled around the hilly back side of their land and found the cattle grazing among some high weeds and grass in an open meadow.

"We're missing a cow," Joseph said. "I'll look for her first thing in the morning."

After a breakfast of eggs, bread, and honey Joseph was saddling his horse near the barn when he spotted movement on the opposite side of the creek. He stopped when he recognized a rider and a cow coming his way. It was Dominik Schuster returning their cow with the Double JJ brand.

"I sure am relieved and thanks for finding her and bringing her back," Joseph said.

"She was mixed in with our cattle and we know you would do the same for us. On this open range, we need to watch out for each other."

"By the way, that looks like a fine horse your riding. Where did you get it?"

"I bought it from Thaddaeus Huber who has a big place just east of Anfang. He's raising some good horses down there along the Bend River."

"I'll have to go see him soon. My horse is dependable but starting to slow down a bit. I need a good, fast horse out here."

"He'll probably have one. I need to head back. By now I'm sure David is wondering why I'm taking so long."

The return of the missing cow left time to start something else. After consulting with Jenell, he left for Timm's house to see if he would help him shear sheep.

He found Timm digging a new posthole next to a broken post. "Timm, I'm shearing a bunch of sheep tomorrow. I can pay you for helping me after the wool is sold and we get our money. Do you have time?"

"Shearing sheep is not my favorite pastime but then I could buy a new saddle sooner. I know you like to start early and that's when I'll be there."

"Jenell, Shadow, and I will round them up today and will have them penned up when you arrive," Joseph said.

Benjamin and Bernadette didn't like being restricted to the porch while the sheep were being rounded up. The sheep were near the creek and were not anxious to leave the short, tender vegetation they had found. With Joseph and Jenell on horseback and Shadow in charge, the weighted down sheep slowly made their way up to the pens. The closer they got to them, the more they tried to escape. When they were finally penned up, Benjamin and Bernadette came down from the porch... they were then warned not to attempt riding any of the sheep.

After Timm arrived the next morning, they greeted the sunrise and started sheering the alarmed sheep. One by one Joseph and Timm grabbed them, held them down, and clipped off the thick wool. Janell was the gatekeeper as the sheep came into the sheering pen and as they left. All three stuffed the wool into burlap bags so they would be ready to be hauled to market. They were then stored in the barn.

When the job was done the Schmidt family, Timm, and the dog went down to the creek to freshen up. The twins played with one of their handmade toys for the first time...a boat moved gracefully in the cool, clear swirling water.

Jenell soaked in the water to relax from the day's hard work. Joseph, while relaxing in a deeper pool of water, was studying the structure of a tall tree at the water's edge...its long, thick limb looked just right for hanging a rope one could swing out over the water and jump in. Timm thanked Joseph and Jenell for the opportunity to earn some extra money and left with a sack of vegetables Jenell had gathered for him.

The remoteness of the Double JJ Farm and Ranch, and the imagination of its occupants, resulted in many homespun toys and activities for the Schmidt twins. Although Bernadette would never outgrow her German made doll she enjoyed running and playing outdoors. Benjamin would never forget his many rides on the wheelbarrow but riding a horse was now much more exciting. Bernadette learned to walk on stilts and Benjamin could juggle three apples at one time. Both enjoyed singing improvised versions of the Schnitzelbank song with their parents where they learned to identify things and places they had never seen.

Meanwhile, after Joseph delivered a wagonload of wool to a warehouse in Anfang and his wife and children to the Miller house, he returned to the Double JJ and packed the provisions for a trip to the land grant. He had a copy of the survey of his tract and directions to it.

Woody was ready to go when Joseph rode up to his house. Together they crossed the Schuster land where Joseph met and asked Eric to have his sons check his livestock as he would be gone for a few days. Eric said he would prefer to do it himself as he wanted to see Shadow, the dog they had given them.

Joseph was glad to have the company of a ranger who had been to many places and had many experiences in Texas. Woody was glad to have someone to talk to as it helped ease the pain of having lost his wife and son to Santa Anna's brutal army.

"What is the purpose of this trip," asked Woody.

"Just curiosity I suppose. I am where I am because I read an ad about free, fertile land in Texas. It turned out very good for us, but I would like to see the place that brought me here. Some immigrants have sold their tracts without ever seeing them. Franz and Carolina sold their grant for a mere hundred dollars."

"Too bad they couldn't wait for better times. The Comanche's have controlled a large chunk of this state for a long time. The forts the United States built in the last few years are making a difference for the settlers and the people moving west, but tribes are scattered all over the place and they keep moving around."

"If everyone would abide by the peace treaty everyone would be better off," Joseph said.

"It did help. Many settlers and Indians are trading with each other and are getting along just fine but there are some that will not abide. The buffalo are still being killed for hides and the raids are continuing. Some never heard of or participated in the treaty. There are many tribes with many chiefs, and I know of no chief that is over all of them. The hostility is far from over."

"You make it sound like we should have some guns for our protection," Joseph said.

Woody laughed and said, "It would help if you would get a six-shooter. I know you are really good with your firearm, but while you are trying to reload, the Indian warrior on his fast horse can pepper you with his arrows."

"I'm aware of the Colt pistol and I know you have one. I'll check into it as I want to keep up with these modern times," Joseph stated.

The discussions continued when the path they were following allowed it. They crossed rivers and streams, went up and down hills, and negotiated brush and cactus.

On the third day they located markers that revealed the corners of Joseph's land grant. It had the shape of a domino with the short ends facing east and west.

Knowing that many thoughts were racing through Joseph's mind, Woody said, "I'm a little hot and tired. I'm going to rest in the shade of that scrub oak tree. When the sun sets, I'll be ready for some jerky, bread, and whiskey but not in that order.

Joseph slowly rode around on the land. It looked a little arid but perhaps it was because a herd of buffalo had grazed and stomped a large swath across it.

He did not find any standing water but there was a draw where rainfall could be trapped. He was startled when a covey of quail blasted out from under some cactus plants.

"What do you think about the land?" Woody asked when Joseph returned to his shade tree.

"I like it. I know some would say it's too rough, but I think it has some potential. It feels good and I'm not going to sell it. By the way, I saw some horned animals through my telescope. They looked like deer but weren't. They spotted me and ran like the wind."

"I'm sure those were Pronghorn Antelope. Did you ever catch one of those Jackrabbits we saw some years ago?"

"Not yet. I've been too busy," he said with a smirk.

"Then for sure you won't corner an antelope. They can leave a Jackrabbit sitting in the dust."

Joseph and Woody took a more westerly route on the way back. It was a bit more rugged than the first and the sun seemed more intense. As they rounded a turn on a seasonal creek, they noticed a bare area that looked like it had been disturbed.

They stopped to see if they could hear anything. They didn't and proceeded to it with their rifles ready and in plain view. They saw no one, but there were tracks of unshod horses and the coals of a small campfire. The coals were no longer warm.

"What are you thinking?" asked Joseph.

"I'm hoping we don't find what I think we're going to find. We'll follow those tracks to where that buzzard is soaring," he answered.

When a small, crude looking house came into view they stopped again to listen. Joseph said, "I think I heard a moan."

Woody whispered, "Let's slowly circle the house from a distance before we go in. I think the varmints are gone, but we've got to make sure."

After they heard another moaning sound that came from behind the house, they found a man lying helpless in some high weeds with two arrows in his torso.

With his eyes half open, he murmured, "My daughter, where is she?"

Joseph said, "We just got here. I'll help you and my partner will look for her."

Then the man, about middle age, gasped for air and took his last breath.

While Woody was looking for traces of a girl, Joseph found a rusty shovel and started digging a grave.

"I think they took her," Woody said. "Judging from some clothing in the house, she's about fifteen years old. I have the man's name from a certificate for this land and I'll make a marker for him. After we get back, I'll report it to the nearest fort and every lawman I can find. She may still be alive somewhere."

When the cross was in place the two men removed their hats and bowed their heads. Joseph led some prayers for this immigrant and his missing daughter.

Joseph and Woody parted when they got to Woody's land. Joseph was welcomed by their dog, Shadow, before reaching his house. After accounting for the livestock, he hitched up the wagon and headed for Anfang.

When he arrived, his wife and children almost knocked him over with joy and exuberance before he could step into the Miller residence. It did not take long for Sarah to serve a snack for all of them.

When they finished, they got into the wagon to see Max at the drug store. They did not interrupt him because he was busy waiting on a group of ill looking pioneers who were coming through on their way to California.

The next stop was the warehouse where Joseph learned that their wool had been sold at a favorable price. After collecting the money, they went to the general store to buy some provisions.

The garden at their house was in good shape thanks to the efforts of the Braun family. Joseph and Jenell were looking it over when Bernadette and Benjamin asked to go swimming.

"That's not a bad idea," Joseph said.

"I want to go too but first we should not disturb the fish. Let's catch some fish so we have something to go with the vegetables," Jenell said.

Jenell found their two cane poles and borrowed two more from the Braun's next door. Joseph with his shovel, broke ground near the riverbank at a moist spot where earth worms often congregated... he found enough for today's fishing.

After what seemed like a long wait, Jenell caught a big perch. The twins caught some too. Jenell was then surprised by a large sized bass she caught. Joseph, who spent considerable time baiting hooks and putting fish on a stringer for the others, finally caught a small catfish and a much longer tree limb.

The swim was fun and refreshing for the whole family. Bernadette and Benjamin did not want to come out of the water, but their parents did...they sat on a fallen down tree trunk to watch their children.

Jenell asked him, "What are you thinking about?"

"About how lovely and gracious you are," he answered. "What were you thinking about?"

"I'm thinking about how considerate and caring you are," she said with a warm smile.

That evening, as the sun went down, the Schmidt family enjoyed a hearty meal of fresh fish, potatoes, corn, and squash that had been cooked over an open fire. After dinner and the fire died out, they turned in for the night.

The next day was full as well. After Sunday mornings church service, Father Matthew commented on how big the twins were getting. Gertrude told Joseph and Jenell that she and Otto would get married someday but that it would never interfere with Otto's ringing of the church bell.

They also noticed Franz, Carolina, and their daughter Anna climbing up on a mule driven wagon.

Joseph said, "I like your mules and wagon, but I guess that means its bad news for Tex."

"Tex and the cart gave out at about the same time. He is in greener pastures now," he answered.

Jenell said, "None of us will ever forget the ox that brought Joseph here, helped me and my parents on the way, and helped build our houses. Come see us sometime and we'll talk about old times."

"That would be fun and a nice change for us. We'll come as soon as we can," Carolina promised.

Later, and as they were approaching their home in the country, Jenell said, "Look at our house from here. It is so nice, and we are so fortunate to have it. It's a great place to raise a family."

"I couldn't agree with you more, but I do have something I want to talk to you about. After the kids are in bed we can sit on the porch and discuss something important," Joseph said.

With a worried sound in her voice Jenell replied, "I'll put the kids in bed while you put up the horses. I hope everything is all right."

After they sat down on the porch Joseph said, "On the trip to the land grant Woody and I came to a house that had been attacked by Indians. We found a man who died as we tried to help him. He was probably a widower and we think his grown daughter was taken away. You and I have heard stories like that but witnessing it makes me think we should be more cautious here and when we ride into town," he said.

"Where does the danger start, and will it ever end?" she asked.

"Like Captain Harris told me once, those are two hard questions to answer. The conditions are worse north and west of here. Woody said we may have been seen by Comanche Indians we never saw or heard. It's the ones that go on raids to steal and create havoc we need to watch out for. Their territory is so large that many sad stories will never be told," he answered.

"My Father says that many of the Indians have suffered from diseases they contacted from the settlers and others coming through here. Their numbers probably have decreased because of it," Jenell said.

"That's tragic and another reason they are upset. I think they're worried about the loss of the land and buffalo that provide them meat and the hides that clothe and shelter them. I am saying that we just have to be more aware of our surroundings and inform our children."

"Maybe we should get another dog to alert us."

"That's a good idea. The Schuster's have a lot. Also, we should have another gun in the house. Woody suggested getting a revolver that holds six cartridges."

"I'm so worried now!" she said.

"Don't be. It just makes good sense for everyone to protect themselves from those, whoever they are, that want to take from you or hurt you."

"I'll talk to the children in the morning. Then I'll get ready for my parents visit. They like coming to see us," Jenell said.

"While you're doing that I'll go and pay Timm for helping us shear the sheep. He'll like that but not as much as the sheep that are much cooler now," Joseph said.

Jenell was busy in the kitchen and getting ready for her parent's arrival. Bernadette was sweeping off the front porch so it would be clean for her grandparents. Benjamin was on his hands and knees searching for doodlebugs in the cone shaped pits that were in the soft dirt under an old oak tree.

Joseph was repairing the barn door when he saw Max and Sarah coming down the road. He knew they would be bringing something, but he didn't expect to see anything jumping up and down in the bed of the wagon.

Jenell and the children stopped what they were doing and rushed down to meet them.

Sarah said, "We picked up this dog on the way. It looked abandoned and hungry."

Max said, "The bad news is that we fed it the liver sausage that we were bringing you. Otherwise she looks healthy."

"We just talked about getting another dog. If you don't want her, we may take her," Jenell said.

"You can have her," Sara said, with a smile.

Joseph said, "Let's get her out of the wagon. By the time you go back to Anfang, we'll know how she gets along with the cat, the dog, the chickens, and we the people."

Sara then said, "Bernadette, I brought a new dress for you since you're growing out of that one. Benjamin, I've got a pants and shirt for you. Let's go in the house and try them on."

Benjamin answered, "I already have a pants and shirt. I want to be outside with my father and my grandfather and the dog."

"Ben" Joseph sternly said, "You go inside with your mother and grandmother.

"How come you call me Ben sometimes?" he asked. "My name is Benjamin."

The adults winked at each other and then Joseph said, "Benjamin, you need the clothes for Sundays. Go inside and try them on. You're grandpa and I will wait for you."

After Benjamin's ordeal of having to try on new clothes, he and the dog followed Joseph and Max down to see the fields. Joseph brought along the wheelbarrow and set it down by the rows of corn.

After they toured the fields for a while Max said, "Your place looks better every time we come out here. It seems a little dry right now, but your corn looks good. With the cattle and the sheep, and the wheat and hay, I don't know how you do it all."

"I enjoy it. I learned it from my father. Jenell spends a lot of time in the garden and soon the twins will find their niche. The plowing, planting, and cultivating takes up a lot of time, but the harvesting makes it all worthwhile. Cutting the wheat with my scythe and tying it in bundles is a lot of work. We are fortunate not to have any debt now but soon we'll get more equipment and farm more acreage."

"Have you heard about the new mill near Anfang?" Max asked.

"Yes, I have. Martin is financing it and Viktor is helping build it. It will be good for the farmers around here," Joseph answered.

"What's next for you?" Max asked.

"Thanks to you we have a good plow. It takes time to borrow and return a harrow so I'm going to buy one soon. Later we'll sow some more grass for the livestock so it will help them through the winter and keep them from roaming too far. In the meantime, I'll harvest the corn since it is almost ready. Our stack of firewood has gone down again, so I'll be out cutting some more...the twins like to help stack it up," he answered.

"Be careful with all that. We saw two rattlers on the way up here. One was in the middle of the road and the other up against some rocks," Max said.

"I'm always on the lookout for them and we keep reminding the twins that they can lurch almost anywhere. Another purchase I'm making is a revolver that I can keep handy," Joseph said.

"That's a good idea. In this day and time, we all should be careful," Max said.

With the help of the children and father-in-law, it did not take long to harvest and load the wheelbarrow with a few early ears of corn. Joseph and Max selected the ones to be twisted off the stalks, and the twins loaded them on the wheelbarrow.

It was very warm in the Schmidt house as Jenell had prepared a meal consisting of mutton steak, potatoes, and sauerkraut. Bernadette and Benjamin recited the blessing as their parents and grandparents bowed their heads.

After dinner, the compliments of it, and the washing of the dishes, it was decided that they would gather on the porch where it was much cooler.

The twins, unable to sit very long, got up to get better acquainted with the new dog.

"You can play with the dog but stay where we can see you," Jenell said.

They were trying to show the dog tricks that Shadow already knew when Benjamin said, "The dog is lucky that grandpa and grandma found her. We are lucky to have her now."

"Yes," Bernadette said with her eyes opening wide. "I think Lucky would be a good name for her. Let us start calling her Lucky before someone else comes up with a name we don't like."

"That's a good idea," Benjamin answered. "I like it. I also have another good idea."

"What's that?" Bernadette asked.

"I think we should load grandpa and grandma's corn in their wagon. If we take our time, we won't have to take a nap. We are seven years old now and too old to take naps," Benjamin answered.

With Bernadette on one handle and Benjamin on the other, the loaded wheelbarrow was slowly moved closer to the wagon. They had to stop a few times to pick up ears of corn that had fallen off.

When they finally got there Benjamin climbed up on the wagon using the spokes and axel of a wheel. With Bernadette reaching up and Benjamin reaching down the ears of corn, one at a time, were neatly stacked on the bed of the wheelbarrow.

They glanced up toward the porch from time to time to see if they were being watched. They did not even notice that Shadow and Lucky were beginning to accept each other as friends.

The parents and grandparents were greatly amused by what they were watching but tried not to laugh when they saw the twins coming back up to the porch with the empty wheelbarrow.

Bernadette was out of breath when she said, "We loaded all the corn on the wheelbarrow so you all could get a rest."

Benjamin with sweat on his brow said, "We also named the dog Lucky because she was so lucky to be found."

Max said, "I think Lucky is a real good name for her."

Sara said, "I agree and bet you are both tired from all that work. Maybe you should take a nap!"

With a painful look Benjamin said, "I'm not tired. I can sleep tonight."

Bernadette followed by saying, "I'm not tired either. I want to see my grandparents while they are still here."

Joseph said, "They did work hard loading all that corn!"

Jenell, with a smile said, "Time did slip away so you can stay on the porch with us. Your grandparents want to get home before dark, and they will be leaving soon."

During the day, Joseph imagined how nice it would be to have the twin's older cousins from Germany, Guido and Franziska, there to play with them. He wondered if they would ever meet each other.

"What are your plans for today?" Jenell asked Joseph early the next morning.

"Going through the corn field yesterday made me realize that I need to buy a new hoe as ours are worn out. I'll also ride out and check on the cattle and sheep.

Tomorrow we can go into town and look for a harrow and one of those revolvers," he replied.

"Since you are so busy, I'll milk the cow and gather the eggs. When we go to Anfang we need to pick up a few supplies for the house," she said.

Joseph toiled in the cornfield all morning. Nearby, Benjamin tried to hoe weeds but accomplished little with a broken hoe. Bernadette followed her mother to the wash line to help her hang the wet clothes. When those chores were finished, Jenell summoned both children into the house for their daily school lessons.

Later in the day, Joseph saddled up to check the livestock. After persistent begging from his son, Joseph saddled another horse so Benjamin could ride along as he had become a good rider. All the sheep and cattle were accounted for except a mother cow and her calf that had wondered across the creek. On their return to the house, they heard Jenell teaching her daughter the lyrics of a German folk song.

The following day, the Schmidt family loaded the wagon and left for Anfang.

"Why do you keep turning around to look back?" Bernadette asked her father.

"We just want to make sure Lucky is not following us because she's supposed to be watching the house. Keep your eyes open," he answered.

"I don't see her, but I'll keep looking," Bernadette said, "Benjamin, you can look on that side and I'll look on this side."

They never saw the dog, but it entertained the twins all the way into town.

After inspecting their house in town, they stopped at the blacksmith shop to see Anton. He said he could make a strong hoe for them and have it finished by the time they would leave town the next day.

Next the Schmidt family paraded into the bank. Martin was busy with a customer but his wife, Beth, was there and brought Jenell up to date with all the happenings in town. The twins were sitting patiently on a bench but had their eyes fixed on a cookie jar sitting on a table near the teller window.

When the other customer left, Martin studied the contents of the cookie jar. He pulled out two and offered them to the twins saying, "These two are the biggest in the jar and they look alike just like you two do. Would you like to have them?"

Benjamin said, "Yes, I like cookies. Thank you."

Bernadette said, "I do too. Thank you, Mr. Banker."

The children devoured their cookies and waited for their parents. They saw them writing something on a piece of paper and then going to the window by the cookie jar where they were given some money.

Having bought a plow from Otto, Joseph thought he would be a good source to find a harrow. Otto didn't have one but directed him to a man named Sid who had accumulated some used implements.

Due to the high weeds, scattered equipment, and large barking dog Jenell and the twins stayed in the wagon. Joseph walked around in the yard until Sid came out of the house.

"I'm looking for a harrow and I'm ready to buy it if it's in good shape and priced right," Joseph said.

"The dog won't hurt you. I've got two harrows in the back yard and I'll show them to you."

One of the harrows had a broken tine. The other was satisfactory so Joseph bought it at the asking price which he thought was fair. After they loaded the triangular shaped harrow in the wagon Bernadette asked, "Why did you buy that? It's rusty and has a lot of dirt on it."

"That's a good question, Bernadette. We can save some money and clean it up ourselves. It will help us break up and smooth out the dirt in the fields before we plant," her father answered.

"I'm going to help you so you can rest some," she replied.

At Alfred's General Store and while Jenell was gathering the many things they needed at the Double JJ, Joseph asked Alfred if he had any Colt revolvers.

"I am sorry I don't, but you can go and see Mr. Graf at the saddle shop. He had one the last time I saw him," he said.

Joseph walked to the saddle shop to inquire about it. Mr. Graf pulled it out from under a counter and said, "One of our citizens who fought in the Mexican-American War was needing a saddle more than his pistol, worked out a deal with me. It's a Colt Percussion Revolver forty-four caliber and has some ammunition and a holster that goes with it. Since you built this good building for me, I'll let you take the revolver with you so you can try it out. If you like it, bring me the money on your next trip into town," the proprietor said.

Joseph looked it over and said, "It doesn't look like I can go wrong. I'll give it a try."

Joseph returned to the general store with the six-shooter and loaded his family and the supplies on the wagon. After spending the night in the small house, they worked in their garden in town and visited Max and Sarah. They were leaving Anfang when Benjamin tapped his father on the shoulder.

"Yes Benjamin, what is it," he asked.

"We forgot to pick up the new hoe at the blacksmith shop."

Everyone chuckled and the wagon turned around.

After their return to the Double JJ, Joseph didn't waste any time in trying out his six-shooter and his family was anxious to watch. They followed him down to the rock fence where he put a small chunk of rock on top of the layers of larger rocks.

He fired one shot and saw no evidence of hitting anything. For him it seemed strange to fire another shot without reloading but the second one hit the larger rock on which the target rock was sitting. "I have to get used to these sights," he told his audience.

The next shot pulverized the chunk of rock he was aiming at. Jenell put a still smaller chunk on the fence and it too was blown to pieces.

"That's enough ammunition for now. The next time we go to Anfang we will stop at the saddle shop and pay for this pistol. I like it," he added.

When Joseph determined that the ears of corn had filled out, he began the main harvest. His family and an occasional neighbor were able to help him out some, but most of the labor fell on Joseph's shoulders due to the remoteness of their location and a tight budget. Soon the corn and stalks would provide nourishment for his family, the marketplace, and the farm animals.

At the end of the day there was enough energy left to go to the creek and swing out on a rope and into the water to get refreshed. The twins could swim but were not allowed to do it unless one of their parents was there. Jenell knew that a combination of the day's work, and the swim, created a powerful appetite.

The raising of cattle and sheep on an open range required a lot of work and presented a lot of risk. The sheep, thanks much to the protection offered by their dog Shadow, increased in numbers although a few were lost due to sickness, the elements, and wild animals. On this day the lamb crop looked good and the sheep's wool was preparing them for the winter ahead.

Although some cattle carcasses had been found in the pastures and four head were now unaccounted for, the size of the herd on the ranch increased. Some newcomers to the vicinity, the Neumann family, had expressed an interest in buying some to start their own herd if they could get the financing.

The stove, fireplace, and an occasional outdoor fire required a lot of fuel, but the early cold spells had depleted the supply on hand. There was plenty of dead and down wood available on the land, but Joseph was now concentrating on a wooded area not far from the creek and rock fence. It was now the middle of November.

The horses and wagon were useful in open areas, but the wheelbarrow proved its worthiness in the dense thickets. Day after day Joseph chopped and split wood and threw it in small piles. When there were several piles, the one-wheeled wheelbarrow and Joseph traveled through the forest with loads of wood to the four-wheeled wagon that had been left in the clearing.

When the wagon was considered full, Joseph drove it to the woodpile near the house. There Jenell and the twins helped unload and stack the wood. On this windy day, however, Bernadette remained indoors because she was not feeling well.

Benjamin looked at his Father and said, "I want to go with you to get more firewood. I'm a good helper."

"I'm not sure that that's a good idea," his mother said. "You might get too close to the axe or a falling tree limb."

"I'll make sure he stays clear when I'm swinging the axe. There is just enough daylight left for one load," Joseph said.

Jenell said, "Benjamin, go in and get your coat. It'll be chilly by the time you get back. I'll be busy making some venison soup that will warm you up when you're finished."

Benjamin rushed in to get his coat, told Bernadette that he hoped she would start feeling better, and hugged his mother. He refused help to get up on the seat of the wagon to sit next to his father.

After they stopped the wagon, Benjamin followed his father on a short trail that led to a dead pecan tree that had fallen among some that were still bearing fruit. Joseph told him not to come too close while he was cutting up the tree and he gave him a small sack so he could gather some pecans.

Benjamin was distracted by an armadillo and some trees he wanted to climb, but he eventually filled the sack. He then said, "Look what I did. I filled the sack and I'm going to put them in the wagon."

"No, you stay here," Joseph said. "I'll soon be finished splitting this log and we'll go back together."

The trunk of the pecan tree was harder than expected and it took longer to cut and break it apart. When Joseph stopped to catch his breath, he looked around but did not see Benjamin anywhere.

After hearing rapid hoof beats, Joseph ran as fast as he could on the trail leading back to the wagon. He saw the first of three Indians on horseback scoop

Benjamin up off the ground and race away in the direction of the creek. The other two raiders were not far behind.

Joseph frantically reached into the bed of the wagon to grab his pistol. A hurried shot at the last fleeing Indian caused the culprit to reach for his side but it did not knock him off the horse.

Joseph ran after them as they galloped across the creek and up the other side in a cloud of dust. They were out of range, but he fired another shot into the air as they raced out of sight.

12

Joseph ran up to the house as fast as his legs could move. He tripped and tumbled over a rock as it was getting dark, but he quickly recovered and kept on going.

"What's wrong? I heard some shots," Jenell shouted standing on the porch with their rifle in her hands.

"Are you and Bernadette all right?" he shouted in return.

"Yes, we are. Where is Benjamin?" she asked.

"They got him. An Indian on a fast horse came and snatched him up near the wagon and sped away across the creek. Two more were behind him and I wounded one of them. I could not stop them," he said, while falling down on his knees.

Bernadette and her parents all hugged and cried in disbelief.

"I'm going to saddle my horse and find Benjamin and bring him back where he belongs," Joseph said.

"There is no moon. You can't see tonight," Jenell said.

"You are right," he said reluctantly. "I'll get some help in the morning and we will track them down."

"It's dangerous but I know I can't keep you from trying. Let's pray they're not hurting him," Jenell said.

After an agonizing and sleepless night, Joseph went to the site of the abduction and saw the spilled bag of pecans that Benjamin had gathered. He followed the horse tracks to where the Indian was wounded and found small traces of blood and an eagle feather.

Next, he went to Woody's house who quickly agreed to escort Jenell and Bernadette to Anfang. After that, he solicited help from neighbors Reinhold, Timm, Eric Schuster, and his two grown sons.

With little preparation the six of them picked up the tracks of the Indians on the opposite side of the creek. The tracks led northward, but they had made some unusual turns as if to confuse any searchers. When they came to a river, the tracks were no longer visible. There they split into two groups of three to try to locate the resumption of tracks on the other side. Eventually, Eric located them downstream and notified the others.

They continued following the tracks and soon came to an area where it was apparent the culprits had stopped. Joseph asked the others not to disturb anything until he had a chance to inspect the site.

Adult footprints were everywhere but he located smaller ones in the sand near a mesquite tree. On it he detected a small broken branch under which a pecan had been placed. He picked it up and showed it to the others as they dismounted to look around.

No other clues were found so they resumed their trek under the threat of some darkening clouds...they watched the clouds pick up speed and coming from the direction they were going. Shortly heavy raindrops announced the advancing rain that was so hard they had to stop and try to get cover under the mesquite trees.

After the downpour, and the resulting shifting sands, there were no tracks left to be found. Joseph searched the horizon with his telescope in every direction and did not see any signs of life. With everyone shivering from the drenching cold Joseph said, "We won't find them now, but I am not giving up. Thank you so much for helping us but now we have to turn back."

Of the six riders, Joseph was the quietest on the way back to their homesteads. The pecan found under the small mesquite tree convinced him that Benjamin was still alive. His mind was crowded with thoughts and methods of finding and getting their son back.

The searchers turned to their respective homes and after Joseph confirmed his house was undisturbed, he rode to Woody's house to see if he was there.

He found Woody cleaning his rifle and pistol when Joseph pulled up. Judging by the look on Joseph's face, he did not ask how the search went.

"Your wife and daughter are safe in Anfang. The news was very hard on Jenell's parents," Woody said.

"I need to go into town and see them. I'll be thinking about what I should do. I want to learn everything I can about the ways and habits of the Indians. Here, this is a feather from one of them."

"That's from a Comanche. Some men liked to braid their hair and attach a feather to one of them. I guess it fell off during their escape."

Joseph thanked Woody for his help and then hurried on to Anfang.

When he arrived at the Miller house, Jenell and Bernadette came running, but stopped when they saw that Joseph was by himself. Again, they held each other and grieved over the disappearance of Benjamin. Max and Sarah came out to console them but got caught up in the sorrow and disappointment.

Joseph knelt down and held Bernadette's hands and said, "I believe Benjamin is still alive. We hope and pray that he is and that we can find him and bring him back to you, and to us, where he belongs."

After Sarah heated and served some stew, Bernadette was put to bed clutching her handmade doll. After she fell asleep, Joseph described to the others the finding of the lone pecan under the broken branch of the mesquite tree.

Max listened intently and then said, "Benjamin must have had some pecans in his pocket because he's seen you do that. It must have been his way of trying to tell you he is okay and knows you are looking for him. I believe your shot in the air when they were fleeing was your signal to him that you would find him."

"We prayed for his return in church," Sarah said. "By now probably everyone in Anfang knows about it."

"Sometimes Indians come to the drug store," Jenell said. "They speak different languages, but I can draw a picture of Benjamin and we can get the message across that we are looking for him. They would try to help us."

Max said, "We know the federal government built a string of forts that stretch up and down the state of Texas to protect the settlers and the pioneers headed west. It seems like they could be of some help."

"Those are all good ideas," Joseph said. "In fact, Woody has already left for the nearest fort to report the capture of Benjamin and the disappearance of Helga Fellman, the daughter of the dying man on the land grant. He should be back by now, so I'll go back and see what he found out."

With tears in her eyes Jenell said, "Bernadette and I will stay here for now. I'll draw the picture of Benjamin and get it circulated. I will write your family in Baumberg. They should know about the capture and their prayers will help us find him."

Joseph returned to the Double JJ but did not stop as he was anxious to see what Woody found out. He located him near his house feathering a large wild turkey gobbler.

"This turkey made a mistake of crossing in front of me on the way back from the fort. It'll make some good jerky."

"What did you find out?" Joseph asked.

"About all I could do was report Benjamin's capture. The lieutenant I talked to said he understood the severity of it, and that they would do what they could to find him. I also gave him the information on Helga Fellman."

"Woody, I sure do appreciate you helping me. I know you've been around a lot and I'm going to ask you some questions. Captain Harris, the man that gave me my telescope, knows I'm not afraid to ask questions."

"Ask me all the questions you want because I too am fond of your children. I was a ranger off and on for a long time, but I can't do that anymore because of my injury. Now, some call them the Texas Rangers, but I can still ride a horse and sometimes help someone out. When the time comes when I can't ride anymore, I'll probably frown a lot, but I'll keep on living the best way I can. I can guarantee that if I was a guard at a jailhouse, no one would ever escape while I'm on duty."

"Did you ever kill anybody?"

"Only when I had to and I will again if I have to, but I never did enjoy it and I never will," Woody answered.

"Finding Benjamin and getting him back alive is always on my mind. From what I've heard, they probably captured him so they could raise him to become an Indian warrior because their numbers have dwindled," Joseph said.

"I think you are right so far. Go on."

"I'm thinking that if he is found, and we attack them with a big posse or an army with guns blazing, that they would have time to hide or harm him. I'm ready to go now, but if I could muster up some patience, they would be less likely to be on their guard. That would also give me more time to prepare for it."

"The element of surprise sure helped us at San Jacinto, but we were more than one."

"More than one would be more detectable," Joseph replied.

"You're a husband and a father and I can't help you make your decision. I will help you do whatever you decide to do," Woody promised.

"In the morning I'm going to check on the animals. Then I'm going back to Anfang to see Jenell and Bernadette."

Joseph found the house and livestock to be okay. He looked again at the area where the abduction occurred to help recall the event and the appearance of the thieves and their horses. While doing so he was distracted by a big buck that was helping himself to the grain he had planted. He quietly crawled up to the rock fence to get closer and then he shot it with his pistol. After field dressing it, he tied it on the back of his horse and headed for Anfang.

When he got to town, Joseph went to see Anton at his blacksmith shop. "I'm sorry that Benjamin was taken," Anton said. "We are all hoping and praying that he is found. What do we have here?"

"This buck got fat on my corn and wheat fields. I'm real busy now so I'd like to give it to you but ask that you set aside some jerky and dried sausage for me. Can you do that?" Joseph asked.

"Of course, I can. You know we can make the meat go a long way. I'll set aside a bunch of jerky and sausage for you," he said.

Jenell and Bernadette were busy cleaning their house when Joseph dismounted. They came running to greet and cling to him.

"Bernadette, your mother and I want to walk down to the river for a short time. Can you wait in the house like a big girl? Then we can go to Alfred's store for some candy," Joseph said.

With tears in her eyes, she said, "Yes, and I'll be good too."

Bernadette watched her parents from the rear window of the house as they strolled down to the water. She watched them talk for what seemed like a long time and then come back up to the house. After that, the three of them left for the general store.

While at the store, Alfred saw Joseph examining a pair of binoculars. He said, "Joseph, that's a good strong set of binoculars. A lot of people have looked at it and put it back down. It's a luxury not everyone can afford. Take it outside and try it and if you want it you can have it at a special price...you have done so much for our community."

He did like it and with misty eyes Jenell nodded her approval. Bernadette got her candy free.

Early the next morning Joseph returned to the Double JJ to check on and feed the animals. As he was scattering some hay for the cattle, Shadow barked to announce that a man on horseback was arriving. When Joseph saw him, he went into the house to heat some coffee for himself and his loyal friend, Woody.

After they settled down Woody said, "I can tell what you've decided to do. Are you taking a pack horse?"

"I thought about that a lot. With a little help from the bank, I'm going to take the best two horses I can find. If one should come up lame, I can use the other one. Tomorrow I'm going to visit Mr. Huber's horse farm because mine is slowing down," he answered.

"Don't forget to take a couple of spikes because you never know where you might have to leave your horses. Not all Indians are warlike, but I would avoid all of them, so word doesn't get around that you are looking for your son. Chances are that they will be camped near a water source. The Comanche braves do the hunting and their squaws do most of the chores."

"I plan on moving very slowly from one spot to another and under cover whenever I can," Joseph said. "I don't want to be seen."

The two outdoorsmen continued their discussion for a long time. Then Woody said, "You are going to have to be smarter and better than anyone out there whether their Indians or not. If you fire a shot for food, or build a fire for warmth, it could be a mistake. Some Indians now have rifles and there is no reason you couldn't carry a bow and arrows on your packhorse...when you are starving, a raw varmint will look good. I can show you how to use one and you can practice until you think you are good at it and then practice again."

"Where can I get one?"

"I knew you would ask so I brought one along. An Indian friend made it for me and gave me some hints on making the arrows."

Joseph followed Woody out to his horse to get the bow and arrows. Woody placed an apple in the dirt twenty steps away and pierced it on the first try.

"Where did you learn that?"

"I have a lot of time on my hands and my arms and back are still working," Woody said as he removed the arrow so Joseph could give it a try at fifteen steps.

Joseph missed the target by a full step. Woody said, "You will get the hang of it and we'll practice it until you get it right. Then we can try a moving target."

Later in the day Woody said, "You catch on quick. You are ready for a moving target. Just make sure you don't hit me or my horse."

Woody put a little gravel in a small burlap bag and tied it up. He then added a long rope and dragged it behind his horse at various distances and speeds. After the ninth try Joseph's arrow zipped through the bag and buried itself in the dirt. Woody whooped and hollered, and Joseph breathed a sigh of relief.

This time it was Lucky that started barking when two riders were coming their way. Joseph said, "That's Eric and Reinhold. They must have a reason for coming here together."

"I invited them here," Woody said. "We have something to talk about."

The four men gathered on the porch and Eric began by saying, "We know you'll be gone for a while and that your wife and daughter are safe in Anfang. Reinhold and I and our three boys are going to take care of your sheep and cattle until you get back. Woody has some good grass left on his land and said we can all graze it since it's been so dry this year. That will help us all out."

Woody said, "I'll spend a lot of time in and around your barn taking care of the chickens, cows, and dogs. From there I could see any marauders that come snooping around your house and then give them a big surprise."

Reinhold said, "You have enough to worry about and you shouldn't have to worry about someone burning down your house and barn. We'll take care of the Double JJ and you take care of yourself. You made a man out of my boy and I will never forget it. I can't read and I don't know much about praying, but I'm going to have Wilma show me how, so you get your boy back."

Joseph was so overwhelmed and choked up that he could barely speak. They all just nodded their heads, shook hands, and parted.

At the crack of dawn Joseph saddled his horse for the return to Anfang. After just a few steps, he turned around so he could view the house, well, and barn that had provided them so much joy and comfort.

Joseph quietly rode into Anfang. He found their little house empty, so he went on to the drug store. Jenell was minding the store so her father could go home for a noon meal.

After their kiss and embrace Jenell said, "I know what's on your mind. When are you going?" she asked.

"I still have to get some things together but first I need two well-trained, fast horses. After I go to the bank, I'm going out to see if Mr. Huber has what I want," he answered.

"I'm going to lock the door here and go tell my parents," she said.

"I want to tell Bernadette later. I'll see you then," he said.

Jenell rushed to her parent's house. Bernadette was not there as she was out taking a walk with Katherine, the blind girl who was now full grown.

"Joseph is leaving," Jenell said.

Sarah paused and said, "I know why he is leaving but I don't know where he is going or how long he'll be gone."

Max said, "I knew he would look for Benjamin sooner or later. Where is he now?"

"He is on the way to the bank to talk to Martin and then he's going out to the Huber farm to see about some horses," Jenell answered.

"I want to go out there with him," Max said. "He knows more about horses than I do, but I think Sarah and I should help him out with the expense."

Max found Joseph before he entered the bank. There the plans were changed, and both of them headed for the horse farm.

Mr. Huber was indoors as he was not feeling well, but he said, "I know your predicament and I've got just the right horses for you. They grew up together, they are well behaved, and three years old. Jude will get and saddle them so you can go for a ride."

Max waited while Joseph and Jude took off on the horses and rode out of sight. There, they exchanged horses before returning to the stables. Max and Joseph then walked around both horses and examined them.

Joseph said, "I have not ridden horses like that since I road Sunrise, one of Mr. Hibner's horses in Germany."

"That's good," Max said. "As soon as you and Jude take off their saddles, we'll take them with us. We worked it all out while you were on your ride."

"I will always be grateful. Thank you so much," Joseph said.

Bernadette saw her Father arriving with two horses and ran outside. "Is one of the horses for Benjamin?" she asked as she jumped into his arms.

"The second horse is for my things because I am going away to look for him. I'll be gone for a while and I may not be back for your birthday, but I'll be thinking about you all day long. Be sure and hug and kiss your Mother for me every day and tell her it's from me," he answered.

"That's easy. I can do that every morning and again when I go to bed."

Early the next day Joseph saddled up the tallest horse and went to the blacksmith shop to see if the jerky and sausage were ready. It was finished and when Anton brought it out, he said, "That's a fine horse you have there. Be careful up in Comanche country because they like horses, and other people's horses even more."

"I'll be on the lookout for them," Joseph answered.

Anton said, "I know you have some knives, but I made a real knife for you because you might need it. Also, Mr. Graf made a sheath for it at his saddle shop. If you get in a hassle with the Indians, they're not going to put you in a comfortable jail cell."

"Maybe they'll treat me right if I give them one of your sausages. You do make better sausage than any blacksmith in these parts," Joseph said.

Anton laughed but then said, "Good luck and I hope to see you and Benjamin real soon."

"Thank you for the knife and the warning. I must go now and do some packing," Joseph said.

Early the next morning Joseph started packing for the search while his wife and daughter watched. While he was doing it, he recalled the packing of his trunk and box in Germany about a decade ago.

"Those are magnificent horses. Do they have names?" Jenell asked.

"I don't know but we can name them ourselves," he said.

"One of them is the same color as that harrow we bought. Why don't we call him Rusty?" Bernadette suggested.

Then Jenell said, "The taller one is dark and gray like the coals in our stove. Let's call him Smoky."

"Rusty and Smoky it will be and that will save me a lot of thinking. I'll be switching from one to the other occasionally and I hope they both get used to having a pack on their back," Joseph said.

Rusty was jittery but accepted the load. The bow and arrows, extra rope, clothing, bedding, and hatchet were carefully packed. The food included the jerky and sausage, boiled eggs, beans, potatoes, apples, and bread. All of it was covered with a large piece of canvas and then balanced and strapped down to prevent shifting.

The binoculars, compass, spikes, and telescope were packed in Joseph's saddlebags where they would be more accessible. Joseph's holster would be near his right hand, the long knife near his left, and the leather scabbard stored his rifle.

When it was time to leave, Joseph said, "Jenell, I have everything I need. I will be thinking about you and our children all the time."

"Joseph, please be careful. Bernadette and I will be praying for you and Benjamin. It would be a blessing if the four of us could be together again," Jenell said.

"I hope you find my brother," Bernadette said as she started crying. "I miss him so much."

It was difficult for the three of them to break up their embrace because of the uncertainty they were facing. When they finally turned each other loose, Joseph mounted Smoky and grabbed Rusty's reins and headed out. Jenell and Bernadette clutched each other and watched Joseph and the horses until they were out of sight.

After only a few hours Joseph had to stop and adjust the supplies on the pack horse because of some slippage and a rubbing noise from within it. When he was satisfied that the load was quiet and secure, he continued in a northwest direction.

Having already visited the land grant, he thought that he had a good general idea of what the landscape would look like and that the Comanche population would be spread out over a vast area. Already he had convinced himself that the pack horse would allow him to take more time to cover more ground. The ground, for now, was his new home.

Joseph had no clue as to where his son might be or if he was still alive. He wondered if the Indians that took him had previously seen him and planned the abduction, or if they just saw him alone and took advantage of the opportunity. Maybe, he thought, they were holding him somewhere and would release him for something they wanted. In any case, it was wrong for them to take him and he would do anything to get him back.

The time of the day no longer mattered to Joseph. Of most importance was to stay hidden and not be detected by anyone that could end his mission. That to him meant not being in the open during daylight time and moving on at night whenever possible.

When Joseph came to a wide riverbed, he felt that the real search was just beginning. Judging by the setting of the sun, he confirmed that the river was flowing in a southeasterly direction like most of the rivers in this part of Texas. The river had some deep looking pools and some clear shallows that made crossing it easy for the horses. During better times, the river would look much more beautiful.

On the other side Joseph turned left and followed the river but at a distance from it so he would not be seen. After spotting a suitable place for the horses to graze, he stopped and removed the saddle from Smoky and the supplies from Rusty. He fell asleep wishing Shadow, their herding dog, was there to guard his camp.

It was cold and dark when he awoke. When he could see well enough, he saddled Rusty and fastened the supplies on the back of Smoky.

In the middle of the morning Joseph arrived at a creek that was draining down into the river. On a hunch, he left the river and followed the creek northward as he felt there would be a better chance of finding a Comanche camp. He rode slowly and deliberately along the thickets but stopped frequently to listen for any unusual noises. Before traveling again, he tended to head to a designated spot to stop, look. and listen again.

At one of those stops, he noticed the sun shining into a small open area. The weeds and grass had been trampled down exposing the soil beneath it. In the middle of the clearing there were the coals from a recent campfire. On a rocky cliff next to it, he found some colorful paintings of horses, Indians, and teepees that looked like they had weathered for many years. Before he continued, he took a tree branch and erased the foot and hoof prints he and his horses had made in the clearing.

As Joseph continued northward, the creek got smaller and he reached a higher elevation. From the highest point he searched his surroundings. His binoculars were best for scanning an entire area and the telescope better for analyzing a more specific object or movement. With the latter instrument he spotted a coyote stalking a smaller animal.

Joseph resumed daytime travel considering the skies were dark and threatening and the first quarter moon might not provide enough light to go further. After nightfall he came to another river, so he stopped to feed the horses and get ready for the storm.

He tied the canvas cover securely to some leaning trees to provide cover from the rain and wind he was expecting. Under total darkness, and while munching on some dry sausage and a raw potato, the wind howled and whipped the canvas back and forth. Surprisingly, it did not rain, and the wind subsided. Joseph put his head on the cradle of his saddle and went to sleep.

In the middle of the night Joseph was suddenly awakened by a loud ruckus coming from where the horses were tied. With his pistol in his hand he crept towards the sound and unexpectedly found himself walking in water. The horses were in much deeper water, so he untied them and led them to higher ground. Next, and in much haste, be cut the cords holding his canvas cover and moved it and all his belongings to where the horses were now staked.

By sunrise the lazy river had quadrupled in width and transformed into a raging, brownish looking river sending logs and limbs downstream. Crossing the river now was out of the question and building a fire to warm up was unsafe, so he packed up and traveled the south fringes of the river. By midday, he came to the area where the heavy rain had fallen.

Joseph wanted to cross the river there but had to wait until the water would drop back into its banks. Waiting was difficult but it did give him time to pick up and shell pecans to eat and take along. He also pulled out the arrow on which he was cutting a small notch for each passing day. This day was December 16th and the birthday of his children. He knew Bernadette was under the care of her loving Mother but did not know if Benjamin was alive or not.

By noon the next day, the water level had dropped enough for Joseph to pack the supplies on the back of Smoky, the taller of the two horses. He examined and reexamined the pack so the swollen river would not jeopardize its contents. Before crossing, he removed the rifle from its scabbard and held it high as he and Rusty entered the muddy looking river. The horses struggled but made it across without a mishap. From there he came to a large open plain. The cover there was sparse, so he headed for a brushy hilltop to spend the remaining daylight hours.

At dusk he moved to the hilltop's edge to glass the area looking west. To his left, he saw some wild hogs uprooting the ground. At a respectable distance from them, some deer were nibbling on short vegetation. To the right, he saw something that did not fit the landscape.

He switched from his binoculars to his telescope and saw smoke, horses, and several people at the foot of another hill. He watched the spot until it was dark but then he saw a small fire. He then crept back into the brush to check on the horses and to eat some of his dwindling food supply.

At morning twilight, Joseph returned to the edge of the hill to see if the fire was still burning. It was not, but he could see some movement in the subdued light...there were horses and riders leaving the camp. He looked around to find better cover as it looked like they would pass by the hill he was on.

When they got closer, he counted nine multi-colored horses and adult riders. They were equipped with an assortment of lances, bows, and shields. By their weapons and winter apparel, he assumed they were Comanche warriors on their way south to conduct raids during the advancing full moon. When they got closer, he concealed his binoculars so they would not detect a reflection. He watched them until they were out of sight.

Joseph took his time getting his horses ready to continue the search as he wanted to make sure the Indians were far away before he would venture onto the open prairie in broad daylight. Since Benjamin's fate and location were so uncertain, he took another hunch and continued in the same northern direction with the aid of his compass.

With little warning, the darkening clouds from the west were an indication that a blizzard was on its way. He stopped near a water hole so Smokey and Rusty could graze before its arrival. He fastened the canvas to some mesquite trees for a wind break and then ate his last section of dried sausage.

Darkness fell and Joseph tried to stay awake during the howling wind. He, however, discovered that he had fallen asleep when he saw snow on his boots. He hurriedly packed and hit the trail again, but he led the horses until the sun made an appearance. Not wanting to be seen during the daytime, he entered a thick cedar break to wait for nightfall.

There with time on his hands, and the small animals out to greet the improved weather, Joseph removed the bow and arrows from his pack. He then crept around the brush and small trees and scored on three of five pulls. He returned to where he had left his horses with a squirrel and two rabbits. He ate some of it but put most of it inside the pack.

Joseph and the horses remained hidden in the cedar break until the sun went down. Now unable to see the needle on his compass, he would have to study the stars to maintain his northward direction. From the looks of a huge mesa ahead, he would have to rely on the instinct of the horses not to make a misstep on its rocky terrain.

Joseph soon determined that the sides of the mesa were not only rocky but were also steeper than he expected...going further would be noisy and dangerous so he and the horses stopped and stayed on a rocky ledge.

In the morning he located a better route to the top by ascending it at a slant. He left the horses on the flat and crept his way to the top of the mesa. The top was long and level and had a lot of brush and small tree cover. He froze when he saw a doe and yearling staring at him. The yearling stepped forward a little bit, but then they both turned around and trotted away.

Joseph slowly walked to the back side of the mesa to get a glimpse of the other side. There was a stream flowing from left to right with water cascading over rocks between larger pools of water. He dropped to his knees as he looked upstream and saw some tepees nestled on this side of the stream. He noticed a few natives mingling around the camp, but at the long distance, he could not get a good look at them.

After he caught his breath, he squirmed away from the mesa's edge and returned to the horses knowing he would be back again with his telescope. At dusk, he scouted for an escape route should it become necessary. On the western end of the mesa he did not see anything unusual. On the east end, he discovered a beaten down path that was most likely the most traveled trail into the camp.

As silently as he could collected rainwater in his hat for his horses from the hillside cavities. After cutting some grass for them, he sharpened the knife that Anton had given him. Next, he wiped his face and beard with mud. Then with the knife, pistol, and a rope, he slipped back to the top of the mesa.

He found a more secluded place to watch the Indian camp below. After studying it, he concluded that it was a newer location for them and that they were still preparing for a longer stay. He watched some braves tending to the horses and squaws hanging meat on poles to dry. There were some older Indians sitting by a small fire, and some children helping here and there, but none of them looked like Benjamin.

Joseph got another indication that the camp was still expanding. Three more horses pulled into the camp and two of them were dragging a travois carrying their things. They were three adults and one infant.

Joseph was disappointed when he returned to his hideout on the opposite side of the mesa. He decided he would saddle and pack his horses first thing in the morning before taking a final look at the Indian camp. From there he would go deeper into Comanche territory.

As planned, he saddled Smoky at daybreak. The pack on Rusty was not as bulky as before, as his food supply was almost gone. When that was finished, he left the horses to climb back up to the top of the mesa one more time.

There was a little smoke coming through the tops of the tepees. When the sun came out, four braves mounted horses, crossed the creek, and disappeared... Joseph thought that they left on a hunt. Some other Indians, probably older men, were busy erecting the poles for another tepee. Some squaws, with and without children, spread out to work on buffalo hides, cook, and to gather nuts and berries.

Joseph concentrated on watching the few children but he did not see anyone who resembled Benjamin. He crunched down some more when he noticed a squaw picking up acorns while working her way downstream. She was putting them into a bag that was held by a young boy with dark hair parted in the middle.

They passed below and beyond him and then she sat down on a boulder overlooking the stream. The boy gave the bag to her and then he tried to skip small flat stones on the surface of the water. Instead they just plunged into the water, so he picked up some round stones that fit in the palms of his hands. He then demonstrated how he could juggle three stones at the same time.

Joseph was stunned and could not believe what he saw. He said to himself, "It's Benjamin. It must be Benjamin. They must have painted his hair black. I've never seen anybody his age, juggle before."

He immediately walked and slid down the back side of the mesa and across the trail the Indians used to get to their camp. The sound of the running stream was to his advantage as he reached over the squaw's shoulder and silenced her with his left hand and held the knife in his right.

The boy looked puzzled because he did not immediately recognize his father because of his beard and muddied face. When he did, he grasped him and said, "Don't hurt her. She helped me."

Joseph said, "Be as quite as you can, take off my neckerchief, and untie my rope."

Joseph looked upstream and didn't see anyone coming...their camp was only partially visible from where he was. He gagged her and tied her hands behind her back. He then shackled her so she could still walk but only an inch or two at a time. He was surprised to see her cooperating. He picked up the telescope and hung it high in a tree where she could see it, but not reach it.

Joseph then led and pulled Benjamin up the side and to the top of the mesa as fast and quietly as he could. They then ran and slid down the other side to where the horses were. Joseph lifted Benjamin up on Rusty and adjusted the stirrups.

Then, as fast as he could, he drew his knife and cut the leather straps that held the canvas covered pack on the back of Smoky. He then threw it aside and jumped on the bare back of the horse and said, "Benjamin, hold on tight because we're going down this steep mesa. When we get to the bottom we're going to ride as fast as we can."

The father and son galloped across the prairie to get as much distance as they could between themselves and any angry Comanche Indians. To the riders, the two prized horses made a loud thundering noise beneath them as they raced away.

When the horses showed signs of exhaustion they stopped to rest. After examining the surroundings with his binoculars, Joseph and his son finally had a chance to greet and hug each other.

Benjamin said, "Thank you for finding me and I can't wait to see my mother and sister. Why did you leave our telescope way up in the tree?"

"I did it because I thought it might give us more time to escape. When your Indian friend got back to the camp and they ungagged her, she may have told them about the shiny object in the tree. They may have been curious and wanted her to show them where and what it was. Let's go now. We have a long way to go before we get to the river."

Joseph hoped for a downpour to wash away their tracks but there were no signs of rain as the duo galloped across the territory that was claimed by the Comanche tribes. The beauty of the landscape on the open prairie was unnoticed by the father and son who just wanted to get home safely.

They, however, were in a large open area when Joseph noticed that Rusty, Benjamin's horse, was struggling. Rusty was favoring his right front leg, so they headed for a small grove of trees that would provide a little cover.

After Joseph inspected the right front leg he said, "Benjamin, Rusty lost his horseshoe along the way and his hoof is in bad shape. He won't be able to continue our pace so I'm going to put the saddle on Smoky and we'll ride together."

Suddenly, Benjamin pointed and said, "Look over there. Someone is following us."

Joseph turned around and saw the movement off in the distance. He grabbed his binoculars and watched five Indians on horseback coming their way. He handed the instrument to Benjamin and said, "Look at them. Do you recognize anything about them?"

"No, I don't."

"We don't know what they want but we will make a stand here because the horses need rest. We don't know if they are from the camp you were at, another raiding party, or believe I kidnapped you because you are dressed like an Indian."

Joseph tied Smoky and Rusty to some trees within the grove and hid Benjamin behind the largest tree. He stood behind another as he watched the warriors coming directly to him. Then at a full gallop they started circling around the grove firing arrows rapidly at him and into the grove. When they came all the way around the grove, he fired his rifle at the one he thought was the leader. It was a hit and he saw the rider sink down on his horse.

After the shot, the other Indians protected themselves with their shields and charged Joseph. This time he drew his revolver and fired twice wounding another warrior in his arm. They looked surprised that he could fire two shots in succession that all of them turned away and fled. When they were out of range, he fired his pistol again as if to let them know he had more shots left.

Benjamin, unharmed in the battle, got up from behind the tree and jumped into his father's arms. Rusty was less fortunate and was squirming around on the ground with a broken arrow protruding from his neck. Joseph placed Benjamin behind the saddle on the back of Smoky and led him out of sight of the fallen horse. The father told his son, "Cover your ears. I'll be right back."

Benjamin soon heard one shot and knew he would never ride Rusty again. On Joseph's return to his son, he found four arrows that had missed their mark...he broke them in two so they would never be used again.

After he reloaded his revolver Joseph said, "It's a full moon tonight and we're going to travel just a bit further. If we get chased by someone you can hang on to my saddle or the rope I just tided around my waist. Today you handled Rusty very well and I am very proud of you. God willing, we'll be back with your mother and sister in a few days."

When they came upon a rocky cliff they stopped to get out of the wind and get some rest. The fatigue allowed Joseph and Benjamin to sleep for a while, but without any provisions they soon woke up to a very cold sensation. Joseph built a fire so they could warm up before leaving under the light of the moon.

By noon they reached the river that had previously flooded and almost washed Joseph away. It was well within its banks now enabling them to follow it downstream for a while and then exit on some rocks that would not leave any hoof prints. A little farther they stopped in a pecan bottom where they picked and ate pecans while Smoky grazed in a clearing.

Before sunset Joseph and Benjamin breathed a sigh of relief when they crossed over some wagon ruts...Joseph assumed that they had been etched into the ground by settlers who had moved to the land grant. After another almost sleepless night, they crossed another river and felt destined to cross the creek at their home on the Double JJ Ranch before it would get dark again.

When they passed by the barn, they heard a loud whoop coming from near the barn door. It was Woody in a great state of excitement because of their successful return.

Joseph said, "I didn't know you could dance. Don't hurt that leg again."

After the joyous reunion between the three, Joseph said, "Thank you so much for helping us but we have one more favor. We're hungry, tired, and dirty. Tomorrow tell the neighbors we're back and then ride to Anfang and inform Jenell and Bernadette that we are safe. We need a day to recuperate and we'll see them in town by noon the day after tomorrow."

"It would give me great pleasure to spread the good news. There's eggs, milk, and bread in the house. I'll see you in Anfang," he answered.

After a long night's sleep and a hearty breakfast, Joseph heated water on the stove to begin the task of cleaning up after a long outdoor adventure. Of most importance was the cutting of Benjamin's hair to make it easier to wash out the black concoction that had been rubbed into it. After Benjamin's bath, the neat and clean clothing that his mother had long ago set aside, replaced the buckskin and buffalo hide clothing that he had been wearing since he was abducted. Then Benjamin watched intently as his father shaved off his beard.

When they finished cleaning up, they ate again and took a long nap. Later they played with the dogs and checked the livestock. Then they cooked a chicken to highlight their evening meal.

Benjamin was anxious to leave the next morning so he could reunite with his mother and sister. He watched his father saddle Smoky for the trip into town. When Joseph started to tie the security rope around his waist he said, "We won't need the rope anymore. Nobody will be after us and I'm already seven years old."

Joseph stopped for a moment and said, "You're right about the rope but your're eight years old now. You and Bernadette's birthdays were on the sixteenth of this December. We can celebrate them at another time."

"That's good and please hurry. I can hang on to the saddle," Benjamin said.

The sun broke out as Joseph and Benjamin departed. The country road that wound up and around the hills of Texas never felt so good. Even Smoky seamed to strut more as the church steeples of Anfang, a town built by the determination of hardworking immigrants, came into sight.

As they completed a turn in the road Joseph said, "It looks like there are a lot of people in town today."

"Stop," Benjamin said. "I would like to sit in front so I could see more."

Joseph smiled, stopped, and chose to walk and lead the horse and his son into town. Benjamin moved up to sit in the saddle. They could see and hear people waving and cheering from both sides of the street. In the center of the street they saw and heard a band playing from underneath the flags of the State of Texas and the United States. On the right were four people sitting and standing on a horse drawn wagon.

Suddenly Benjamin slid off the horse and with his father rushed to meet Jenell and Bernadette for a family reunion with hugs, hearts open wide, and tears of joy. Jenell's parents soon joined the foursome for these precious moments.

Joseph then helped Benjamin up on the saddle and Bernadette behind him. In her right hand Jenell held the reins of Smokey, the tall dark gray horse that had served them so gallantly. In her left hand she held the right hand of her brave husband who had rescued her son.

Max and Sarah, now back in their wagon, followed them and unknowingly started the formation of a parade. As they moved forward, the spectators followed by peeling away from the sides of the street as they moved further down the street. Old and new friends, including Indians, joined in the procession.

The businesses they passed were decorated for Christmas but were closed for the special event. By appearance, Benjamin was the proudest and happiest of all as he was waving both hands to both sides of the street. When Joseph saw Woody watching and leaning against a tree he shouted, "You sure know how to spread the news."

When the parade got closer to the town square, the participants could hear the Schuster brothers ringing their big cow bells to let everyone know they were invited to the pavilion at the town square for refreshments. The band played on as the four members of the Schmidt family mingled among the crowd. No one asked Joseph about the details of Benjamin's rescue, but it was apparent that it lifted the spirits of everyone in town.

That evening the pleasant aroma of beef stew filled the little house on the banks of the Bend River. When they finished eating Benjamin asked, "When are we having our birthday party?"

Bernadette asked, "Can we have a Christmas tree next year?"

Their parents looked at each other. Then Jenell answered for them by saying, "Tomorrow we'll hook up the wagon and find the nicest tree in the woods...it's not too late to do that. After that I'll bake a big birthday cake."

"Those are great ideas and we'll invite your grandparents," Joseph said. "It might get a little crowded in here but to me this house feels like a castle."

"Me too," Benjamin said.

On Christmas morning, Jenell started a fire in the wood stove to warm up the house. She shook the others and said, "It's time to get up for church. We need to look our best."

The clothes for all of them were neatly arranged and hanging on pegs in the corner of the room. When Joseph finished getting ready, he went outside to hook up the wagon. Benjamin went to the shed to get the axe they would need to harvest a Christmas tree.

Bernadette pulled on her Mothers dress and whispered, "I think they will be surprised." Jenell smiled and nodded in agreement.

The Schmidt family were among the first to arrive at St. Anne's Church on Christmas day. Father Matthew, who was greeting the arrivals, watched them as they came up to the door of the church. He said, "You have heard me speak many times, but at this moment, I cannot describe how happy I am to see the four of you together again. I would like for you to sit in the front pew today."

"That won't be necessary," Joseph said. "We know it will be crowded and we can stand to make it easier for the ones that aren't able to."

"This time I wish you would sit up front because it is a special, special day," the priest said while turning away to greet others.

As suggested, they walked up to the first pew. Joseph and Benjamin were surprised to see Max and Sarah already there saving the space for them.

Before the time the church bell rang, the church was filled. The mixed choir sang as the nativity scene was reenacted by small children. The Christmas message was eloquent and the service inspirational. After the final prayer, Father Matthew welcomed Bernadette to rise and stand in front of the congregation.

All was quiet as everyone watched as she began singing "Silent Night, Holy Night." Her clear, beautiful voice filled the church and the hearts of the people.

CPSIA information can be obtained
at www.ICGtesting.com
Printed in the USA
LVHW042231130821
695214LV00005B/164

9 781632 933126